SECRETS TOLD

THE SECRETS SERIES - BOOK 1

TINA HOGAN GRANT

TINA HOGAN GRANT BOOKS

REVIEWS

"I LOVED all her other books and just knew I would love this one. There are some authors you buy books from without even reading what they are about. And this is one of those books." *Agnes Shapario*

"I couldn't turn the pages fast enough to find out! I absolutely loved this story. My emotions were all over the place." - *Darlene Johnson*

"More importantly, it is the story of love, family, roots, redemption, and deception. Read this story and discover how someone you love can distort your perception of reality for their own selfish reasons. You will learn about true love and family and how good old-fashioned values can put everything into perspective.

As always, Ms. Grant manages to put some of her love of the water, fishing, and boating into the story.

Be careful what you wish for. Everything has a cost. Are you willing to pay the price?" - *Kris Rubi*

""The Devil Wears Prada" meets "Steel Magnolia" 5-Star novel. Can Bryce's compassion sway Patricia's evil ways or will she forever live on the dark side alone?" - *Author, Ashley Cobb Post*

CHAPTER 1

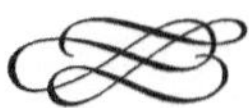

From her desk, 33-year-old Leslie Williams heard the prominent footsteps marching across the marble floor in the reception area on the other side of the heavy double glass doors. Only the Gucci black-heeled pumps worn by her boss, successful and powerful Manhattan criminal defense attorney Patricia Levenick, would make that fearful sound.

Leslie quickly sat up straight, opened the top drawer to her left, and slid the donut and napkin inside before hastily closing it. Being Patricia's legal assistant, her desk was the closest to Patricia's office overlooking downtown Manhattan from the 57th floor. Leslie brushed back her shoulder-length blonde hair with her hand and looked over at her five co-workers sitting at their desks, shifting things around to make their work area look more organized. Some of them quickly yanked headphones out of their ears, and they all turned around in their seats, switching their focus instead to their computer screens.

"It's 9:00 am; the dragon lady has arrived," Leslie laughed, followed by loud laughter from the others.

Seconds later, carrying an armful of files, dressed in a Gucci black pencil skirt and matching lapel blazer, her short, chestnut brown hair layered away from her face, 39-year-old Patricia marched past Leslie's desk, her footsteps silenced by the carpet in this part of the building.

Without looking at Leslie but instead turning to unlock the double mahogany door to her office, she hollered in a sharp tone. "Leslie! I need the Jacob files on my desk pronto. I'm due in court this afternoon."

Leslie rolled her eyes. "I put them on your desk last night before I left."

Patricia abruptly stopped before opening the door to her office and slowly turned her body to face Leslie, giving her a piercing stare. "You did? Why didn't you tell me? I could have taken them home last night and studied them instead of being rushed this morning."

Leslie swallowed the lump in her throat that had quickly formed. "I did. I thought you heard me."

Patricia placed a hand on her hip and rolled her eyes in a demeaning manner. "Did I reply? Or say thank you? If I did not, then you obviously need to pay more attention and not just assume everything."

Leslie lowered her eyes to the floor. "I'm sorry, I honestly thought you'd heard me."

"Well, next time get clarification. How many times have we had this conversation, Leslie? Now, I need you to hold all my calls, and I want no interruptions whatsoever unless the building is on fire. Do I make myself clear?"

Leslie cowered from her stare. "Yes, understood." She breathed in a heavy sigh of relief when her boss entered her office and closed the door behind her. The tension in the room quickly lifted and chatter amongst the others started up again. Leslie calculated in her head and whispered to herself. "Six more months and I'll have a year under my belt at this friggin' place. Then it will be time to start looking for another job where I'll be appreciated and treated far better." She opened her top left drawer and took a bite of her now almost stale donut. She was determined to stick it out. Having the law office of Patricia Levenick on your resume was guaranteed to take you places, and it seemed that a year was sufficient according to previous legal assistants that had moved on to higher and better positions.

With her hands still full of files, Patricia embraced the silence and solitude of her spacious office. She felt a sliver of guilt for the way she'd talked to Leslie, but she didn't get where she was today by being nice. She had learned to grow a tough skin in the business and had worked hard for all her achievements, and it had paid off. She was highly respected in her field, had her own law firm, and was among the top ten best lawyers in New York City.

After placing the files on the only free corner of her desk, Patricia walked behind her desk, slid her black leather purse off her shoulder and placed it on the floor next to her leather desk chair before taking a seat.

As she did every morning, she smiled at the framed picture of her two daughters. Her eleven-year-old, Savannah, and her young, nine-year-old munchkin, Jewel. She would miss them this weekend. Her ex-husband Bryce would be picking them up from their private school this afternoon and taking them for the weekend to his awful 200-acre dairy farm in Connecticut, something he did once a month; a place Patricia had no desire to visit and also hated the thought of her two girls out there in the middle of nowhere, when they could be with her, playing tennis, practicing ballet, or having violin and piano lessons. She shuddered at the thought and picked up the phone handset from her desk and connected the outside line.

"Bryce, it's Patricia. I wanted to make sure that you'll be picking up the girls this afternoon?"

"Yes, Patricia, we talked last night, and I confirmed then. Why would you think I'd forget to pick up my daughters? I count the days until it's my weekend every month. As soon as they've left, I'm counting the days again. Geez Patricia, have more faith, will you? Have I ever forgotten?" he said in his prominent English accent with a cocky tone.

"No, you haven't; I just worry when they're not with me. Call me after you've picked them up if you don't mind?"

"Patricia, I'm their dad. I know how to take care of them, okay?

And yes, I will call you like I always do. We've been doing this for five years since our divorce."

"And don't be late dropping them off on Sunday," she barked. "They have school on Monday, and Bryce, please make sure they take a bath before they come home after being on that filthy farm of yours for two days."

"I don't know why you hate my farm so much. I've never been happier, and you know as well as I do the girls love it here. Jewel loves fishing in the pond. In fact, I bought her a shiny new red tackle box to match her fishing pole. It's a surprise."

Patricia gasped. "You bought our daughter a tackle box? Why couldn't you buy her a nice dress or a new pair of shoes for heaven's sake?"

Bryce cracked a loud laugh. "She can't wear that stuff on the farm. They have a wardrobe of jeans, t-shirts, and sneakers here, and honestly? They can't change into them fast enough when they get here. Savannah spends most of her time riding her pony, Cleo."

"Oh please, I've had enough of hearing about that damn pony. Savannah won't shut up about it. You should have talked to me first before you bought it for her."

"Now hang on a second; since when do I need permission from you before buying my daughters a gift? You should have been there three months ago when I gave her the pony. She was crying, I was crying. Heck, even Jewel was crying. It was beautiful. You really should come up here and watch her ride, Cleo. She's a natural Patricia, and she has the biggest smile I've ever seen when she rides. It's a beautiful sight. I'm telling you; you're missing out."

Patricia rolled her eyes and shook her head. "I honestly don't want to get into this. I have work to do. I need to be in court this afternoon. Just call me after you've picked them up, okay?"

"Fine, but you really should make some time to come out here, Patricia. Like it or not, our girls love being in the country and communing with nature. Maybe one day you will, too."

"Not a chance," Patricia hissed, hanging up the phone.

CHAPTER 2

Dressed in faded blue jeans, a black-and-white checkered shirt and brown work boots, 45-year-old Bryce left his dairy farm in Easton Connecticut in his white Ford 250 pickup truck at noon for the 90-minute drive to the Upper East side of Manhattan to pick up Savannah and Jewel from The Brearley All-Girls School. Even though they didn't get out until three, he always gave himself plenty of time in case of accidents and unexpected traffic on the I-95 interstate.

He had plenty of hired help on the farm and wasn't worried about not being there for half a day, including his younger brother Darren, who'd left England where they both grew up to help him run the place after Bryce had purchased it five years earlier.

Darren was 37 at the time, three years younger than Bryce, and still single with no kids. He had been working on a sheep farm in Yorkshire, England for the past 20 years after their parents, who'd passed away, lost the dairy farm they'd grown up on shortly after the brothers had left home. Darren was content sticking to what he'd known all his life and had never ventured out of England, living the simple life, working off the land. It's what he knew best.

Bryce wanted more and ventured into real estate, and at the age of

23 he moved to New York to work for a company in commercial real estate. He was told the Americans loved the English accent and along with his charm he'd go places. They were right. When making a deal, Bryce laid on his thick accent; within minutes his clients melted like butter in his hand. Just like Patricia did when they first met fourteen years ago in 2004 at a snobby function in some fancy hotel. Two years later they married when he was 33, and Patricia, a young 27, much to her Aunt Cassie's dismay, who believed their marriage would interfere with Patricia's career and success.

Bryce noticed Patricia immediately when he walked into the large ballroom and saw her from across the room dressed in a long black gown and white pearls. She looked stunning, wearing a radiant smile that latched onto his heart immediately. Her hair was much longer back then, cascading down the middle of her back. Other than her brilliant smile, it was her thick, long mane of hair that caught his eye, and he was shocked one day when she returned home with her hair cut short and away from her face.

"What the hell did you do to your hair?" he'd gasped with a dropped jaw, his English accent thick.

Patricia nervously ran her fingers through her now short hair, seeking approval. "I had it cut."

"Cut? More like chopped!" he shrieked. "Why on earth did you go and do a thing like that?"

"So that I'll be taken more seriously. I'm going places Bryce, and I need to present myself in a more professional manner, and I felt my hair was a distraction." She raked her fingers through her hair again, tugging on the ends. "Please tell me you like it," she pleaded.

Bryce paused; he was going to have to lie. "Well, it's going to take some getting used to, but I'm sure it'll grow on me." He never did get used to it, and missed running his hands through her long, wavy hair and pulling it away from her face when he made love to her. But he never confessed his true thoughts to her.

Driven by the wealth of Manhattan, Bryce wanted a piece of it. Sucked into the corporate world of arrogant, selfish people, Imani suits and flashy cars, Bryce soon turned into one of them, and within ten years became a commercial real estate tycoon, making millions in the market.

After exiting onto FDR Drive in Manhattan from the I-278, heading towards the school on 83rd street, Bryce strained his neck at the tall buildings surrounding him, many of which he'd done business with and knew the area like the back of his hand. He pitied the people still trapped here where money and power were the most important things to them, including his ex-wife, Patricia. She was still caught up in the city's web. But he wasn't giving up on her. There was still time for her to make a change - if not for herself, for their daughters. He hated the thought that they were being raised in such a world. Thank goodness he was able to break them away for just a few days a month and bring them to his farm where they could defuse and be kids.

He smiled to himself while driving through the congested streets of Manhattan, thinking about one instance when Jewel caught her first trout last year on his farm. It was with her first fishing pole, a shiny red one that he had bought her for her birthday. She couldn't wait to put on her shiny green rubber boots and head down to the pond. He and Savannah quickly followed her, and within minutes, Jewel had hooked a good-sized trout. After watching her sister, Savannah wanted to try. Previously she had refused, but after seeing the fun Jewel was having, she eagerly took the second pole he'd conveniently bought, and, after showing her how to bait the hook, she dropped the line into the water. Within minutes, like Jewel, she caught a fish almost immediately.

"Nothing in the city could even come close to seeing my two girls standing in the mud at the edge of the pond reeling in a fish they'd caught and then eating it for dinner. It was moments like that that will stay with me forever," Bryce thought to himself. It saddened him that Patricia would never experience it.

"Daddy!" Jewel squealed, dressed in her black skirt and white shirt uniform as she raced to her dad when he walked into the classroom. Bryce knelt and greeted her with a huge smile and open arms, brushing her long dark hair away from her face, which was the same color as their mother's

"Hey, Munchkin." A nickname both he and Patricia had given her. "I've missed you," he said, hugging his daughter. He held her in her arms and squeezed her tight. "Are you ready to spend a weekend on the farm with your old man?"

"You bet I am. I want to help Uncle Darren milk the cows," she said, playing with her father's curly blonde hair.

Bryce laughed. "You can help him with the second round. You're never up for the first one at 5:00 am," he said, tickling her side. "Come on, let's go get your sister."

Dressed in the same uniform as Jewel, her dark hair also like her mother's braided into a ponytail, Savannah greeted her dad with the same excitement. Bryce called the valet on his cell phone a few blocks away and instructed them to bring his truck to the front entrance of the school, then took the hands of his two daughters and exited the building.

Once in the truck with the girls buckled in, Bryce called Patricia's cell to let her know he had their daughters, only to be greeted by her voicemail. She's probably in court, he thought to himself as he waited for the automated message to end before speaking. "Hey Patricia, I picked up Savannah and Jewel. They're in the truck with me."

"Hi Mommy!" The girls yelled from the back seat.

Bryce laughed before continuing. "See, I'm not lying. Anyway, no need for us to stick around in this congested place. We're heading out to the farm. Have a good weekend and we'll see you Sunday. Bye."

"Daddy, can we go fishing tomorrow?" Jewel shouted from the back seat; her voice full of excitement.

"Don't we go fishing every time you come to the farm, ever since I bought you your very own fishing pole?"

"Yes, but I was just checking," she answered, wearing a big smile.

"I want to ride Cleo," Savannah insisted. "I miss her every day and I wish she could come home with me," she added.

"And where would she stay?" Bryce asked, looking at her through the rearview mirror. "You don't have a yard, Savannah, and you can't keep her on one of the balconies of the apartment. She needs fields to run around in and a stable."

"I know. I just miss her."

"Well, you'll get to see her in less than an hour. I'm sure she missed you too, sweetheart."

Twenty minutes into their drive, Bryce became more relaxed when the traffic began to lighten and the concrete buildings became fewer, replaced with open fields and trees. Leaning back in his seat, he switched the tunes on the radio from country to Taylor Swift, which the girls always requested. They knew every song by heart and sang along cheerfully from the back seat.

An hour later, they were pulling into the three-car garage of Bryce's extravagant farmhouse, adorned with apple and pear trees providing plenty of shade. There was a two-story grey, planked colonial style five-bedroom home with white trim, two upper balconies and a large wrap-around lower deck overlooking the 200 acres of grassland. To the left a few hundred yards from the house was a large pond that Bryce kept well stocked with trout just for Jewel.

Leaving New York with millions, Bruce had spared no expense when he bought the property and tore down the original 100-year-old farmhouse and rebuilt it. When he asked Darren if he'd like to come to America and help run the farm, he had a small cottage built for him on the property. Darren had shown no interest in the corporate world when Bryce had asked him to come on board and work at his firm in Manhattan many years ago, but when he learned about the farm, he didn't hesitate to leave England.

Jewel was the first one to exit the truck and was immediately greeted by one of Bryce's dogs, a three-year-old female Golden Labrador.

Jewel stopped running up the walkway to the house and squealed. "Goldie! I missed you," she said, hugging the dog as Goldie wagged her tail ferociously and smothered Jewel's face with affectionate dog kisses.

Savannah caught up with her sister, knelt beside her, and joined in petting Goldie. "I love that she remembers us," Savannah said between giggles as Goldie tickled her face with her tongue.

Bryce stood behind them and chuckled. "She'd never forget you;

she loves you," he said, petting the top of Goldie's head. "Look at her. I think she missed you both."

Savannah nuzzled her face into Goldie's and kissed the top of her shiny wet nose. "I wish we could have a dog. Mom said the building where we live doesn't allow pets, and she reminds me of that every time I ask for a dog, and that we don't have a yard, either." She frowned. "Just like I can't have Cleo at home. I hate not having a yard. I can't have anything," Savannah whined, folding her arms in a disgruntled manner.

"You do have a dog, sweetie. In fact, you have two. Goldie is your dog and so is Jack." Bryce scanned the area where they stood. "Where is that bugger anyway?"

Jewel stood up and spun around staring out at the fields. "Jack! Where are you? We're here," she yelled.

"He's probably with Darren. He loves to go to work with him." Bryce rubbed the top of Jewel's head. "I'm sure they'll show up at dinnertime." He took Jewel's hand and smiled. "Come on, let's go inside."

"Yes! I want to get out of this uniform and put on some jeans. The only time I get to wear them is when I'm with you, Daddy," Jewel said, racing towards the front door.

"Me too!" Savannah echoed as she took her dad's other hand, and together they skipped into the house with Goldie following closely behind, her tail still wagging ferociously.

"I'll be back, Daddy," Jewel hollered as she ran through the large foyer adorned with a grand pine bench and a matching mirror hanging on the wall behind it.

Bryce laughed as he watched his daughters race through the house and up the stairs to their bedrooms, anxious to change their clothes, with Goldie close behind.

There was no better sound than that of their sweet voices echoing through the house. It was the only time the farmhouse felt like a home. The silence after they left and returned to New York was deafening. The only thing missing was their mother making a home-cooked meal in the massive kitchen complete with the latest stainless-steel appliances, white cabinets, and a large pine table with matching chairs. But who was he fooling? He'd never known Patricia to cook a meal, even when they were married; they always ate out, spending hundreds of dollars at fancy restaurants so they'd fit in with the elites and what the rest of the corporate world did. From what the girls had told him, their nanny Letti cooked all their meals while Patricia worked through the night.

His wishful thoughts were interrupted by the sound of footsteps descending the stairs. Bryce looked up and smiled, his elbow resting on the banister at the bottom. "Well, that was fast. Feel better?" he asked both his daughters as they raced into his arms, now dressed in jeans and t-shirts, almost knocking him over.

"Yes!" Jewel shouted out. "Savannah wants to see Cleo. She really misses her when we're not here."

"Well, it's time for her feeding, and I'm sure she'd like a carrot or two. Why don't you both go grab a handful and we'll walk out to the stable."

"I want to see the chickens, too," Jewel hollered as they headed out the door. "And I want to gather the eggs in the morning," she added.

Bryce laughed at her enthusiasm. "We will do all of it, Munchkin. We have two whole days together to do everything you've missed."

Savannah quickly walked ahead, almost running, excited to see her light chestnut-colored pony. Her smile grew as they entered the stable and Cleo immediately raised her head and greeted her with a happy neigh, her tail swishing from side-to-side.

"Cleo, I've missed you so much!" Savannah squealed as she petted her face and gently kissed her before handing her a carrot.

Bryce smiled at the love oozing from Savannah's eyes for Cleo and the bond that had formed between them. Not for a second did he ever regret buying the pony, even after Patricia scolded him for it. After paying for riding lessons prior to buying the pony, Bryce saw what a natural she was and what joy riding brought her. Sadly, Patricia had never witnessed it. Savannah turned and looked at him. "Can I ride her, Daddy?"

"Sure, she hasn't had her exercise today. Judy knew you were coming this weekend, so I told her not to come until Monday to take her out, but she may pop by before then; she wants to see you ride Cleo."

"I love that she takes care of Cleo when I'm not here. She was great at teaching me how to ride."

"Yes, she's great with horses. You have nothing to worry about, Cleo is in good hands." Bryce patted Cleo's face. "Let's get her saddled up and walk her out to the corral so you can ride her," Bryce suggested.

Bryce let Savannah saddle up Cleo on her own. It was good practice for her, and she knew the procedure well, thanks to Judy. While waiting for Savannah, Jewel decided to entertain herself by playing fetch with Goldie outside the stable. Her giggles warmed Bryce's heart.

Once they were in the corral and the gate was closed, Bryce helped Savannah mount Cleo as Jewel watched from outside the corral, sitting on the ground hugging Goldie. When Savannah took the reins and gave Cleo a little nudge and a gentle shake of the reins, Bryce stood back, beaming with pride as Savannah slowly walked Cleo around the corral. It was a beautiful sight, and a memory that he knew Savannah would carry with her for the rest of her life. That's what this place was doing - creating priceless memories for his daughters that Manhattan could never provide.

For the next 20 minutes, Bryce watched his daughter reconnect with her pony, wearing a smile that warmed his heart. He decided to take a few pictures with his phone and send them to Patricia in hopes of enticing her to come and experience the moment in person, but her response was always the same; she was too busy and had to work. But that didn't stop him, he was going to keep trying.

He looked out beyond the corral at the hundreds of acres of green pastures and blue skies dotted with puffy white clouds. As he looked at the glistening pond to the left of the house where Jewel had caught her trout and the shade trees gently swayed in the breeze, he thought to himself, "how can this not be better for his daughters?" All the while not taking his eyes off Savannah.

CHAPTER 3

$\mathcal{P}$atricia listened to her voicemails in her Lexus after leaving the courtroom and headed back to the office. After skipping the numerous clients' messages which she planned to listen to in their entirety once behind her desk, she paused when she heard the familiar voice of Bryce, and relaxed when he said he had the girls.

Patricia planned to work late into the night at the office. It's what she always did when the girls were with Bryce for the weekend. She hated going home when they weren't there. She'd find herself moping around missing them terribly, and had already given Letti, the nanny, the weekend off. At least she could lose herself in her work, order take-out and not be reminded how lonely she really was without her girls.

Since she and Bryce divorced five years ago, she hadn't dated. She didn't want to get wrapped up in another disappointing relationship, so instead consumed herself in her work, expanding her client list and her staff – it had paid off. She was recognized and respected by some of the top elites in New York who paid well to have her firm represent them and was invited to many important and highly publicized functions weekly.

In her mind she was the responsible parent, raising Savannah and Jewel with the best education money can buy, including music, dancing, and learning other languages, living in a beautiful 5,000 square-foot corporate apartment overlooking Central Park in one of the most prestigious areas in Manhattan.

She rolled her eyes as she pulled up to the valet outside the West Chase building that housed her office when she thought about Bryce, who, on a whim, had packed up and left their marriage and bought a dairy farm in Connecticut. "I still can't believe it," she hissed as she exited her car and gave a forced smile to Harry, the valet who'd been working at the building for as long as Patricia could remember.

Standing stiffly wearing black pants, a white dress shirt and a royal blue vest and white gloves, he stood to attention holding her car door open. He nodded and smiled. "Good afternoon, Mrs. Levenick."

Patricia forced a smile. "Hello, Harry," she said, grabbing her briefcase and cellphone off the passenger seat and approaching Lester the doorman, another longtime employee of the building, dressed in a black tailcoat and hat.

Lester smiled, holding the door open to the building. "Working late again I see," he said, wearing a professional smile.

Patricia returned the smile. "You know I always do Lester, when Bryce has the girls."

"Have a good evening," Lester said as Patricia strolled past him towards the elevator.

It was after 5:00 by the time Patricia returned to her empty office. Everyone had gone home for the day, and she felt a little envious knowing they'd all be with their families and loved ones for the weekend.

She released a heavy sigh as she unlocked the double doors to her office and entered the dismal quiet room. After she dropped her briefcase on the nearby brown leather couch, she sat in her desk chair and contemplated calling Bryce to see how the girls were doing, but then decided against it. She already knew the answer. Savannah would only go on and on about her pony, and god knows what Jewel had been doing besides catching fish, milking cows, and looking for chicken eggs. She dreaded to think. All the etiquette and manners she'd worked so hard to teach them were instantly thrown out the window when they spent a weekend on that awful farm with their father. And just when she'd gotten them back into their normal routines, it was time for them to visit Bryce again. For Patricia it was frustrating and annoying. She had tried to express her concerns with Bryce that she didn't think it was good for the girls to be tramping around in mud and chicken coops, and she was afraid that Savannah could get seriously hurt while riding her pony. But Bryce had only laughed at her, his only response being, "lighten up, Patricia. Let them be kids for Pete's sake."

She looked at the brass clock sitting at the head of her desk and saw that it was 6:30. And even though she'd only had a bagel for breakfast, she wasn't hungry or in the mood to eat alone and reached for today's mail piled on the corner of her desk.

She combed through the envelopes, putting the manila envelopes aside, knowing they were legal papers that she'd deal with tomorrow. She opened a couple that looked to be official invites to more functions. She would have Leslie, her legal assistant, check her calendar and reply accordingly.

After making a pile of letters she wanted to take home to work on, her phone dinged with a text message. She immediately saw it was from Bryce and stopped going through the mail and picked up her phone. She leaned forward, her forearms resting on her desk and opened his text and saw he had sent a picture of Savannah on her pony. She rolled her eyes. Why does he keep sending me these? She had mud on her face and a hole in the knee of her jeans as she zoomed in on the pictures. Patricia shook her head in disgust.

The second picture was a picture of Jewel sitting in the dirt hugging Bryce's Labrador. "Good lord! She's filthy, and that dog may have fleas. Does Bryce even consider that? Of course not," she said aloud, her voice laced with disgust. She continued to scroll through the numerous pictures and gasped when she came to a picture of Jewel and Savannah who looked to be sweeping out a chicken coop. What puzzled her the most was that both girls were smiling. "Good grief, Bryce! Our girls are not free help on your farm." She immediately hit reply and began typing at lightning speed, fueled with anger.

Bryce, why are you having our girls do your dirty work? This is not the idea of fun for any little girls. This is horrible. Why do you continue to make them do these filthy things? They are dirty and look like poor children. May I remind you that you're the one that loves to live on a farm. Quit trying to persuade Savannah and Jewel to like your ridiculous lifestyle.

Unable to concentrate on her task of going through the mail any longer, Patricia impatiently drummed her fingertips on the edge of the desk, waiting for Bryce to reply with an apology. She was instantly disappointed when she read his next text two minutes later that began with two laughing emojis, fueling her frustrations even more.

Relax. Can't you see the bloody smiles on their faces? They're having a ball. Do they ever smile that big when they're with you?

Patricia slammed down the phone, refusing to reply to his nonsense and leaned back in the chair, her nostrils flared. "When would he come to his senses? I thought this farm thing was going to be a temporary fad of his, but it's being going on for years," she hissed, pushing her chair back with force, and marching over to the mahogany bar to pour herself a glass of brandy.

After taking a large sip she closed her eyes, allowing the soothing liquid to slide down her throat and help suppress her anger. She turned to the large floor-to-ceiling window that spanned one entire wall of her office and looked down at the still busy streets below at Manhattan. "Why would anyone leave this amazing city? There are fortunes to be made here and I'm just getting started." She took another large sip of brandy and smacked her lips with satisfaction after swallowing. "Why did you give all of this up, Bryce? I don't understand it. I've never understood it. And you wanted me to drop everything I've worked so hard for and follow you to go live on a dairy farm." She released a loud laugh. "Ha! It's the most ridiculous idea you've ever had, and you've had a few."

Patricia shook her head and laughed again before pouring herself another glass of brandy and returning to her desk.

For a few minutes, feeling calmer, her anger diminished, she leaned back and sipped on her drink, savoring the flavor as it coated her mouth and throat, trying not to think of the pictures of Savannah and Jewel being subjected to filth.

After composing herself and shaking her head a few more times, she set down her glass on the desk and resumed going through the mail. She paused when a letter with the return address of an attorney in Alaska caught her attention. She wasn't representing anyone from that state and was puzzled that an attorney would be contacting her. She reached across the desk for her gold-plated letter opener and carefully slid it along the lip of the envelope. She pulled out the single-page letter and began reading. After perusing the first paragraph of the introduction, she leaned forward, her jaw dropped, and her eyes grew wide, like she'd just seen a ghost. Her face turned pale, and her hands shook as she continued to read the letter, shocked by the news. "You have got to be kidding me," she whispered under her breath.

CHAPTER 4

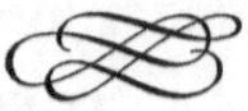

After riding Cleo for at least 30 minutes, Bryce walked with Savannah as she led Cleo to one of the pastures where she could roam for the next hour before being taken back to her stable as Jewel skipped a few yards behind, chasing Goldie.

"Can we go see the chickens now?" Jewel pleaded after Cleo was released into the green pasture and trotted away.

Bryce laughed and took her hand. "Yes Munchkin, we can go see the chickens now, and I have a surprise for you."

Jewel's eyes lit up. "You do! What is it?"

"Well now, if I told you, it wouldn't be a surprise now, would it?" Bryce let go of her hand. "Come on, I'll race you to the chicken coop." He looked over his shoulder at Savannah as he began to run. "You too, Savannah. Let's see if you can outrun your old man."

Savannah immediately took on the challenge, tucked in her elbows and sprinted past her dad at high speed.

"Dang girl. Where did you learn to run so fast?" Bryce yelled, slowing his pace so Jewel wouldn't be left so far behind.

"At school," Savannah yelled as she continued to race. "I'm on the sprint team."

They reached the chicken coop a few minutes later, all of them panting, bending over, and holding their knees while catching their breath. Jewel was the first to stand up straight and quickly ran over to the redwood fence surrounding the coop. She stepped onto the lower plank of the fence so she could look over the top at the 30 chickens of different varieties, from Rhode Island Reds, Golden Comets, Leg Horns, and Plymouth Rocks.

"Where's Lucy?" Jewel asked, scanning the chickens pecking at the feed on the ground.

Lucy was a Leg Horn that Jewel had become attached to and had even named her. Bryce was thankful that he only raised chickens for eggs and not meat. Having to explain to his daughter why her prized chicken was no longer around is something he'd never wanted to do, even though she knew where her chicken dinner came from.

After catching his breath, Bryce joined Jewel at the fence and scuffed her hair with his hand. "Lucy may be inside the coop sleeping." He walked over to a red metal can and removed the lid. "Let's go inside the coop and you can make your famous click-click sound that Lucy knows, and I'm sure she'll come greet you like she always does," Bryce told Jewel as he scooped feed into a large plastic container.

"Good idea, Daddy!" Jewel said, jumping off the fence and taking the container of feed from her dad's hands so he could fill another one for Savannah.

Once behind the closed gate of the coop, Jewel and Savannah shook their containers as they sprinkled feed onto the ground. They were immediately surrounded by clucking chickens, eagerly pecking at the food. Jewel began making her calling sound that the chickens had come to know and associate with food, and as she continued to make the friendly sound, more chickens joined the flock from the sheltered nesting boxes.

"Lucy!" Jewel shouted when she saw her favorite chicken racing towards her, and held out a handful of seed for Lucy to feed from.

Bryce matched his daughter's smiles as they stood amongst the chickens, throwing more feed on the ground. "After you've fed them, we'll gather up the eggs and deliver them to the restaurants in town tomorrow morning," Bryce told them.

When it comes to Cleo, Savannah's pony, Bryce hands over the caring, feeding, and exercising to her when she visits and is impressed with how well she is doing. She genuinely enjoys the responsibilities that come with having a pony. The same applies to the chickens and his two Labradors, Goldie, and Jack. The girls eagerly feed the chickens and dogs, and even help Bryce clean out the coops. To his surprise, the girls don't squirm when shoveling chicken poop and are eager to help. He wonders what chores or responsibilities they have at home with Patricia? Patricia has a housekeeper, nanny and a cook, and most days the girls are driven to school by a chauffeur. "What's left for the girls to do?" Bryce often asked himself. When they're with him one weekend a month, he can at least teach them some good ethics.

"Do you want to see your surprise?" Bryce asked before filling up Savannah's canister a second time.

They both jumped up and down at the same time, their eyes bright and wide with anticipation. "Yes!"

"Okay, put down your cans and follow me," Bryce instructed. He laughed when he saw Jewel scatter a trail of feed in front of her favorite chicken Lucy, who gladly gobbled it up and followed her as they walked over to the redwood chicken house at the back of the coop.

Bryce stopped at the door, his hand resting on the handle, turned his head and looked at his daughters. "Okay, don't let any of the other chickens in as we walk through the door."

Jewel nodded, turned her head, and looked down at Lucy who had continued to follow her. "Lucy, you have to stay here. I'll be right back," she ordered the chicken.

Bryce slowly opened the door and led the girls into a dimly lit space and over to a pen illuminated by red glowing heating lamps. Both girls gushed and squealed when they saw the many baby chicks huddled under the lamp chirping baby chick sounds.

"Daddy! We have new baby chicks!" Jewel squealed. "Can I go inside and pet them?"

Bryce approached the gate and opened it. "Yes, you can. But be ever so gentle with them, and I suggest you sit down on the ground and handle them with care."

Savannah and Jewel entered the pen and slowly took a seat on the ground covered with straw. The baby chicks immediately became louder and began climbing over their legs and hands. "Daddy, they are so cute!" Savannah said with a big smile as she cupped one gently in her hands.

Jewel watched her big sister and copied her actions, gently scooping one up in her hands and kissing it softly on its head.

"I want to take one home," Jewel begged, kissing the baby chick again.

Bryce chuckled. "You know you can't take any of the animals home. We've already been through this, but you can visit and take care of them as long as you want while you are here."

After kneeling next to his daughters, he scooped up a baby chick and placed it on Jewel's knee. "Speaking of which it's getting late in the day, and, as you know, we never rest on the farm. We need to clean out the coops, collect eggs, bring Cleo back to the stable and feed the dogs before the sun goes down."

"Can we make Scotch eggs for dinner?" Savannah asked, picking up another chick.

"We sure can. You've become quite an expert at making them. Have you made them for your mom yet? You said you wanted to."

Savannah shook her head. "No, Mom doesn't want me to make a mess in the kitchen."

Bryce shook his head. "Well, maybe one day she'll let you cook and then she'll find out what a dang good chef you are," he said, patting her head.

"Can you ask her?" Savannah asked with pleading eyes, crushing Bryce's heart.

Bryce released a heavy sigh, his smile diminished. He wished the girls were allowed to do more when they were with Patricia, but his hands were tied. He patted Savannah's knee. "Sweetheart, when it comes to your mother, I don't interfere with anything. I've tried that before. I suggested she'd get you an indoor cat if you can't have a dog, and I've also suggested that she allow you to help Letti cook in the kitchen. I think you're old enough, but she's stuck in her ways and won't agree with any of my ideas. I can't convince her to change. I'm sorry."

Savannah looked down at a baby chick walking across her thigh and released a sigh. "It's okay Dad, I know Mom will never let us do what we can do here."

"I'm afraid not." He patted her leg again. "What do you say we get our chores done and go mess up the kitchen and make some Scotch eggs."

"Okay, Dad," Savannah said, wearing a large smile that instantly cheered up Bryce and matched her smile as he stood up.

I'll even send your mom a picture of you and your sister cleaning out the coops. That should freak her out," Bryce said with a loud laugh as he closed the gate to the pen.

CHAPTER 5

$\mathcal{P}$atricia read the letter over and over, not believing what she was reading. "He's dead," she whispered under her breath before picking up her glass and finishing the remainder of her drink in one large gulp. She looked at the empty glass in her hand. "I need another one," she confessed, her hands shaking. She quickly dropped the letter she held in her other hand onto the desk, stood up, and returned to the bar, where she struggled to pour herself a double shot of brandy as her hands continued to shake. Before returning to her desk, she took a large swig and closed her eyes. "I knew he would die eventually, everyone does, but I honestly thought he would have been dead by *now...*" she mumbled under her breath, returning to her chair to pick up the letter and read it again.

"Maybe it's a prank?" She tried to convince herself, but quickly dismissed the idea. Everything they stated in the letter was correct. She was his daughter, but it was something she hadn't thought about in decades. She had never said his name or spoken of him since she arrived in Manhattan when she was just eighteen years old, 21 years ago. She tried to calculate in her head how old he would have been by now and came to the assumption that he would have been close to 80.

She thought back to that time of her life. It seemed so long ago, and she immediately thought of her Aunt Cassie, her mother's sister. She needed to call her. Cassie was the only one that knew about her father. Even Bryce didn't know.

Without hesitating, she picked up her cell phone from the desk and noticed the time. It wasn't too late, so she located Cassie's name in her contacts and made the call.

After a few rings she heard her aunt's familiar voice. "Patricia, darling! How are you, and how are my beautiful nieces? I've not heard from you in such a long time. Just the other day, your Uncle George and I were reading about you in the paper. You won another case – congratulations, sweetheart! We're so proud of you. We miss seeing you and dining with you and the girls. We'll make it to Manhattan soon, I promise. We try to make it back there at least twice a year since we left. But you must come and see us in California soon. I know how busy you are, but I hope you can make it out here soon. It's absolutely heaven out here. You can't beat the weather, and I know Savannah and Jewel would love it. I can't wait to take them to Beverly Hills for lunch and Rodeo Drive shopping."

Patricia decided to cut her off by using a hint of urgency when she spoke. Cassie had a habit of rambling on, not allowing her to get a word in. On previous calls she'd allowed it, but not this time. "Cassie, that's all very nice, but Savannah and Jewel are just fine and they're spending the weekend with Bryce."

"On that ranch!" Cassie shrieked. "I don't know why you allow them to go there, Patricia. It can't be good for the girls. All those germs on that filthy farm. You're a lawyer, one of the best I might add, and their mother. Isn't there something you can do?"

Patricia was losing her patience. "Cassie, not now, okay? We have this discussion every time we talk. No, there's nothing I can do. Bryce is their father. That is where he lives." She released a heavy sigh; thankful Cassie was silent and that she had the floor. "I'm calling because I just found out One Eye has died." It felt strange saying his name after not uttering it in decades. He had become a distant memory. There was silence. "Cassie did you hear me? One Eye has passed away," Patricia repeated.

"Yes, I heard you. What do you expect me to say? That I am saddened by his death, and he will be missed? How did you find out anyway?" she asked, speaking in a sharp tone. "You've not spoken to that man since you came to live with us in Manhattan. At least that's what I've assumed all these years. Have I been wrong? Have you been in contact with that man? Patricia? I sure hope that is not the case. If it wasn't for him - my sister - your mother, would still be alive today. You know that."

"No, I've not spoken to him or even thought about him in years until I got this letter today."

"Who's the letter from?" Cassie asked.

"An attorney in Alaska," Patricia replied, staring at the letter as she spoke.

"So, he never left. God, I'm so glad I got you out of that awful place. You do realize that you'd still be there today if I hadn't, and you'd not have the success you have today. That's no place for a young girl. I saved you, Patricia. I hope you know that."

"Yes, I know that, Cassie."

"So why is this attorney contacting you? And how did they find you?"

Patricia released a sarcastic laugh. "Cassie - I'm not that hard to find. I happen to be one of the most successful lawyers in New York City, if not the entire east coast."

"You've got a point," Cassie agreed. "But you've not had anything to do with that man in decades, why would they contact you?"

"Because I'm his daughter. His only daughter, I might add."

"Okay, so he's dead. They sent you a letter to let you know. Now you can throw it away and forget about it." She paused. "Wait. Are you upset that he's dead?" Cassie didn't wait for her to answer. "You didn't know the man, Patricia. Look at the life you were living before I got you out of there?"

"To be honest, I don't know how I feel or what I'm supposed to feel for that matter. Am I upset? No, it's like you said, I never knew him, but he was my father and now I no longer have one. No matter how much I want to pretend that he didn't exist, this letter reminded me that he did and now he doesn't."

"Oh, Patricia, don't get all mushy when it comes to that man. He's not worth it. Now throw the letter away and do whatever you were planning on doing this evening and forget about it."

"I can't, Cassie. There's more."

"What do you mean there's more? The man is dead. What more can there be?"

"They are requesting that I call them to discuss his estate."

"What estate?!" Cassie shrieked. "The man had nothing."

"I don't know. But it's the weekend, so I won't be able to get ahold of anyone until Monday. I'll call first thing and let you know what this is all about."

CHAPTER 6

It took Bryce and the girls a few hours to clean out the coops and gather up the eggs, placing them in baskets to take to the house where they would then fill up the egg cartons.

The last chore of the day was to bring Cleo back to her stable, which Bryce let Savannah do by herself as he watched with pride, making sure she took off her saddle and bridle, rewarding her with a carrot.

When they arrived back at the house, Jewel raced through the door hoping to find her Uncle Darren. Her face lit up when she saw him standing at the stove, holding a stainless-steel kettle.

"Uncle Darren!" she screamed, racing to the kitchen and into his arms.

Darren quickly set the kettle down on the stove and embraced Jewel in his arms. "Hey Munchkin, I've missed you," he replied, wearing a big grin, his English accent thicker than his brother's who'd been in the states much longer.

"I've missed you too, Uncle Darren. Did you see all the eggs we gathered?" she said, her face beaming with pride as she pointed to the three baskets that Bryce and Savannah had placed on the counter.

"I sure did. It looks like you and your dad will be heading into town tomorrow to give them to the restaurants." He released his hold on Jewel before turning around. "Hold on a second love, let me put the kettle on. Your Uncle Darren needs his tea. I'm sure your dad will want one, too."

A few minutes later, Savannah and Bryce came through the front door, followed by the two dogs, Goldie, and Jack, both wagging their tails and chasing each other as they ran through the door.

Savannah laughed as the dogs barked playfully before picking up a large red rope toy and indulging in a game of tug-of-war. "I guess they've missed each other," Savannah said, laughing and quickly dodged out of the way to avoid getting knocked over by one of them.

"Yeah, they do this every night. Jack hangs out with your uncle for most of the day on the farm, and Goldie likes to laze around the house, keeping guard. You'd think they hadn't seen each other in ages the way they carry on every night," Bryce joked, walking into the kitchen.

"Kettle's on," Darren said, taking a seat at the large pine table to remove his rubber boots.

"Thanks, mate. Nothing like a good cuppa to end the day. Maybe one day my daughters will grow to love tea." He turned and smiled when he saw that the dogs had settled down and his daughters were now kneeling on the floor petting them. "Hey girls, let's put these eggs in cartons, then we can start making dinner. What do you say?" Bryce asked the girls.

Jewel was the first one to jump up. "Yes! I want some Scotch eggs," she yelled, racing over to the table where Bryce sat removing his boots.

"Okay then, why don't you bring a pile of cartons from the pantry to the table, and Savannah, can you bring the basket of eggs? We can fill up the cartons here and your Uncle Darren can help."

"Okay Daddy, Jewel said, skipping towards the pantry and returning with a pile of egg cartons.

Bryce leaned back in his chair and stared at the boxes of eggs. "Well, we have three days of eggs to deliver tomorrow. We'll be able to visit a few restaurants, give them some eggs, then afterwards I'll take you out for breakfast." He patted the edge of the table and pushed back his chair. "Okay, let's feed the dogs and then it will be time to make Scotch eggs."

Both girls cheered as they left the table and grabbed the dog bowls sitting on a shelf by the back door. They had a system. Bryce remained seated as Savannah led the way to the bag of dried dog food in the laundry room, proceeding to fill each bowl that Jewel handed her with two cups of food. Jewel called the dogs by name to their mats by the back door and placed their bowls in front of them, petting them on the head before walking away and leaving them to eat.

"The dogs are eating, Daddy," she said, returning to the table.

"Okay, both of you, go wash your hands while me and your uncle get everything, we need to make dinner."

When the girls returned from the bathroom, the table was set with rolls of sausage meat, twelve hard boiled eggs that Bryce always kept on hand in the fridge for a quick snack, breadcrumbs, flour, and a dish with four beaten eggs.

Savannah and Jewel had made Scotch eggs many times and knew the recipe by heart. Joining their dad and Darren at the table with an empty plate in front of them, the girls eagerly grabbed an already peeled egg and placed it on their plate while Bryce cut them each a thick slab of sausage meat. Bryce laughed aloud as he watched Jewel struggled to wrap her egg in the sausage meat, but she never gave up or got impatient. It took her a little longer than Savannah to completely wrap the egg, but she succeeded every time. Normally Savannah would make three eggs in the time it took Jewel to make one.

After all twelve eggs were successfully wrapped in sausage meat, the girls proceeded to roll the eggs in the beaten eggs and bread-crumbs while Darren heated up the deep fryer sitting on the counter.

While the wrapped eggs cooked in the deep fryer for the next ten minutes, carefully monitored by Darren, Bryce sat at the table with the girls, and helped them chop lettuce, tomatoes, and cucumbers for a salad.

"I love cooking with you, Daddy," Jewel said, kneeling on one of the pine chairs, tossing the salad into a wooden bowl.

"Did you used to make Scotch eggs with your mom?" Savannah asked, adding cheese as Jewel continued to toss the salad.

Bryce leaned back in his chair and smiled. He loved sharing stories of his childhood with his daughters. He had many from growing up on a farm in England, and wanted to make sure that his girls knew the history of his side of the family and be proud of being half English. Little was known about Patricia's side, mainly because she refused to talk about her parents. The only thing she'd ever told him was that they'd died, and she didn't want to talk about it. Bryce respected her wishes and never pursued the subject, but it saddened him that Savannah and Jewel would grow up with no grandparents, and at least talking about his childhood gave them a little insight into the grandparents they never knew on his side.

"Oh yes, every weekend your Uncle Darren and I made Scotch eggs with our mom, just like we're doing tonight. They were our school lunches for the week. We'd make two dozen - that lasted the week. Our dad loved them too, so mom always made enough for everyone. She would cut them in half and wrap each half in foil. One half we would eat for lunch and then the other half we ate on our walk home from school."

"I remember you telling us you walked to and from school every day, Dad," Savannah said, adding the last of the cheese to the salad. "Wasn't it a long way?" she added.

"We didn't think so because we had no choice. We'd walk three miles to school and then three miles back home," Bryce told her.

"That's six miles in one day!" Jewel shrieked.

Bryce laughed. "Yes, it was, and we did it every day, even in the rain and snow, and let me tell you, young lady, we lived in Yorkshire, and we got a *lot* of snow."

"Why didn't you have a snow day?" Savannah asked, her brow furrowed.

Bryce laughed again. "There was no such thing as a snow day when

I was a kid. Our mom just bundled us up with an extra sweater, a scarf and a beanie and waved us out the door."

"Did our mom used to walk to school too?" Savannah asked.

Bryce paused. "I don't know sweetheart. I didn't know your mom when she was a little girl, you'll have to ask her."

"I asked her once if she had a dog when she was little."

"And what did she say?" Bryce asked, intrigued because he didn't even know the answer.

"It was weird. She told us that what she had when she was a child didn't matter. I had asked her because she had said we couldn't have a dog."

Bryce kept his opinion to himself. He thought it strange that Patricia never shared anything about her childhood with their daughters. Not only did she refuse to talk about her parents, but he was now learning that she never discussed her childhood with Savannah and Jewel. Unsettling thoughts began to stir in his head, and for the first time, he wondered if she was hiding something and found himself questioning how well he actually knew her, the mother of his daughters.

Bryce felt chilled from the sudden awareness that had come to light; questions about his ex-wife couldn't be answered. Where was she born, did she have siblings, what did her parents do for a living? From the time they'd met, they were both focused on their corporate careers and were consumed with climbing that ladder of acceptance within society, and when the girls were born it was all about them. Patricia had to have the best childcare, clothes, and schools for them, and raise them in a molded lifestyle dictated by the elites.

Bryce was thankful he eventually woke up and was able to break the mold and escape the lifestyle that was choking him, but sadly Patricia was still trapped, and his daughters were now caught in that web. As much as he tried to free her, Patricia refused to leave what she called the only world she knew. But was it? Bryce now found himself asking that question. She came from a place she refused to talk about, and he wanted to know why. The corporate world was protecting her from a place she'd left behind for some reason. Bryce wanted to know what that was.

CHAPTER 7

Patricia, numb from the news, sat silently in her chair after ending the call with Cassie. She wasn't surprised by her aunt's reaction; she hated the man, and Patricia understood why. Cassie was correct - her mother Louise would probably still be alive today if she hadn't met One Eye.

Patricia found herself thinking back to that devastating day when her mother was tragically killed in the accident, realizing she hadn't thought about it in decades. She was only eight years old when she'd lost her mother, and since that terrible day her Aunt Cassie had been the only mother figure in her life.

Not wanting to go back to those terrible memories, Patricia shook her head vigorously in an attempt to erase the memories that she'd successfully suppressed for many years until that damn letter arrived today. She picked it up and read it again. "To discuss his estate," she mumbled under her breath. "What is there to discuss?" she said, puzzled, rolling her eyes. "It's like Cassie said, the man had nothing," she stated aloud.

After reading it a few more times, Patricia concluded that it was just a formality letter. Legal documents needed to be signed by next of kin or an immediate relative to finalize the death, and as far as she knew, she was the only next of kin. She had no other siblings, and her father had no brothers or sisters. Comfortable with her assumptions, Patricia soon found herself beginning to relax and believed she had nothing to fear.

No matter how hard she tried to convince herself that she had no feelings for the man that was her father, someone she didn't know, she couldn't shake the emotions she was experiencing; she left him over 20 years ago when she was eighteen, vowing never to return. She suddenly remembered his last words as she walked to the departure gate at Anchorage Airport with a single suitcase. *"You will be back. It's where you belong, Patti. I can guarantee it."*

Determined to prove him wrong, she'd never looked back, never called, and never spoke of her childhood to Bryce or their daughters. She'd removed herself entirely from her father's world and rebranded herself amongst the elites, accepting only the best life had to offer for her and her girls.

Now here she was, two decades later, returning to her past because of some stupid letter. She wondered what One Eye had been doing for the past 20 years. Did he remarry after her mother's death? If he did, then she must have died too, because she would have been the one to finalize his death. She made a note on a nearby piece of paper to ask the attorney about it when she called him.

Sitting at her desk in silence and realizing how much time had passed since she'd left and come to New York, she had so many unanswered questions about her father, and for the first time, felt a hint of guilt. She had no idea what her father looked like when he died. Did he age well? How did he die? Was he alone? These questions never crossed her mind and she never cared about them before learning of his death. Her guilt increased when she had the somber realization that she'd never be able to ask her father anything, and for the first time she felt a chilling void.

For many years she'd successfully avoided any discussions about her childhood or parents and hated to admit it, but unbeknownst to Bryce, he deserved some of the credit for her achievement. When they first met, he'd asked questions about her younger years; she had immediately shut him down, using a vicious, sharp tone, telling him she never wanted to discuss her parents or even mention their names. Being the gentleman that he was, he respected her demands and never brought the subject up again during their entire marriage, or even after the divorce. "Thank you, Bryce," Patricia whispered under her breath, staring at the letter.

But recently, with the girls getting older and asking more questions, especially Savannah, who constantly wanted to compare her childhood with her mother's, Patricia often struggled to give her satisfactory answers. But she stood firm, wanting only the best for her daughters, giving them wealth, success and a life surrounded by the elites. The life she'd left behind could never provide that. It was something Patricia reminded herself of often.

Patricia never believed her past would eventually catch up with her. She'd hidden it so well. She'd done everything possible to erase it and remove herself completely from its existence, but the letter reminded her that she was still his daughter, and that was something she could never change.

Again, she hoped the phone call to the lawyer on Monday would be a simple, easy formality that she'd be able to wrap up in a few minutes and handle secretly, not involving anyone else, especially her daughters and Bryce. She had no intention of telling them. How would she explain the secrets she'd had been keeping? That they'd had a living grandfather that she'd purposely kept from them? The possibilities of their reaction petrified Patricia. No, she could never tell them. They'd never understand that she was only trying to protect them.

Trying to erase the guilt sweeping through her, for the first time in decades Patricia questioned her choices and the decisions she'd made in the past, wondering if they'd been the right ones. She quickly convinced herself they were. If she hadn't fled, she'd never have met Bryce or had Savannah and Jewel. Yes, it was definitely the right choice.

When her thoughts shifted to Bryce, she shuddered. She must keep this from him at all costs. She wouldn't know where to begin with an explanation. She'd kept so much from him for good reason and must keep it that way.

Patricia shook her head and wiped her moist brow with the palm of her hand. She refused to dwell on her concerns any longer and not allow them to ruin the rest of her weekend. She flipped the letter over, preventing the words from jumping out at her, leaned back in her chair and closed her eyes for a moment to settle her mind and think good thoughts. Monday she would take care of the daunting task and continue on with her life. A terrifying thought suddenly crossed her mind; knowing how much her Aunt Cassie liked to gossip, she quickly picked up her cell phone and hastily texted Cassie.

Please keep this to yourself. I don't want anything accidentally getting back to the girls or Bryce. Thanks.

Cassie quickly replied.

I have no intention of telling anyone. Not even your uncle. You should know that, Patricia.

"Yeah right," Patricia whispered under her breath. "I just stopped you before you could," she added, relieved she'd texted her in time.

Satisfied she had pulled in the reins on Cassie before any damage was done, Patricia felt the need to hear the voices of her daughters, Savannah, and Jewel. They were the only ones that made any sense in her life right now.

CHAPTER 8

After the Scotch eggs had cooled on a plate, Darren set them in the middle of the table next to the bowl of salad and handed Savannah four plates from the cupboard. "Here you go. Set these on the table sweetheart, and I'll grab the silverware," he told her.

Goldie and Jack took their usual places underneath the table in the hopes of catching a crumb or two as everyone took their seats.

"Wait! We're forgetting something," Jewel hollered, racing to the front room. "I'll be right back!" she shouted.

Bryce looked over his shoulder from his chair and watched her open the cupboard where he kept all the board games.

Jewel returned a few minutes later, carrying the Yahtzee game, placing the box on the table before taking off the lid. "We always play this when we eat dinner," she said, smiling and handing everyone a score card and pen.

"You're right, Munchkin. Maybe this time you'll let me win," Bryce said, followed by a wink as he pinched Jewel's side.

"No, it's *my* turn to win," Darren said, nudging Savannah sitting next to him. "I've not won in ages because you two girls keep beating me. You gotta give this old man a break," he chuckled.

Jewel laughed. "The dice don't like you, Uncle Darren."

Jewel was right, it had become a family tradition on the farm to play Yahtzee over dinner and on Sunday mornings Before taking the girls home, they'd take turns picking other games to play over breakfast. Savannah's favorite was Monopoly, and Jewel's was Sorry.

Bryce knew the only time they played board games was when they spent the weekend with him. He had asked the girls before what games they'd play at home with their mom. He wasn't surprised when they told him that they only play games on their tablets in their room before going to bed. He remembered the disappointment on Savannah's face when she'd said, "Mom is always too busy to play games."

Only having the girls one weekend a month, Bryce devoted every free minute to them. He hired extra help on the weekend they visited, and was thankful Darren took on extra chores so he could be with his girls. They were growing up so fast. He saw it each time they came, and wanted to cherish every moment with them before they suddenly realized they were becoming too old to hang out with their dad.

After throwing a single Yahtzee die to see who went first, Jewel cheered when she had thrown the highest one and would go first.

"You always go first," Savannah laughed, "but I'm going to beat you this time."

The game connected everyone over dinner, creating laughter, cheers, and unity. In the middle of Savannah's turn, Bryce's cell phone rang, and he was surprised to see Patricia's name on the screen. She never called when he had the girls, and he immediately became concerned.

"Hang on a second," he said, picking up his phone. "Your mom's calling."

Savannah and Jewel had the same surprised look on their faces and sat in silence While their dad answered the call.

"Patricia, to what do we owe this honor?" Bryce said in a cocky tone.

"What do you mean, Bryce? Can't I call to say hello to my girls?" Patricia snapped.

Bryce cracked a laugh. "You never call, Patricia. Text yes, but calling, nah. I think this is a first." He looked at Savannah and Jewel and threw them a wink before he spoke." So, what's up? We're having dinner and playing Yahtzee right now."

"Yahtzee? I didn't know that was still a thing," Patricia admitted.

"There's a lot you don't know Patricia, and *yes*, Yahtzee is still a thing. The girls love the game. How come they don't have it at home?" Bryce asked. He loved putting her on the spot whenever he had the chance.

"We don't have time to play games, Bryce. We're terribly busy here in the city. The girls have a full schedule, you know that."

Bryce hated it when she used her schedule as an excuse for the girl's absence from activities and called her on it every time. "No Patricia, *you're* too busy. Why can't you just come out and say it?"

Bryce sensed her anger when she spoke in a sharp tone. "Look, I didn't call to argue with you. I miss my girls and just want to hear their voices. Is there anything wrong with that?"

"No Patricia, there's nothing wrong with that. I just find it odd as you've never called before." He stopped joking and instead showed genuine concern. "Is everything okay?"

There was a pause before she spoke again. "Yes, why wouldn't it be?" she snapped. "Now, can I please just talk to Savannah and Jewel?"

Bryce wasn't buying it. He knew Patricia well and sensed that she wasn't being truthful with him but didn't want to pursue it with the girls present. He'd get to the bottom of whatever was bothering her over a private phone call he planned to make later. "Yeah sure, here is Savannah," he replied, handing his daughter the phone.

"Hi Mom," Savannah said, smiling. "Are you okay?"

Bryce had put the call on speakerphone and noticed the surprise in Patricia's voice when she spoke. "Yes, of course I'm okay. You sound like your father. He already asked me that." She paused. "I just wanted to hear your voice."

"I know he did, but Dad's right. You've never called us on the phone when we're here."

Bryce chuckled at his daughter and mumbled under his breath. "That's my girl."

"Well, I'm calling you *now*. It's quiet here, and I thought I'd call to say hi and tell you and your sister that I miss and love you very much."

"Where are you at?" Savannah asked.

"I'm at the office. I'll be going home soon, but I wanted to call before I left. You might be in bed by the time I get home."

"No, we won't. We always watch a movie with Dad and Uncle Darren before we go to bed. Tonight, we're going to watch E.T. I love that movie," Savannah said, excitedly. "Have you seen it? Dad watched it when he was my age he told me."

Again, a question about her childhood came into their conversation, shifting Patricia's mood to frustration. This was not what she wanted right now and replied hastily, quickly changing the subject. "No sweetheart, I've never seen that movie. What is Jewel doing?" she asked, trying desperately to change the course of their conversation.

"She's waiting to throw the dice. It's her turn next." Then Savannah asked another question. "Have you ever played Yahtzee, Mom? Dad said he played it with his mom and dad in England."

Patricia rolled her eyes. She was tired of hearing about what Bryce did when he was a child. Why did he constantly have to tell the girls those things? Doesn't he realize that they'd of course want to know about her childhood? She was certain Bryce was doing it on purpose to make her look bad. Why else would he keep bringing up his childhood? What both of us did back then was irrelevant. How can the girls benefit from it? What she thought was important for the girls is guiding them to having successful futures, not what we did and didn't do in the past. "Savannah, I've never played Yahtzee, okay?" Patricia replied impatiently.

Much to Patricia's dismay, Savannah pursued her questioning. "Well, what games did you play, Mom?"

Patricia tried again to take control of the conversation and restrain herself from showing frustration in her voice. "Sweetheart, I don't want to talk about me. I called you and your sister because I miss you both and wanted to hear your voices. It's incredibly quiet when you're not here and Mommy is lonely. I'm looking forward to watching you play the piano in the school play on Monday night. Have you been practicing?"

"Yes Mom, I practiced at home Thursday, after school when you were at work. I told you already."

"Oh, that's right sweetheart, you did. I'm so sorry, I've just been so busy lately."

"You're always busy, Mom," Savannah said, followed by a heavy sigh. "Here's Jewel," she added, passing the phone to her sister.

"Hi Mommy, we're playing Yahtzee. I think I may win this game. Dad is throwing lousy," she laughed.

"That's wonderful sweetheart. I can't wait to see you when you come home Sunday."

Jewel ignored her comment. "Tomorrow we're going into town and giving the restaurants a bunch of eggs. We gathered them up this afternoon," she said, excitement bursting through her voice. "Mommy, we have tons of eggs to give to them," and added, "and Daddy got a bunch of new baby chicks. They are so cute and tiny."

Patricia didn't know what else to say and repeated herself. "That's wonderful, sweetheart."

"Hey Mom, I gotta go, it's my turn. Bye!" and then the line went silent.

Holding the phone and looking at the blank screen, Patricia's heart sank. "They don't even miss me," she mumbled, setting the phone down on her desk. She reflected on the brief conversation she'd had with her daughters that she'd hoped would have made her feel better, but instead all she heard was daddy this, daddy that. "Damn him!" Patricia hissed. Just then her phone rang, and she was startled when she saw Bryce's name flash across the screen. "What the hell does he want now?" she barked loudly before grabbing the phone and accepting the call.

"What?" she snapped.

"Wow! Someone's having a bad night. What's going on Patricia? I stepped outside to call you, so tell me, the girls are inside."

"Nothing is going on, Bryce," Patricia snapped again.

Bryce cracked a loud laugh. "Bullshit! You seem to have forgotten that we were married for five years, and I've known you for fourteen years. I know when something's bothering you. Not once have you ever called here when I have the girls, there's a reason why you did. Yes, I know you miss them, but there's more to it than that, so what is *it,* Patricia? Why the sudden need to talk to them? You obviously called because you needed to feel better. Our girls always cheer us up, I know that. So, what upset you so much that you turned to Savannah and Jewel for a pick-me-up?"

Shit, he's good, Patricia thought to herself before replying. "God Bryce, stop with this nonsense," she said defensively, her voice edgy. "I'm fine, and I'm sorry I called to talk to my daughters, okay? It won't happen again."

Bryce cracked another laugh. "Oh, so now we're playing the pity card. Do whatever you want Patricia, but you can't blame me for calling you out when you do something unexpectedly. Even the girls were shocked you called."

"Look, I have to get back to work. I'll see you Sunday when you drop off the girls."

"Yeah, of course you do. Go hide behind your work, Patricia. That's what you've always done isn't it? Even when we were married, you never talked about genuine issues. I was always the emotional one in the relationship; you were and still are like a bloody brick wall. Enjoy your weekend. I hope whatever is bothering you sorts itself out. I'm sincere about that and talking about stuff really helps - maybe one day you'll figure that out."

Bryce abruptly ended the call, and with tears welling in her eyes, Patricia's lips trembled as she mumbled into the now silent phone. "You don't fucking understand. No one understands," she cried, leaning back in her chair, and letting her tears fall.

CHAPTER 9

Patricia slammed her phone down on the desk and stormed over to the grand window overlooking Downtown Manhattan. She pressed her forehead against the pane of glass as she looked down at the bustling streets filled with cars and people walking in droves on the sidewalks. It was nighttime and the buildings were lit up like Christmas trees, illuminating the skies and streets below. Patricia wondered how many others like her were in their offices rather than at home with their family.

"There's almost two million damn people in this city, and there's not one that I can talk to or confide in," she hollered loudly. "Yeah, Bryce, talking may be good if you have someone to talk to," she yelled, spinning around, and marching over to the bar where she poured herself another generous serving of brandy. She headed over to the couch, placing her drink on the glass coffee table before flopping her body down on a cushion, feeling sorry for herself.

She leaned back, closing her eyes, feeling her head spinning from the copious amounts of brandy she'd consumed in the last hour. Yet again, alone on the weekend, she already knew she wouldn't be going home tonight. It had become a familiar pattern when the girls were with Bryce. She'd dig herself into a depressive state, drink too much to the point where she didn't feel safe driving home. Going home was too depressing anyway. It just reminded her how lonely her life had become. A sad reminder that she really didn't have any friends, just associates and business acquaintances. Every dinner function and trip revolved around some sort of business. There was no fun in her life. She regretted calling the girls; it had been a huge mistake, only adding salt to her wounds and depressive state.

Leaning forward, Patricia ran her hands through her disheveled hair and picked up the brandy glass from the table. She stared at her reflection in the glass before taking a sip. "You need to stop feeling sorry for yourself," she moaned, drawing the glass up to her lips and taking a large gulp. With her head continuing to spin, she glanced around her grand office. "Look at this place. I built it from nothing. People look up to me and respect me. They are jealous of what I have and what I've accomplished. My name is known up and down the east coast as one of the best criminal defense attorneys, and they all want to be just like me," she hollered at the top of her voice as more tears flooded her eyes. She shook her head and took another swig from the glass. "So why am I so god damn depressed?" she cried aloud. She continued to shout as she returned her drink to the table. "This is all your friggin' fault, Bryce! I only feel this way when you have my girls, because when they come home, all they talk about is the grand old time they had on your stupid farm." She released a sob, burying her head in her lap. "We had a good life Bryce, and you had to ruin it by leaving me and buying that awful place. You messed up our lives Bryce, not me - *you* did this! You're why I get in this state every month, and it's because of you that I will be spending my weekend alone in this office, so I don't have to go home to an empty house." She sniffed back her tears and yelled. "It's what I do every god damn month! We were a family, Bryce, and you broke it. Why?" She cracked a loud sarcastic laugh and slurred her words. "You said you couldn't do it anymore. That you were tired of living a lie and pretending you were happy." She laughed again and tossed back her head. "You had the audacity to tell me you needed more! What more could you possibly want? We had everything! A lovely home, nice cars, good education for our girls, money and two successful businesses. I still have all of that by the way, and what do you have, Bryce? A friggin' dairy farm! That's what you have."

She got up and spun around with her arms spread like an eagle and yelled. "You traded all of this for cows! Are you happy now, Bryce? Did you get what you wanted?" She continued to spin her body, standing between the couch and the coffee table, her anger elevated, until she could no longer keep her balance and lost control, feeling her body tumbling toward the floor. Failing to break her fall with her hands, she screamed when her forehead hit the edge of the glass table, and from where she lay face down, she felt the warm liquid of blood trickling down her face. Wedged between the couch and table, she felt a throbbing pain in her arm which was trapped underneath her stomach, twisted in an uncomfortable manner. She tried to push the coffee table away using her body weight to give her some room to move but being solid glass as well as the added solid brass legs, it was too heavy. She managed to turn her head slightly and the blood from her forehead began to trickle at a faster pace until she felt the taste of her own blood on her top lip. "Help me," she whimpered, still unable to move her body, the pain in her arm increasing. She held her breath and tried to inch her arm away from her stomach that was crushing it, but immediately cried out from the excruciating pain she was experiencing. "Oh my god. I need help. I can't move," she sobbed. Again, she tried to move the coffee table with her body weight. She just needed a couple of inches, but she was feeling weak and didn't have the strength to continue. Her efforts were hopeless, and now, out of breath, she soon gave up.

For the next few minutes, she lay motionless on the floor, her head tilted slightly to one side, her head spinning from the alcohol, and her chest heaving from the pain and anxiety she had from not being able to move. "God, this can't be happening," she cried. "What more can go wrong? Please!" she screamed at the top of her voice, trying to ignore the pain from her throbbing arm. "I need help!"

Unable to move, her head now throbbing, adding to her pain, she continued to sob until her cheeks were drenched, her nose runny and her eyes puffy and red. Feeling helpless and drained, she closed her eyes where she was greeted by darkness. She drifted off into a deep sleep, passing out from the alcohol and the wound to her head.

CHAPTER 10

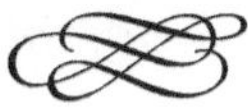

*B*ryce returned to the house after abruptly hanging up on Patricia, frustrated that she didn't confide in him about what was truly troubling her.

He pushed open the back door to the kitchen and forced a smile as he entered the room where he found everyone still sitting around the table. Maybe he had been a little hard on Patricia, but damn it, she always brought out the worst in him. Not once since knowing her had he ever known her to speak from the heart and be completely honest with him. Everything she does is for display and to gain a recognized status in the corporate world.

"It's your turn, Daddy," Jewel said, looking over her shoulder and smiling.

Bryce took a seat next to her and scuffed the top of her head with his hand. "Okay Munchkin, let's see if Daddy can beat you."

After talking to Patricia, Bryce was now distracted throughout the game and tried his best to hide his concerns from his daughters. Cheers erupted from Jewel when all the scores were tallied, and she was proclaimed the winner.

Darren retired to his cottage shortly after the game, and with the two dogs settled in for the night curled up on their beds in the living room, Bryce joined Savannah and Jewel on the couch where they cuddled under blankets and watched the movie E.T.

The next morning, Jewel, as always, was the first to wake up around 6:00 am and came charging downstairs dressed in her black and white polka-dot pajamas, joining her dad in the kitchen who was on the phone with Darren. He raised his hand to hush her and continued his conversation with Darren who'd just completed the first round of milking the cows with the hired help and was about to head into town for supplies. Jewel approached the table and seated herself in her father's lap, wrapping her arms around his neck, waiting for him to finish his phone call.

"Okay Darren, that sounds good, I'll see you in a few hours," Bryce said, ending the call. "Hey Munchkin, how did you sleep?"

Jewel rocked herself in her dad's lap. "Good. I'm hungry and I want to go feed the chickens and see the baby chicks."

Tired from a restless night due to his concerns over Patricia, as well as feeling guilty about the way he'd spoken to her, Bryce found himself forcing a smile.

"One thing at a time, Munchkin. Your sister is still sleeping. Let's get some grub in that stomach of yours and then we'll go wake up Savannah if she hasn't come down already. Then we can all go feed the chickens together after she's had some breakfast."

"Okay, Daddy," Jewel replied, leaving her dad's lap, allowing him to stand and grab some boxes of cereal.

While pouring Jewel a bowl of Captain Crunch, Savannah made her entrance, also dressed in pink pajamas, and joined them at the table.

"Can I ride Cleo this morning?" Savannah asked, taking a spoonful of cereal.

Bryce leaned back in his chair and smiled. "We can only do so much in a day, girls. You can ride her this afternoon after we've delivered the eggs to the restaurants in town, but you can feed her this morning after we've fed the chickens. Darren already fed the dogs and has taken Jack into town with him. We can take Goldie in the truck with us."

"Yay!" Jewel screamed. She looked at Goldie laying at her feet. "You want to go for a car ride, Goldie?" she said excitedly, which instantly brought the dog to her feet, her bright eyes shiny with joy and a wagging tail that would knock you over if you crossed her path.

"Jewel," Bryce said in a harsh tone. "Now why did you do that? We're not leaving for a few hours. Now Goldie thinks we're leaving soon." He looked at the overexcited dog making circles by the back door. "Come lay down, girl. We're not leaving yet." He motioned with his hands. "Come on Goldie, lay down."

With sad eyes, Goldie's tail drooped down between her legs, and with her head hung low, she obediently returned to her bed.

Jewel looked at her dad, unable to hide the guilt she felt. "Sorry Daddy, I just love it when Goldie rides with us."

Bryce immediately sensed her guilt and smiled. "It's okay, Munchkin. When we're ready to go you can be the one to tell her and lead her out to the truck."

Jewel's eyes quickly lit up. "Thanks, Daddy. Can I get dressed now?"

"Yes." He turned and looked at Savannah. "Are you almost done? The sooner you two are dressed the sooner we can get our chores done and head into town."

"Two more bites, Dad," Savannah replied with a mouthful of milk and cereal.

After the girls had raced up to their rooms anxious to begin their day, Bryce, now alone in the kitchen, took the opportunity to text Patricia, thinking it was too early to call her.

You sounded pretty upset last night. Just wanted to make sure you're okay this morning. Shoot me a text. Me and the girls are off into town to deliver eggs.

Feeling somewhat better that he'd attempted to make amends and wasn't expecting a reply for a few hours, he slid his phone into his back pocket and left the table to go grab his jacket from the hook by the back door. Even though he knew Patricia was angry with him (which wouldn't be the first time), she'd always made sure to ease his mind with a text or phone call when he'd expressed his concerns for her.

With his jacket on and Goldie by his side waiting to follow his lead, Bryce was soon joined by his daughters dressed in blue Levis, checkered shirts and tennis shoes, eager to feed the chickens. Smiling at the girls he held open the back door as they skipped by followed by Goldie, wagging her tail.

After feeding the chickens and checking in on the baby chicks, which ended up taking almost half an hour because the girls had a tough time pulling themselves away, Bryce intervened and hurried them along.

"Come on, girls. We have to go," Bryce insisted, opening the gate to the pen, and ushering the girls out.

"Can we go say hi to Cleo?" Savannah pleaded.

"Yes, but we need to make it quick. We still have to grab the eggs from the kitchen," he reminded them.

Savannah wore a large grin as she skipped ahead toward the stable and was already petting Cleo and kissing her face when Bryce, holding Jewel's hand, entered the stable.

"She looks happy to see you," Bryce said smiling as he joined Savannah at the stall.

"I can't wait to ride her later. Can I give her some food before we go?" she asked.

Bryce nodded. "Sure, me and Jewel will wait outside and round up Goldie."

After placing the baskets of eggs on the backseat next to Savannah, Jewel sat in the front with her dad and Goldie in between.

"You may have to sit next to me, Munchkin. Goldie likes to put her head out the window and feel the wind in her face when we drive."

Jewel quickly changed places with Goldie and laughed when she immediately stuck her head out the window as Bryce fired up the truck and headed toward the main road for the 20-minute drive into the town of Easton.

Bryce leaned back in the bench seat, rolled down his window and breathed in the fresh air gently caressing his face. He never got tired of this drive on the quiet country road surrounded by endless beautiful scenery of farmland and miles of shade trees, scattered farmhouses, and fields of cows, sheep, and the sights of wildlife. He loved the openness of the land and how everything was spread out. Not only would he and the girls be dropping off eggs at a local store and two restaurants, but they also had enough to drive over to Trumball and donate them to a few more restaurants and local stores.

Since arriving in the states and falling headfirst into the corporate world in Manhattan, Easton had been the first place where he had a sense of belonging. Life had slowed down immensely. No longer was his only mission being to bleed clients dry of their money to enrich his own. Looking back, he was ashamed to admit that he had used people and quickly discarded them when he could no longer benefit from them. He had become a heartless man with no morals. Greed fed him, and he'd lost all sense of value until he had a rude awakening.

He had sold a business to what would be his last client in the corporate world. Bryce knew the business he was selling was unstable but didn't share his findings with his client. His only concern was the healthy commission coming his way. His client, an elderly man looking to secure a future for his sons, poured his life savings into the deal. Within a year the business collapsed, and the man lost everything.

Bryce received a phone call from one of the sons. That call changed his life. Sitting at his desk, his body became numb when he listened to the son tell him how distraught his father had become and had tried to kill himself. Thankfully, he'd failed, but the remorse of making the deal with Bryce and spending all his savings haunted him, and he felt like an utter failure. The son went on to tell him how he blamed everything on Bryce and that he was solely responsible for ruining his father's life, and how Bryce would have to live with that for the rest of his life.

Listening to the son speak, his voice shaking and at times spitting his words out in anger, tore at Bryce's heart. Everything the son was saying was true; he *had* destroyed the man through his own greed.

That night Bryce couldn't sleep. While his family slept, he paced his luxurious home taking inventory of items that no longer had any meaning to him. The finest area rugs from India, crystal chandeliers in every room, rare artwork adorning every wall and rooms furnished with Baccarat and Ralph Lauren furniture. The best money could buy. But it was all for show. They had to preserve an image that was acceptable to the elites, but that night he realized it was all fake, a mirage, and he no longer wanted any part of it. This wasn't him; this was not what he wanted. Where was his big comfy chair with the cushions that were worn just right and molded to his body when he sat down? Or the two-family dogs laying at his feet. That was a big no-no. Patricia had made it clear that she wanted no pets because they left hair everywhere and destroyed things. His wardrobe consisted of Dior suits. Where were his jeans and sweatpants? When was the last time he felt comfortable when dressed? He wasn't going to live the lie anymore and nor was his family, and after a sleepless night and after the girls had been chauffeured to school, he confronted Patricia while she was being served coffee in the exquisite dining room as she tapped the keys on her laptop.

Bryce took a seat across the table from her. "Patricia, we need to talk," he said in a stern voice.

Without looking up she brushed him off with her left hand. "Bryce, I'm busy, we'll talk later."

"No, it can't wait. I don't want to do this anymore." He shook his head at using the wrong word and quickly corrected himself. "Us! I don't want us to do this anymore."

Patricia ignored him and still didn't look up, but instead continued to type. "Do what?"

Bryce grew impatient, hating that he was being ignored. He reached across the table and slammed her laptop closed. "Damn it, Patricia! I'm talking to you. Can you give me five minutes of your bloody time?"

Patricia gave him a hard stare and hissed her words. "What in heaven's name has come over you? How dare you interrupt me when I'm working."

"That's just it, Patricia, you're always bloody working. You never have any time for me or our daughters. I'm sitting here telling you, I don't want us to do this anymore and you just don't care, do you?"

Patricia rolled her eyes. "I have no idea what the hell you're talking about. Do what?"

Bryce quickly stood up and spun around, his arms spread like an eagle. "This! I don't want to live like this anymore. In this fake world where there are no conversations and every damn thing that we own, which I hate by the way, are all for show." He pointed to a five-foot T McKinney statue in the corner of the room. "That is the most hideous statue I've ever seen. Why do we even own it? What a waste of $15,000." He laughed and shook his head. "I know why. Because it's the best, and if you want to be a part of the elites in this godforsaken city, you have to own crap like that."

Patricia's jaw dropped. "What is the matter with you? You told me you loved that piece?"

Bryce placed his hand on the back of one of the Baccarat dining room chairs, squeezing it tightly until his knuckles turned white. "I lied. Everything I do is a bloody lie. I want to live like a real family."

"What do you mean? We are a family. We have two daughters. You are the father, and I am the mother." Patricia barked. "Last I heard, that was a family," she said sarcastically.

"Those are just titles, Patricia. I want to have home cooked meals, eat around a table where we actually talk to each other. Ask about each other's days. Play games and watch family movies."

Patricia creased her brow. "What? We do have cooked meals. Letti is a fabulous chef and cooks for the girls every night."

"And where are we when they eat? We are at work, and when we come home, most nights they are asleep because we're too busy kissing up to potential clients so we can buy more of this bloody crap," Bryce yelled, waving his arms around the room. "I'm done Patricia, I want us to move away from this city that has turned us into strangers in our own home. I never see you or my kids. We never do anything together, and I'm sick and tired of pretending to be someone I'm not. I grew up on a farm with parents that cooked for their family, took me and my brother places, making memories that I am thankful for. What bloody memories are we making for Savannah and Jewel? What are they going to tell their kids when they are parents? That we sent them to boring ballet and violin classes because we were too damn busy to teach them anything ourselves?"

Patricia jaw dropped at his words. "How can growing up on a farm be better than this? We give our girls everything they need and more than any other girls their age I might add, and that this apartment is in one the most prestigious parts of Upper Manhattan. Many people only wish they had the life we live; you're being ridiculous."

"There you go again. Everything we do or have has to be better than anybody else, but you know what, living on the farm with my parents was real. We sat around the kitchen table, we talked to each other, laughed, and joked. My brother and I washed the dishes after every meal. Every day we were up before the sun and expected to help on the farm before heading to school. My parents taught me the value of a pound and treating people with respect and having good morals. New York has stripped me of all of that and I want it back. I want my daughters to grow up with the same values I was taught and not with a god damn silver spoon in their mouths. This is not how I want to raise my girls."

Patricia raised her voice; she'd had enough of his nonsense. "You're being ridiculous, I think you're going through a mid-life crisis. Now sit down and let me finish my work. I have to meet a client in an hour. I don't know what's caused you to act this way, but I hope it will pass soon."

Bryce ignored her request. His hands in his pockets he began pacing the room. "You want to know why I'm acting this way? Because yesterday I found out I ruined a man's life because of my greed. He lost everything because of me and then tried to kill himself. Do you have any idea how that makes me feel? I was so blindsided over the commission I'd be making if the deal went through that I had no compassion for the fact that the man was pouring his life savings into the deal. Money he'd worked hard for his entire life. When his son called me and told me how distraught his father had become, it made me realize what a monster I had become. What if my next victim is successful and actually kills himself because of my dishonest business practices? I could never live with myself. I can't take that risk, and I'm putting an end to it right now!" Bryce hollered, slamming his palms on the table. "I'm going to give that man a check for every dollar he invested and give him back his life, and then we're going to take our lives back and move the hell away from here!"

Bryce now had Patricia's full attention. "You're serious, aren't you? Because *you're* going through some sort of meltdown, you expect me to give up everything I've worked hard for and follow you on some ridiculous notion that we need to change our lives and who we are. Well, let me tell you something, Bryce Levenick, *I like who I am*, I'm proud of what I've achieved, and I won't change for anyone, not even you. I'm not going anywhere. I'm not uprooting our daughters or their lives to accommodate you. If you decide to follow through with this crazy notion that you need to leave, you will be leaving on your own. The girls and I will not be going with you."

It was at that moment Bryce knew his marriage was over. After the awakening he'd had, he couldn't go back and pretend anymore. He still had feelings for Patricia but knew if he continued to stay, he'd never be happy.

As hard as it was for him to leave, it brought him to Easton, and at least once a month he was raising his girls the way he wanted to, making memories with them. He had no regrets; he was genuinely happy living on the farm. He'd found his heart and morals again, donated to the library, schools, police, and fire department every month. He was on the board for the local festivities: Easter, 4th of July and Christmas, when the entire town came together. Here it was the simple things that mattered: family, community, respect, always watching out for others and loving one's neighbor. Bryce finally felt he was home after leaving England.

CHAPTER 11

By noon Bryce and the girls had made good timing and had delivered the last six dozen eggs to the restaurant, Kittie's Kitchen. Everyone was famished, and Bryce decided they'd all have breakfast before heading home, plus it would give him a chance to try and give Patricia another call. He'd tried three more times since being on the road, had heard nothing and was beginning to get concerned. It wasn't like her not to return his calls or text in a timely manner. Always within a few hours.

He'd also checked in with Darren, who was now back at the farm and had everything under control. "You enjoy the girls, mate; we have plenty of hired help today," Darren told him.

Bryce smiled and leaned back in the seat of the booth as Kittie, the owner of the restaurant, chatted with Savannah and Jewel for a few minutes, asking Savannah about her pony. "I bet you're riding her really good now," she asked her, smiling.

Savannah grinned. "She's such a good pony."

Kittie placed menus on the table. "Maybe one day when you're visiting your dad, I'll try and get away from this place and come watch you ride her."

Savannah's eyes lit up. "That would be awesome."

"Well, I'll do my best. Your daddy does nothing but talk about how good of a rider you are. Now girls, what can I get you to drink?"

"I want orange juice," Jewel replied.

"Me too," Savannah said, picking up a menu.

"And I'll have coffee," Bryce added before reaching for the last menu.

After their order had been placed and the girls were occupied sipping their beverages, Bryce picked up his phone from the table and tried calling Patricia again. After five rings it went to voicemail, and again, he left a message for the fourth time. After ending the call, he located Patricia's housekeeper's number in his phone which he had in case of emergencies when it came to the girls. After two rings she answered.

She spoke with a heavy Spanish accent. "Hello, this is Letti."

Bryce was relieved she answered, "Letti, it's Bryce. I'm trying to reach Patricia but she's not answering her phone. Are you at the apartment? Is she there?"

"No, Mr. Levenick. I am not at the apartment. Mrs. Levenick gave me the weekend off because the girls are with you."

"So, you don't know if she made it home last night?" Bryce asked.

"No, I do not. I'm deeply sorry."

"That's okay Letti, thank you."

Bryce ended the call, his concerns raised.

The girls had obviously overheard his conversation. "Is Mommy, okay?" Jewel asked.

Bryce forced a small smile and patted her head. "I'm sure she's fine. I'm just having a tough time reaching her."

"She's probably at her office," Savannah mumbled, sipping her juice.

"But it's the weekend. She'd be at home, don't you think?" Bryce questioned.

Savannah shook her head. "She's always at her office, whether we're home or not. You know that, Dad."

His daughter made a good point. Why hadn't he thought of that? Still, he was puzzled about why she wasn't answering her phone. He decided to call the direct line to her office and quickly found the number. Holding his breath he counted the rings; after six rings it went to voicemail whereby, he left yet another message. He couldn't deny that he was now worried about Patricia and wouldn't be able to relax until he'd heard from her.

"Mom isn't at the office?" Savannah asked, taking a bite of her pancake.

Bryce shook his head. "I honestly don't know. She's not answering any of her phones," he said, trying not to let his concern show. While eating his hash brown and eggs, Bryce found it hard to engage in a conversation with the girls, his mind consumed by who else he could call to locate Patricia. He drew a blank. There was no one else, no family or friends. It was pointless to call her aunt in California, whom he rarely spoke with anyway. She was too controlling when it came to his daughters, and shared the same disapproval as Patricia when it came to his farm. Patricia really did lead a lonely life.

"Dad, can I go fishing today?" Jewel asked, interrupting Bryce's thoughts.

He turned and smiled at his daughter, her question reminding him that he hadn't given her his gift yet, the tackle box. He quickly decided he'd give it to her when she retrieved her fishing pole from the garage. "Yes, of course sweetheart, after Savannah has ridden Cleo, okay?"

After paying the check and saying goodbye to Kittie, who gave Savannah and Jewel a sucker, they headed out to the truck, where they were greeted by Goldie sitting on the front seat, her head leaning out the window and, tail wagging rapidly.

"Goldie!" Jewel squealed, climbing into the truck next to her and patting her head.

Before getting into the truck himself, Bryce had an idea; even though he thought it was a long shot, he had no other options.

He leaned into the truck on the driver's side, his palms resting on the seat and looked at Jewel and then Savannah who was now seated in the back. "Hey girls, I'm going to make a quick phone call, keep Goldie company until I get back."

"Okay, Daddy," Jewel said, kissing Goldie's snout.

Bryce walked away from the truck, retrieved his phone from his back pocket and called the front desk of the building where Patricia's office was located. No matter what day of the week it was, there was always someone at the front desk.

A deep male voice came on the line. "West Chase Building, how may I help you?"

Bryce took a deep breath. "Hi, I'm trying to get in touch with Patricia Levenick on the 52nd floor, but she's not answering her phone."

"Well sir, it is the weekend. Maybe she's at home. Have you tried her cell phone?"

"Yes, I have, and her office phone. To be honest I'm a little concerned. It's not like her not to return my calls, especially when I have our daughters. I'm her ex-husband. Are you security?"

"Yes sir, I am."

"Is it possible for you to see if her car is in the parking garage, or if she has even signed out since her last visit?"

Bryce knew from working in corporate himself that everyone that enters all workspaces, especially in buildings with thousands of people, that signing in and out was a mandatory procedure for security and safety reasons in case of evacuations, and he also knew there were cameras everywhere in the parking structures.

"One moment, sir. What did you say her name was again?"

"Patricia Levenick. She has the law firm on the 52nd floor."

"Oh yes, we all know Mrs. Levenick. I'll check to see if her car is here as well as the log. Give me one moment please."

"Sure," Bryce replied before being put on hold.

A few minutes later the security guard came back on the line. "Yes, her car is here in her parking spot, and it looks like she used her keycard to enter her office yesterday evening, but I don't see it being used since then. I guess she's been working through the night, sir."

Bryce gasped. "So, she's there! Well, something isn't right. I've called her a dozen times. She's not answering her phone or returning my calls. Is there any way you can go up to her office and check on her? I would really appreciate it."

"Yes, of course, sir. Can I reach you at the number you're calling from?"

"Yes, please do. I'll be waiting to hear from you and thank you."

"My pleasure, sir."

After ending the call, Bryce returned to the truck to check on the girls and found them singing songs to Goldie while she lapped at their faces with doggie kisses. "I'm waiting for a phone call and then we'll be on our way, okay?"

Savannah nodded, "Is it Mom?"

"No, I'll be back in a minute."

Bryce quickly ushered himself away from the truck and anxiously waited for the security guard to call him back, pacing the parking lot while holding his phone tightly.

~

After talking to Mr. Levenick and sensing his concerns, Joe the security guard reached for his communications radio on the desk and called Billy, whom he knew was doing his rounds.

"Hey Billy, it's Joe, you got me?"

A few seconds later Bill replied. "I gotcha, Joe."

I need you to go check on Mrs. Levenick on the 52nd floor. She's in suite 5208, Levenick's Law office. I got a call from Mr. Levenick who's been trying to reach her with no success. Her car is here, he just wants verification she's okay."

"Will do. I'm nearby on the 55th floor; I'll get back to you as soon as I know something."

"Thanks, Billy."

Joe returned his radio to the desk, picked up his cell phone and began killing time waiting to hear from Billy by scrolling on Facebook, checking out the travel groups he belonged to. Living on his small salary and supporting a wife and two kids under six didn't allow him to travel, but he sure loved to dream, and perhaps one day he'd be able to take his family to some faraway exotic place for a vacation.

He wasn't sure how much time had passed, but his dreams were interrupted by the sound of Billy's voice in a panicked state over the radio. "Hey Joe, you need to call 911 right away. I used my master key to access her office and found Mrs. Levenick lying on the floor, hurt and delirious. I see blood on the carpet."

Joe quickly dropped his phone and picked up the radio. "Is she conscious.? Where is she hurt?"

"She's fading in and out. I don't want to move her."

"Stay with her until help arrives. Keep talking to her. I'm calling 911, then I need to call Mr. Levenick back. He's waiting for my call."

"Okay, I'll standby," Billy replied, then added, "I wonder how long she's been laying here?"

"I don't know, but I'm calling 911 right now."

After giving all the information to the dispatcher at emergency and receiving confirmation that an ambulance was on its way, Joe quickly ended the call and immediately called Mr. Levenick.

Bryce didn't know how much time had passed when his phone suddenly rang, but it seemed like a lifetime. He quickly answered after the first ring. "This is Bryce," he said anxiously.

"Mr. Levenick, this is security at the West Chase Building. Mrs. Levenick is in her office, but she's hurt. An ambulance is on its way and one of my staff is with her until they arrive."

Bryce's chest heaved. "She's hurt! What do you mean she's hurt?"

"I'm not sure, sir. The guard said she was passed out on the floor, fading in and out of consciousness. He's not sure of her injuries. I'll know more when the paramedics arrive."

"Good grief. Do you have any idea what happened? Did she tell the guard?"

"No, sir. Like I said, she's not fully conscious. I can call you back as soon as I know more."

Bryce shook his head. "No, I'm going to drive to Manhattan. I'm an hour and a half away. Call me as soon as you know more and what hospital they're taking her to. I'll drive straight there," Bryce said, his voice rushed.

"Will do, Mr. Levenick."

Bryce held his phone tightly as he walked back to the truck, contemplating how to break the news to his daughters without upsetting or worrying them too much. This was the first time he'd had to deal with a situation like this. Since he'd known Patricia and throughout their marriage, he couldn't remember her ever getting injured or being admitted to a hospital.

He forced a smile as he approached the truck, but the girls knew him well and immediately sensed his anxiety.

"Everything okay, Dad?" Savannah asked, her hands clasped together in her lap.

"It seems your mother's been hurt. One of the security guards found her in her office passed out."

Savannah's eyes grew wide. "Will she be okay?"

"Mommy's hurt!" Jewel cried from the front seat, hugging Goldie.

"I'm sure she'll be okay, but an ambulance is on its way, and they'll probably take her to a hospital to check her out."

"I want to see Mommy," Jewel pleaded, tears pooling in her eyes.

Bryce slid into the front seat of the truck and took his daughter in his arms. "I want to see her too, sweetheart. I think we should drive to Manhattan and go see her. What do you say?"

Both girls echoed the same response. "Yes! We want to see Mom."

CHAPTER 12

After dropping off Goldie at the farm and giving his brother the rundown on Patricia, Bryce had Savannah and Jewel pack their bags while he packed one for himself, unsure if he'd have to spend the night in Manhattan. After Darren reassured him that everything was under control on the farm, Bryce and the girls set off in the truck for the 90-minute drive. If the traffic was good, he hoped to reach the city by 3:00 pm.

When he was 30 minutes out, Bryce called Joe the security guard at Patricia's building. He answered right away, greeting him by his name, obviously recognizing his number from earlier. "Good afternoon, Mr. Levenick, I've been waiting for your call."

"Hi, we're about 30 minutes out of Manhattan. How is Patricia doing? Did they take her to a hospital?"

"Yes, sir. They told me they were taking her to Mount Sinai Hospital on 1st Street. She has a broken arm and possibly a broken wrist. She also has a head injury and is suffering from a severe concussion."

"Oh my god!" Bryce gasped. "Do you have any idea what happened?"

"I'm afraid not, sir. The paramedics believe she somehow experienced a nasty fall and became trapped between the coffee table and the couch, unable to move, then eventually passed out from exhaustion and emotional stress."

"Do they know how long she'd been there before she was found?" Bryce asked.

"They do not, sir. They tried asking Mrs. Levenick, but from what I understand she was in so much pain their questions were not answered. I'm sure once they've stabilized her, they'll know more."

"Thank you. I have our daughters with me and we're heading over to the hospital now. I appreciate everything you've done."

"You're welcome, Mr. Levenick. I do hope Mrs. Levenick will be okay."

"Thanks, me too," Bryce replied, sighing heavily.

After ending the call, Savannah leaned forward from the backseat. "Will Mom be okay? Where is she?"

"She's been taken to a hospital. Apparently, she broke her arm," Bryce said, trying to keep his voice calm so as not to alarm his daughters.

"How did she break it?" Jewel asked.

"I have no idea sweetheart, but we're going to head over to the hospital right now. Your mom will be fine, she's in good hands."

"What about her head?" Savannah asked. "I heard the man say she had a head injury."

"I'm not sure. I'll know more after I've spoken to the doctor," Bryce told her, frustrated by all the red lights he had to stop at. Another thing he didn't miss when he moved to Connecticut. He could drive for hours on the open roads without hitting one red light.

By the time they reached the hospital, the receptionist at the front desk said Patricia had already been admitted and was resting in a room on the 21st floor. She told him that she'd broken her arm and wrist and had a severe concussion as well. After giving him directions to the ward, Bryce and the girls were greeted by a friendly nurse at the desk across from the elevator when they stepped out.

"Hi, how may I help you?" she asked, showing her pearly white teeth.

"Hello, I'm Bryce Levenick and these are my daughters Savannah and Jewel. I believe their mother, my ex-wife Patricia Levenick, is on this floor. She was recently admitted," Bryce said.

"Yes sir, she was admitted about an hour ago. Let me call the doctor for you."

"Thank you. I appreciate it."

The nurse picked up the handset of a white phone on her desk. "Give me just one minute," she said before making the call.

Bryce nodded and took Jewel's hand as they waited.

After a brief ten minutes of talking to the young brunette nurse at the desk who basically told him what he already knew, a middle-aged, slender female doctor with short blonde hair approached the desk.

The nurse behind the desk spoke. "Dr. Allen, this is Mr. Levenick. He is here to see Mrs. Levenick."

Dr. Allen extended her hand to Bryce. "Good afternoon. Your wife is doing fine."

Bryce smiled. "She's my ex-wife." He turned and smiled at Savannah and Jewel. "These are our daughters. They've been staying with me this weekend, and we drove here from Connecticut as soon as I found out. Can you tell me what happened?"

Dr. Allen reached out and gently touched his elbow, guiding him away from the girls. "Let's talk over here."

Bryce looked at Savannah and Jewel and said, "I'll be right back. I'm going to talk to the doctor." He pointed to a lime green couch and four matching chairs near a TV. "Why don't you wait for me over there."

Savannah led her sister to the seating area. Once they were seated, Bryce followed Dr. Allen to the far end of the desk.

"So, can you tell me what happened?" Bryce asked again.

Dr. Allen slid her hands into her white coat pockets. "It seems your wife, I'm sorry, your ex-wife, fell in her office which resulted in her breaking her arm and wrist. When she fell, she also hit her head on the coffee table. Your wife is conscious, but a bit drowsy from the pain medications. She told me she fell last night and was laying on the floor next to the couch all night and into the morning until the security guard found her. We set her arm and wrist, and it's now in a cast. We found no severe brain injuries or bleeding on the brain, but, as a precaution, I'd like to keep her here for a few days and monitor her closely."

Bryce's jaw dropped. "Yes, of course." He paused and breathed in heavily. "My god, she must have been there for over ten hours if not more. Did she tell you how she fell? Did she trip on something?"

Dr. Allen hesitated before she spoke and rested her hand gently on Bryce's arm. "Mr. Levenick, I don't want to assume anything, but there was alcohol in her system."

"Are you saying she was drunk and fell?"

"I'm not saying anything. I'm telling you what we found."

"Did Patricia say she was drunk when she fell?"

"She did not, and I have not mentioned the alcohol in her system. I think it's best you discuss it with her."

"Thank you, I will. Can I see her?"

"Yes, I will take you and your daughters to her room."

CHAPTER 13

Holding his daughter's hands, Bryce followed Dr. Allen down the hallway. After turning left, she stopped at room number 2321-B and gently knocked on the door.

They heard a faint "come in," from inside, and Dr. Allen slowly opened the door. "Patricia, you have visitors." She turned and smiled at Bryce. "I'll leave you alone so you can have some privacy."

"Thank you," Bryce said, entering the room with Savannah and Jewel close behind.

"Who is it?" Patricia said from her bed, her voice weak.

Bryce approached the bed; Patricia's eyes were closed. Her right arm was on top of the sheets in a cast up to her elbow, and the right side of her face was swollen, especially above her eye where he noticed stitches and some bruising.

"It's me and the girls," Bryce whispered.

Patricia slowly opened her eyes and squinted to focus. "Bryce, what are you doing here?"

Jewel spoke next, her hand resting on the bed blanket. "Hi, Mommy. How did you hurt yourself?"

Patricia managed a weak smile for her daughter's sake. "Hi, Munchkin. Mommy fell at her office, but I'll be okay." She shifted her stare back to Bryce. "How did you know I was here? There was no need for you to come or bring the girls for that matter. I don't like them seeing me like this."

"We were worried about you, Mom," Savannah said, standing next to Jewel and holding her dad's hand. "Does your arm hurt?" she added.

She lied, not wanting to worry her daughters. Her head was pounding, and her arm ached. "No, sweetheart. I'm just tired."

Bryce squeezed Savannah's hand as he looked down at Patricia. He'd never seen her looking so helpless. "I got worried when you didn't answer any of my calls or texts. I felt bad after our call last night and wanted to apologize. It's not like you, even when we've had some silly argument, not to call back, especially when I have the girls. After not hearing from you I made some phone calls; Savannah was the one that said you might be at the office, so I called the building and had security go find you. You were passed out on the floor. What happened, Patricia? How long had you been lying there before they found you?"

Patricia rolled her eyes. "This is so embarrassing. I don't know how it happened. All I remember is that I got up from the couch and somehow fell, and I guess I broke my arm and wrist on the fall."

Bryce wanted to ask her about the alcohol but held back because their daughters were present. "Well, I'm glad you're going to be okay. Dr. Allen told me they want to keep you in for a couple of days to monitor your head injury. I can take care of the girls, so don't worry about them. I'll make sure they get to school on Monday."

Patricia released a heavy sigh of frustration. "I'm supposed to be in court Monday, I can't stay here."

Bryce smirked. "You don't have a choice. Like it or not, you're going to be out of commission for a while. That arm of yours is going to take some time to heal. You need to set back all your court dates for the next month at least."

Patricia gasped. "I can't do that! My clients are depending on me."

"Then ask someone on your team to stand in for you."

"Oh, this is such a mess. I need to make some phone calls." She scanned the room. "Where's my phone and briefcase? Did they bring it from my office?"

Bryce looked around the room. "I don't see your briefcase here, or your phone." He opened the cupboard next to the bed. "Aah, here's your purse."

"Hand it to me," Patricia demanded, holding out her good arm.

Bryce set it on the bed next to her.

"Do you want me to look for your phone?" Savannah asked.

"Yes, would you sweetheart?" Patricia said, laying her head back on the pillow.

"I want to help," Jewel said, rummaging through her mother's purse with her sister.

"It's not here," Savannah said, returning a pack of mints to the purse.

"Damn it," Patricia hissed. "I need my phone and briefcase."

"We can go to your office and get them," Bryce told her. "Is there anything else you need?"

"No. You'll need my key card; it should be in my purse. What about my car?"

"I'll let security know what's going on. It should be fine there until you're released, and you'll need to hire a driver. You can't drive with your arm in a cast."

"I can't believe this has happened. I'm too busy for this." She was interrupted by Jewel; her words shocked her.

"Is Daddy going to stay at the apartment with us while you're here in the hospital?" Jewel asked.

Jewel had a good question, Bryce thought. It hadn't occurred to him where he'd stay. His main concerns were helping Patricia and taking care of the girls while she was laid up in the hospital. He hadn't thought about where he would take care of them.

"I'm not sure. That's up to your mom," Bryce replied, looking over at Patricia, who couldn't hide her surprise by Jewel's question.

"Well, if he's going to make sure we get to school on Monday, then he needs to stay at the apartment so he can help us get ready. Letti's not there this weekend, so there's no one there to watch us," Jewel announced.

Bryce shrugged his shoulder. "She has a point. I don't mind staying at the apartment with the girls if you're okay with it."

"I guess I don't have a choice, do I?" Patricia replied, her tone flat. "The keys are also in my purse."

"I'll get them," Savannah offered, reaching for her mom's purse on the bed.

"Okay, so the girls and I will head back to the office and grab your briefcase and phone. In the meantime, you get some rest and we'll be back here in an hour or so."

Tears welled up in Patricia's eyes. "I think I left my phone on my desk, and Bryce," she paused.

Bryce looked at her. "Yes?"

"Thank you for coming here."

Bryce took her hand and smiled. "Hey, we may have our differences, but I still care about you, and not only were Savannah and Jewel worried about you, but I was, too."

Caught up in her emotions, Patricia let her tears flow. "God, I hate for you to see me like this. I'm not used to depending on people for help."

Bryce chuckled. "You'd better get used to it. You're going to be laid up for a while, and like it or not, you're going to have to ask for help. I know how stubborn you can be, but now is not the time."

Patricia nodded. "I know." She took his hand, which surprised Bryce. "Like you said, we have our differences, and we now live different lives, but you're a good man, Bryce Levenick. Thank you."

Bryce gave her a caring smile. It wasn't too often he heard Patricia speak from the heart. He found it attractive but kept that to himself. "Pity it took you to break your arm to realize that," he joked. "Me and the girls will be back as soon as we can. In the meantime, get some rest."

CHAPTER 14

$\mathcal{E}$ven though the hospital was less than five miles away from Patricia's office, it took almost 30 minutes to get there because of the congested traffic and endless traffic lights they had to endure.

After parking in the guest parking area, Bryce made his way up to the lobby with Savannah and Jewel where he met the friendly security guard in person.

Bryce rested his arms on the marble counter as Savannah and Jewel studied a statue of a lion in the lobby. "Hi, I'm Bryce Levenick, are you the person that found my wife Patricia Levenick?"

"No sir, my colleague Billy did. My name's Joe, I'm the one that talked to you on the phone. How's she doing?"

"She's doing okay, resting in the hospital with a broken arm and wrist. Thank you so much for your help." He looked over his shoulder to check on the girls and saw they were still occupied by the statue. "She's going to be in the hospital for a few days. Will her car be okay here? She'll probably have a driver come pick it up in a few days when she's home."

"Yes, of course sir. It will be fine here. I'll make a record of it in the log."

"Thanks. I'm going to grab some things from her office. It was nice meeting you."

"Likewise, sir. Let me know if I can be of any assistance," Joe said, shaking Bryce's hand.

"I think we'll be fine, thank you." He turned and looked at Savannah and Jewel. "Come on girls, let's go."

It had been a while since he'd last been in the building, but he still remembered the way. He'd come here to pick up the girls after he was delayed due to a car accident on the I-95, and Patricia had to pick them up from school and bring them back to her office. That was over a year ago, and, since then, he'd left home much earlier when it was his weekend to pick them up in case of an unexpected incident on the road.

The office looked just like he remembered it except for a few new paintings on the walls of a black panther, as well as a scenic landscape by artists he didn't recognize.

Savannah and Jewel immediately ran over to one of the floor-to-ceiling windows and looked down at the street below.

"We are so high up, Daddy!" Jewel squealed.

"We sure are, Munchkin," Bryce replied. He began scanning the office while the girls giggled and occupied themselves with the view. The first thing he noticed was the empty glass on the floor by the couch, then he saw the dried blood on the carpet by the coffee table. He looked over at the bar and saw the opened bottle of brandy on the brass-and-glass bar. "I wonder how much she'd had?" Bryce mumbled under his breath.

He looked over at the desk and saw Patricia's black briefcase on the floor next to it and began to walk towards it when he heard a phone ring.

"That's Mom's phone," Savannah called, looking over her shoulder. "It's coming from her desk."

"I'll get it," Bryce said, quickening his pace towards the desk. He had no intentions of answering her calls, assuming it would be business, and would let the caller leave a voicemail, but when he saw it was her Aunt Cassie, he changed his mind. No matter what he thought of the woman, she had a right to know what had happened to her niece.

"Hello, Cassie."

There was a moment of silence on the other end. "Bryce? Is that you?"

"Yes, Cassie, it is."

"I thought so. I don't know many people with an English accent. Why are you answering Patricia's phone? Is she there with you?"

"No, I'm afraid not. She's in the hospital. Me and the girls are here at her office grabbing some things for her, one of them being her phone."

Cassie gasped. "Oh, my goodness! What happened? Is she okay?"

"Yeah, she's fine. She took a nasty fall here at the office yesterday and broke her arm and wrist. She had a bad concussion and they're keeping her in the hospital for a couple of days so they can keep an eye on her."

"How did she fall?"

"I'm not sure. I wasn't here, but I'll tell her you called, and she can call you back and tell you what happened."

"Oh, would you please?" Cassie pleaded. "God, I wish I were in New York. She's going to need help. Will you be leaving the girls with Letti while she's in the hospital?"

"No, Letti, has the weekend off; I'll be staying with the girls at the apartment and making sure they get to school on Monday."

Cassie couldn't hide the surprise in her voice. "You'll be staying at the apartment with the girls; well, whose idea was that? Yours, I assume."

"Actually no, it was Jewel's idea."

"And Patricia is okay with that arrangement?"

"Yes, why wouldn't she be, Cassie? I'm their dad."

"Yes, of course you are." She quickly changed the subject. "Well, have Patricia call me as soon as she can. Thank you."

"Will do. Bye, Cassie."

After ending the call, Bryce picked the briefcase up off the floor to put her phone inside but discovered that a code was needed to open it, so he instead slid the phone in his jacket pocket before sitting down at the desk for a minute before leaving.

It was then he noticed a letter on the desk, face down, opened and out of the envelope. Being the curious sort, Bryce leaned in to take a peek and flipped the letter over. Within seconds of reading the first sentence he quickly picked it up to read more, checking first to see that the girls were still playing at the window. He was relieved to see that they were.

As he quietly read the letter, he gasped when a sentence jumped off the page and threw his head into a tailspin. He whispered the words aloud, not believing what he was reading.

"We regret to inform you that your father, Billy Matts, has passed away."

He read it again, his brow creased. "What the fuck?" he said, shocked by what he'd read.

Savannah looked over her shoulder at him. "What did you say, Daddy?"

Bryce quickly looked up, realizing he had just cussed aloud. "Oh, nothing sweetheart. I'm just getting some things together for your mom."

He looked at the letter again and checked the date - it was a week ago. *Why did she tell me her father was dead many years ago? Why did she lie?* Feeling his temper rising from the thought that Patricia had deceived him, Bryce folded the letter and slid it into his jacket pocket. "She's got some bloody explaining to do," he hissed under his breath. His anger continued to rise and before he could stop himself, he slammed his hand down on the desk. "And she's going to tell me tonight!" he barked, suddenly standing up.

Startled by her father's outburst, Savannah jumped back from the window. "Dad, are you okay?"

Regretting his sudden outburst, he walked over to the window and smiled at Savannah before patting her on the shoulder. "Yes, I'm fine. I'm just thinking about tonight," he paused. "I'm not sure how long I'll be at the hospital with your mom, and I think I should call Letti and ask her to meet us at the apartment so she can stay with you."

The part he didn't tell his daughters was that he wanted to have a serious conversation with their mother about her father, their daughters' grandfather, whom they'd been told was dead by their mother for their entire lives. Bryce clenched his fists at the thought - not only did she lie to him, but to their daughters, too.

He took a deep breath to calm himself and patted Savannah's shoulder again. "Let me give her a call, okay?"

"Okay, Dad," Savannah said. "I'm getting pretty tired and I'm sure Jewel is too," she said, looking at her sister, lost in her own world, humming a tune and dancing around the office.

Bryce returned to the desk, pulled out his phone and called Letti who answered after two rings.

"Hello, Mr. Levenick, did you find Mrs. Levenick?"

"Yes, I did. She fell in her office and will be in the hospital for a couple of days."

"Oh, no!" Letti cried. "Will she be okay?"

"Yes, she'll be fine, but I have the girls with me. I need to take Patricia some things from her office, but the girls are getting tired and I'm not sure how long I'll be at the hospital. Could you possibly meet me at the apartment and stay with them?"

"Yes, of course. I'll leave right now," Letti told him.

Bryce was thankful that Letti was single and had no obligations at home, not even a pet. "Great, we'll leave now; I should be there within 30 minutes. Thank you, Letti."

CHAPTER 15

*A*fter parking in the guest parking spot at Patricia's apartment, the doorman, whom Bryce didn't know, greeted him, and smiled at Savannah and Jewel, who he obviously knew.

"Hi, Jeff!" Jewel said with a big grin, skipping toward the steps of the building. "This is my daddy."

Jeff nodded. "Good evening, sir. Is Mrs. Levenick with you?"

Bryce gave the doorman a friendly smile. "No, she's not. She's in the hospital, I'm afraid. Nothing serious, I might add. I'm going to be dropping off the girls with Letti and then heading back to the hospital. I'll be back later and will be staying here while their mother is in the hospital. I'll be using Mrs. Levenick's parking space."

Jeff gave an approving nod. "Very good, sir, and I'm sorry to hear about Mrs. Levenick. I will call Miss Letti and let her know you're on your way up."

Bryce was thankful that Letti was waiting at the door of the apartment when they exited the elevator. He hadn't been in the apartment since he left and wasn't ready to deal with those emotions right now. Not only that, but he was also anxious to get back to the hospital and have a serious talk with Patricia.

Without entering the apartment, he smiled at Letti and kissed his daughters goodbye.

"I'll see you tonight. Now you be good for Letti," Bryce said, hugging Savannah and Jewel before returning to the elevator.

Alone in the car, Bryce changed the music to country. He'd had enough of Taylor Swift and drove a little faster, racing the lights and weaving through traffic, the letter he had found constantly on his mind. "How could she lie to me?" he said aloud, his hands gripping the steering wheel tightly. "What the hell is going on, and who the hell is my ex-wife?" he questioned, still not believing what he had read.

When he reached Patricia's room with her briefcase in hand, her phone in his pocket and the letter in his other pocket, he knocked lightly on the door.

"Come in," Bryce heard from inside the room.

Bryce opened the door and was surprised to see Patricia sitting up in bed sipping on a glass of water through a straw.

"Hi, you're awake," he said, approaching the bed holding up her briefcase. "I have your briefcase. Where shall I put it?"

"Oh, great! Over there on the end table would be good, where I can reach it. Did you remember my phone?" she asked.

Bryce pulled it out from his back pocket and held it up. "Yes, it's right here," he replied, setting it on the table in front of her.

"Fantastic. Now I can make some phone calls and get some work done." She looked beyond where he stood. "Where are the girls?"

"They were pretty tired and hungry I'm sure, so I called Letti and she's watching them at the apartment."

"That was probably a good idea. How are they doing? Are they okay? I didn't like them seeing me like this," she confessed.

"They're fine. Now, don't you worry." Bryce took a deep breath and pulled the letter out from his back pocket, setting it down on the table next to her phone. "I also brought this; it was on your desk." He looked at her, his eyes narrowed. "I wasn't sure if you needed it."

Patricia picked up the letter, her brow creased. "What is it?"

"You tell me," Bryce replied, his voice flat.

Bryce waited patiently while she read the letter, noticing the obvious changes in her body language, realizing what she was reading. Her eyes couldn't hide the guilt. The guilt someone feels when they've been caught in a lie. He also noticed the slight tremble of her hand holding the letter.

"Dear god," she whispered.

"I thought your father was dead," Bryce hissed, his jaw tight, his lips narrowed. "But according to that letter, he just recently passed away. What the hell is going on, Patricia? You told me your parents were dead. You friggin' lied to me."

Patricia let the letter fall from her hands onto the table. "I never lied to you," she yelled. "I told you my mother had died, and you never asked about my father, so I never brought him up," she snapped in her defense.

Bryce rolled his eyes, tossing his head back in disgust. "Because you never talked about your father, I assumed he was dead, too. The one time I did bring him up you immediately shut me down by telling me you didn't want to talk about him or your parents, and me, being the thoughtful guy that I am, obeyed your wishes instead of insisting you tell me." He folded his arms, giving her a hard stare. "Well, not anymore, Patricia. I'm done being Mr. Nice Guy. We are going to discuss your parents. You're going to tell me what happened to them and why you had me believe they were both dead!"

Patricia slammed the palm of her good hand down on the table and raised her voice. Her cheeks flushed. "God damn it, Bryce! I didn't lie, I just didn't tell you."

Bryce unfolded his arms and placed his hands on his hips. "Why? Why did you not want me to know about your father? And why would you deprive our daughters of their grandfather? My parents are dead, and I try to tell them as many stories as I can remember about them, so they know a little about their heritage, but you, you've not told them anything. They know nothing about your side of the family. In fact, none of us do." He shook his head. "I'm standing here not knowing who the hell you are. I know nothing about you Patricia, and we were married for five years. How is that bloody possible?"

Patricia released a nervous laugh. "Of *course* you know me. You're being ridiculous. I was your wife, and I'm the mother of our two beautiful daughters."

Bryce shook his head, placing his hands in the front pockets of his jeans. "No, I don't. I only know what you want me to know and what you've told me, which I find now is not a hell of a lot. If someone asked me where you grew up, I couldn't tell them. If they asked me where you went to school, I would have no idea. Did you have any family pets? I could go on, Patricia. I know nothing about you." He gave her a hard stare. "But do you wanna know something?" He raised his hand and pointed his finger at her. "You're going to tell me. I have a right to know." He threw back his head and rolled his eyes. "Shit, our daughters have the right to know. So where do we start? I'm not leaving this room until I know something about your parents and your childhood." He gave her a sarcastic grin and rolled his eyes. "As strange as this may sound, I feel like I'm meeting you for the first time."

Patricia tightened her jaw and matched his stare. "I don't have to tell you anything," she hissed. "It's none of your god damn business. Now leave me alone, I'm tired."

Bryce refused to let her off the hook this time. "Wrong! It is my business because like it or not, you're the mother of my daughters. I want to know for their sake. I don't give a rat's ass where you're from. I'm not married to you anymore."

Patricia raised her good hand up to her brow and closed her eyes. "Damn it, Bryce, will you please just leave me the hell alone? I don't want to do this," she barked.

"Too bad Patricia, you owe it to me and our daughters. There are plenty of things I don't like about my childhood, but it's a part of me and who I am. I hated working on the farm every morning when it was freezing ass cold, walking miles to school, sometimes starving because we had so little food in the house. But my parents did the best they could, and I love them for that." He pulled his hands out of his pockets and folded his arms again. "Let's start with where you were born and where you grew up. I have a feeling it wasn't Manhattan." He shook his head. "Yet another lie you led me to believe. So where were you born, Patricia?"

"For the last time, it wasn't a lie!" she snapped. "You've never asked where I was born."

"That's because I was forbidden to talk about your childhood. Well, I'm asking you now, and I want an answer."

Patricia turned her head away from his piercing stare and remained silent.

"I've got all night, Patricia. Letti is with the girls, and like I said, I'm not leaving until I get some answers from you. If you want to lie there and say nothing, thinking I'll go away and never bring the subject up again, you're wrong." He walked over to the chair against the wall, dragged it to the side of the bed, took a seat and folded his arms in front of his chest. "I'll just sit here until you want to talk to me."

Patricia slammed her good hand on the bed, turned her head and yelled. "Alaska, okay? I was born and raised in Alaska. Are you satisfied? Will you leave me alone now?" she added, turning her head away from him again.

Bryce's jaw dropped. "Alaska? What the hell?" he said, stunned. "You grew up in one of the most amazing places on this planet and you don't want to talk about it? So *that* explains why the letter came from Alaska. Your father still lived there?" He released a sarcastic laugh. "I am *definitely* meeting you for the first time. I don't know you at all."

Patricia turned her head and looked at him. "Stop saying that."

He ignored her remark. "Well, let me see, I do know your mother died when you were young. You at least told me that. So, what happened to her? How did she die?"

Patricia closed her eyes. "Do we have to talk about this right now? I'm really tired."

Bryce shook his head and waved his hand at her. "Oh no you don't. You've avoided this conversation for years. It's time to come clean and let me know who the hell you are."

Patricia leaned her head back on the pillow and closed her eyes as she spoke, knowing she had no choice but to tell him. She took a deep breath. "My mother died in a car accident. She was coming home from work, it was nighttime, and she skidded on some ice, hit a tree, and died instantly. That's all I know."

"I'm sorry to hear that. What was her name and what did she do for a living?"

Patricia looked up at the white ceiling from her bed, her voice flat. "Her name was Louise, and she was a waitress."

Bryce gasped. "A waitress? So, your parents weren't rich?" he said, flabbergasted by what she'd told him.

"No, they *weren't*, okay?" Patricia snapped.

Bryce ignored her outburst. He wanted to know more. "Do you remember her? Was she a good mother? What did she look like?"

"Oh god, Bryce! Can't we have this discussion when I'm home and feeling better?"

"Answer those three questions and I'll be satisfied for now. At least I'll be leaving knowing more about your mother." He pointed his finger at her again. "But we are nowhere near done. I want to know everything."

"Fine," Patricia moaned. "I remember little about my mother. She worked a few nights a week, the rest of the time she sewed quilts and I think sold them to the locals. She homeschooled me in the winters and for the rest of the year I went to public school."

"Sounds like my parents. She did the best she could. That's nothing to be ashamed of. Do you remember what she looked like? I want to know if you look like her?" Bryce asked.

"I don't have any photos of her, I don't know, Bryce." She shrugged her shoulders. "I guess I do. Her hair was the same color as mine. That's all I know." She looked at him. "Are we done?" she pleaded.

"For now, yes, we're done. I'll let you get some rest." He paused and picked up the letter. "So, in this letter the attorney is asking you to call him. When are you going to do that?"

"I don't know," Patricia replied, unable to hide her frustration. She just wanted the conversation to end. "Soon, I guess."

"How about tomorrow? You can then tell me what they said." He gave her a hard stare. "And no lies - you tell me everything." His eyes widened. "In fact, I want to be here when you do. I'll come here tomorrow at noon. You can call them then."

Patricia returned the hard stare. "I don't want you here!" she shrieked.

"Too bad. You've kept me in the dark long enough. Well, not anymore. I'll see you at noon." He thought about bringing up the alcohol content in her blood the doctor mentioned, but he could see she was tired. Her eyes were now closed, and he told himself that there would be plenty of time to have *that* discussion. With his hand on the doorhandle ready to leave, he suddenly remembered her Aunt Cassie and turned to look at Patricia. "Oh, by the way, Cassie called when I was at your office," he told her.

Patricia opened her eyes and raised her head. "My aunt?"

Bryce nodded. "Yes. How many Cassie's do you know? I told her you're in the hospital and that you'd call her later."

Patricia's face turned a shade of white, like she'd seen a ghost. Her eyes wide. "You talked to her?"

"Yes, I saw her name on the screen of your phone and thought she had a right to know where you were. I didn't want her to worry. Is there something wrong with that?"

Patricia quickly shook her head. "Er, no, it's fine. Thank you; I'll call her in a little while."

"Okay then, get some rest and I'll be here tomorrow," he said, leaving the room.

CHAPTER 16

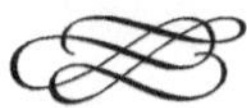

*a*fter Bryce had left and Patricia was alone, she covered her face with her palms and closed her eyes, feeling utterly angry with herself and her carelessness. "Damn it! Why did I leave that stupid letter on my desk?" Then she remembered that she'd moved to the couch and stupidly gotten drunk and then fell. She suddenly had a horrendous thought, opened her eyes, and quickly sat up. She feared Bryce had mentioned the letter to Cassie? Maybe he knows more than he's letting on and is testing me, to see how much I'll tell him?" she said aloud. "I wouldn't put it past him," she hissed, pulling herself to an upright position. *I need to call Cassie*, Patricia said to herself as she searched for her phone, finding it on the nightstand.

She quickly grabbed her phone and located Cassie's number.

After three rings Cassie answered. "Patricia! What in heaven's name happened to you? Bryce said you were in the hospital."

"I am, but I'm fine. I took a fall in my office, broke my arm and wrist, and had a slight concussion. It's nothing serious."

Cassie gasped. "You broke your arm! How on earth did you manage to do that?"

"I don't know, Cassie. It just happened." She quickly changed the subject. "What did Bryce tell you?"

"Just what you told me. I was surprised when he answered your phone. I knew something was wrong straightaway."

"Did you talk about anything else?" Patricia asked, holding her breath, anxiously waiting for Cassie's reply.

"No. We weren't on the phone for more than a minute."

Patricia released a heavy sigh of relief and rested her head back on the pillow, massaging her forehead with her hand that was free of a cast. "Thank god."

"What's that's supposed to mean?" Cassie asked.

"He knows about One Eye. He saw the letter on my desk and brought it here."

"He read your mail?" Cassie asked in disbelief.

"I left the letter unfolded on my desk, and he read it. He now knows One Eye recently died, and he also asked about my mother. He's so angry."

"He asked about Louise? Well, he's known for years that she passed away when you were a child. You've never kept that from him. How much did you tell him about One Eye? It's none of his business by the way, now, is it?" Cassie remarked, her tone sharp.

"Not much. He started asking questions about my mother."

Cassie quickly interrupted. "What kind of questions?"

"Just the basics. Her name, the color of her hair, things like that."

"And what about One Eye? What did you tell Bryce about him?"

"Nothing. I told him I was tired and managed to avoid his questions. But he insists on being here tomorrow when I call the attorney in Alaska. When I objected, he made it clear that I had no say in the matter. Then he also demanded that after the call with the attorney I tell him everything. I've never seen him so angry. You know how laid back of a man he is. It takes a lot to fuel his fire." Patricia released another heavy sigh. "What in heaven's name do I tell him? I'm not prepared for this," she confessed, her anger rising. "You're right, it's none of his damn business, but he thinks it is." Patricia's tone became sharp. "He said that he has a right to know, and that the girls should know the history of where they came from." Patricia held her hand up to her forehead again, kneading it with her fingertips, digging her nails into her skin. "Oh, this is such a mess. I should have known my past would catch up with me eventually. When the girls find out that their grandfather was alive all this time, they'll probably hate me."

"Now, don't you say that," Cassie snapped. "You're their mother. They're not going to hate you. You did what was best for them and I'm sure they'll understand. That's what mothers do."

"How would you know? You aren't a mother," Patricia reminded Cassie.

"That's a little cruel, Patricia, and uncalled for. George and I wanted children, but after my third miscarriage we stopped trying. We just couldn't put ourselves through anymore heartache. Your uncle and I have accepted the fact that we'll never be parents, but you, Patricia, have been like a daughter to us, and we've always wanted what's best for you."

A rush of guilt swept through Patricia. "I'm sorry. I don't know why I said that. You have been incredibly good to me."

Cassie resumed their previous conversation. "So, just how much are you going tell Bryce?" she asked, sounding concerned.

"As little as I can. Just enough to satisfy his sudden thirst for my life," Patricia confirmed.

"Will you call me when you have a chance? I want to know everything that was said," Cassie pleaded.

"Yes, of course, but I'm not expecting it to be a very pleasant conversation. I just want to get all of this bullshit over with and get back to my normal life."

"Well, I'm going to let you get some rest," Cassie told her. "I will be anxiously awaiting your call."

"I'll call you as soon as Bryce leaves. I can't talk to you while he's here." She raised her voice and added, "and whatever you do, *don't* call me. I have no idea how long Bryce plans on sticking around. He's so unpredictable; I mean, look how he left me. One day we were a family, happily married, and then poof, the next day he was gone. No warning of any kind. I'll speak to you tomorrow."

After ending the call, Patricia rested her head on her pillow and closed her eyes. For the first time in decades, visions of her mother entered her mind. She hadn't thought about her since she'd left Alaska. Once she'd left for New York, it had become easier to forget about her. She was no longer in the home where everything around her reminded her of her mother, and she no longer had to listen to her father talk about her every day, listening to all his stories as he brooded over their photos after her death. Once in New York, the images of her mother and the sound of her voice soon began to fade over the years.

Patricia was too young to realize just how heartbroken her father had been over her mother's death and how much he loved her. She'd never thought about it until now, but her mother had given up her life to be with him. She loved him just as much as he loved her. She never knew how they'd met until she arrived in New York to go live with her Aunt Cassie.

Cassie had told her the story, and that there was nothing she could do to persuade Louise to come home. She had fallen head-over-heels in love with the man.

She told Patricia that she had taken Louise on a cruise to Alaska for her birthday. It was the first time the sisters had taken a vacation together. It was before Cassie met her wealthy husband, George, and for Cassie, the trip was a time for her and Louise to bond, but that never happened. To this day Cassie regrets taking her sister on that cruise. It was the last time she saw her, because Louise never got back on the ship or left Alaska. Cassie returned home alone.

Docked for a few hours in the small coastal town of Whittier, the two sisters took advantage of the time to go explore. Louise had bumped into Billy while looking at a map of the area as they walked through town.

"That was his real name. One Eye came later," Cassie had told Patricia. "I'll tell you how he got his nickname another time," she added, and carried on with the rest of the story. "I could tell immediately that Louise was smitten by the man. I can't for the life of me understand what she saw in him. He was dressed in blue jeans, a red and black plaid shirt and rubber boots. His hair was a dark chestnut color, medium length that almost reached his shoulders, and he wore the ugliest black beanie on his head. I don't think he'd shaved in a couple of days, either. I'll never forget how Louise looked at him with her big brown eyes when they first met, curling the ends of her hair around her fingers, and flirting a big smile." At that moment Cassie had taken Patricia's hand, her eyes pooled with tears. "That was the day I lost my sister," she said, and went on. "Within ten minutes of the two flirting with each other, and me standing there rolling my eyes and being totally ignored, he invited us for lunch at a local cafe. Of course, Louise didn't refuse, and I had no choice but to tag along."

Cassie told Patricia how she watched her sister's infatuation with the man from across the table. "Louise couldn't take her eyes off him. She laughed out loud at his stupid jokes, looked at him with dreamy eyes, and constantly brushed her body up against his. She was acting like a teenager who had a high school crush," Cassie told Patricia. "And by the end of our meal, she was resting her head on his shoulder as he cradled her in his arms, telling her he hadn't believed in love at first sight until he'd met her. I wanted to vomit, but Louise took his words seriously, and when I stood up to head back to the cruise ship, Louise announced she wasn't going, and looked at Billy with those dreamy eyes of hers and said she wanted to stay in Alaska and live with him if he'd have her. I thought it was the most ridiculous thing I'd ever heard and hoped that she was joking, but she wasn't, I could see it in her eyes. After Louise's announcement, Billy cupped her face in his hands and kissed her hard on the lips, then jumped up from his seat and danced a jig around the table as Louise looked on, giggling like a child."

Cassie told Patricia with tears in her eyes that traveling back to New York alone on the cruise ship without Louise was one of the hardest things she'd ever had to do. She wanted to be happy for her sister but couldn't. Cassie thought Louise had lost her mind, and no matter how hard she tried to talk her out of the ridiculous life-changing decision that she'd made in haste, it was useless. Louise was suddenly, foolishly in love, and was going to throw away her entire life for a man she'd known for less than two hours. Cassie decided to let her have her fling, assuming that in a week she'd realize what a mistake she'd made and board the next cruise ship back to New York. Content with her decision and mindset, Cassie helped Louise gather her things, pretending to be happy for her, holding back her tears and waving at her sister and newfound love from the ship as they stood arm-in-arm on the dock.

But Cassie's predictions never happened. Louise called her every week for the next few months, telling her how happy she was and what a wonderful man Billy was. They were married soon after and then Patricia was born. The calls became less frequent, and Cassie never saw her sister again.

After reminiscing on the story of her mother, Patricia squeezed her eyes shut to stop the tears from flowing. She didn't know how to handle the flood of emotions she was experiencing. Up until now she'd locked them up, prevented them from escaping. But now they had control of her, and it was overwhelming.

"Oh my god, I can't believe this is happening," she whispered under her breath, then talked to herself aloud. "I have a week of court cases coming up that I'm going to have to push back, and I don't need this shit in my life right now." She shook her head vigorously, trying to pull herself together, refusing to allow her emotions to control her when she needed to focus on her clients - something she'd been able to do for the past 20 years. She shifted her thoughts and reached for her briefcase. It was time to get to work and make some phone calls.

CHAPTER 17

Relived to be out of Patricia's room, Bryce marched down the hallway of the hospital towards the elevators. His fists were clenched, and his anger had peaked. If he had stayed any longer, he wouldn't have been able to control what came out of his mouth. He was still in shock that for the past fourteen years, five of which he thought were a decent marriage. He'd no idea who the mother of his daughters was. How was he going to explain this to Savannah and Jewel? Wait! No, it wasn't up to him. This was Patricia's mess, and she could damn well clean it up herself, Bryce thought as he waited for the elevator.

"Good night, Mr. Levenick," the nurse called from her desk, waving her hand, and smiling.

Bryce turned his head and forced a smile. "Good night."

When he reached his truck, he welcomed the solitude and silence, refraining from starting it up for a few minutes as he leaned back in his seat. He closed his eyes and collected his thoughts. He had so much he wanted to ask Patricia, but just hearing about her mother, Louise, was all he could manage to focus on. She was their daughter's grandmother that Patricia had purposely kept from them. He slammed his right palm on the steering wheel. *How could she?* And he had a feeling he had just scratched the surface. How much more was there? He wanted to know everything about her. Bryce felt so betrayed. His chest heaved and his breath was rapid. He needed time to let the news of the estranged relative sink in before asking Patricia about her father, whom he'd discovered had been alive the whole time since they'd met, and she bloody knew it. It was obvious - she had never shared her life with him. She'd never informed her father of their wedding, the big reception at the Waldorf Hotel, or even the birth of his granddaughters. "Why!" Bryce yelled aloud, slamming his hand down on the steering wheel again. "It makes no bloody sense."

Shaking his head in disgust, Bryce started the truck and put it in reverse. As he drove along the streets of New York, illuminated by the night lights of the buildings, he reminded himself that he also needed to have a talk with Patricia about her alcohol consumption.

Traffic was much lighter on the way to Patricia's apartment, and he managed to hit every green light, putting him in somewhat of a better mood. After parking his truck in Patricia's parking space, he managed to reprogram his thoughts and adjust his sour mood before reaching the apartment.

Before unlocking the door to the apartment and entering, he took a deep breath and composed himself. On entering, the scent of Patricia's perfume lingered in the air. "The place still smells like her," he whispered to himself.

He closed the door behind him and stood quietly in the foyer. It was like he'd never left. Everything was exactly how he remembered. The same paintings hung on the walls. Photos of the girls and Patricia adorned the glass and white metal console table with a grand decorative mirror hanging on the wall above it.

Bryce picked up a picture of Savannah playing the piano with her mother looking on proudly. He noticed his daughter's smile didn't seem genuine, compared to the many joyous ones she expresses when staying at the farm. Another photo of Jewel caught his attention, and he picked it up. She was at the dance studio doing ballet. Patricia stood next to her beaming with pride, but Jewel had her arms folded and wasn't smiling. "God, our girls don't like doing this stuff," he mumbled. "Can't you see that, Patricia?" he hissed.

Hearing footsteps behind him on the black-and-white tile of the foyer, Bryce looked over his shoulder and saw Jewel running towards him.

"Daddy, you're home. We just had dinner."

Bryce returned the picture he was holding to the console and greeted his daughter with open arms. "Hey, Munchkin. What did you have?"

Letti fixed us my favorite, spaghetti, and meatballs. She made a lot. Do you want some?"

"Sure, I'm famished. Lead the way," he said, taking her hand.

Jewel squeezed her father's hand and skipped in front of him to the kitchen, where he found Letti loading the dishwasher. She stood up straight, still holding a plate, and smiled.

"Oh, Mr. Levenick, you're here. How is Mrs. Levenick?"

Bryce returned the smile. "Hi, Letti. Patricia is doing fine. She'll be home in a couple of days, so, I'll be staying here with the girls and getting them off to school. I'll stay out of your way and let you do whatever you normally do when you're here," he laughed.

Letti chuckled. "Oh, you won't be in my way, and I'll be here to help Mrs. Levenick when she comes home."

"Thank you, Letti, I appreciate you coming in on such short notice." He turned and looked at Jewel who had grabbed an apple from a white porcelain bowl on the glass table. "Where's Savannah?" he asked.

Jewel took a bite of her apple before answering. "Probably in her room on her tablet."

"Can you go tell her I'm here and we'll play a game before you go to bed."

"We don't have any games here, Daddy," Jewel replied. "Mommy doesn't like playing games."

"Okay, then we'll watch a movie."

"Oh, goodie. Mommy doesn't like watching movies either."

Bryce rolled his eyes. "What do you do?"

"Mom works, I watch TV most nights for an hour before bed, and Savannah is always on her tablet," Jewel told him.

"Bloody hell," Bryce hissed under his breath. "Well, tonight is movie night. Go get your sister," he ordered Jewel, angered by what she'd told him.

After eating his plate of spaghetti, Bryce headed to the living room to wait for Savannah and Jewel to join him. Like the foyer and kitchen, the living room was exactly how he remembered it. Time had also stood still in this room. The white grand piano sat in front of the large floor-to-ceiling windows that overlooked Central Park and the Manhattan skyline, with pictures of the girls on its polished surface. Like the rest of the grand six-bedroom, five-bath apartment, two of the walls were floor-to-ceiling windows filling most of the rooms with natural light. The remaining walls and all the furniture, including the couch and area rug on the hardwood floors, were white. Just like all the other rooms it was pristine, everything in its place. For Bryce it felt more like a showroom than a place where family would gather.

The girls came down the ornate spiral staircase, both dressed in their white silk pajamas and furry white slippers, joining him on the couch.

"We're really having movie night?" Savannah asked.

Bryce stretched out his arms across the back of the couch, embracing both his daughters, one on either side.

Bryce grinned. "We sure are. Where does your mother keep the remote?"

Savannah pointed to the white coffee table. "In that white box."

Bryce chuckled; he should have known it had its own little box. Patricia hated any kind of clutter and tried to keep all surfaces clear of any unnecessary items. He leaned forward, opened the lid of the box, and grabbed the remote. "Let's see what's on," he said, aiming the remote at the flatscreen TV mounted on the wall.

After a few minutes of scrolling the channels, they unanimously decided to watch Beethoven. Snuggled together on the couch, his daughter's heads resting on his chest, Bryce squeezed their sides.

"Hey, we should have Letti bring us some popcorn," Bryce suggested.

"We're not allowed to eat in here, only the kitchen," Savannah told him, her head still resting on his chest.

Even though the rules were still the same, Bryce had an idea. "Then I guess we'll watch the movie then get a snack in the kitchen before you go to bed."

Savannah and Jewel smiled, cozying closer to their dad where they remained for the entire movie. After it ended, Bryce gave them a gentle squeeze and smiled. "How about we go eat some ice cream and then I'll tuck you both into bed."

"Yes! I want ice cream," Jewel squealed, standing up quickly. "Come on, let's go," she shrieked, skipping through the living room towards the kitchen.

"Okay, we're coming," Bryce said, laughing at her excitement.

"We never have ice cream this late," Savannah said, taking a tub of chocolate-flavored ice cream from the freezer. "Mom won't let us eat anything past 7:00 pm."

"Well, your mom isn't here, and Letti has already left and won't be back until 10:00 tomorrow morning."

Jewel clapped her hands. "Goodie! I like it when you stay here, Daddy."

Bryce opened one of the cupboards that he remembered housed the dishes; sure enough, they were still in the same place. He grabbed three white bowls, waited for Savannah to put the tub of ice cream in the middle of the table, then scooped some into each bowl.

"Okay girls, eat up and then it's bedtime after you've cleaned your teeth," Bryce told them.

"But I cleaned them earlier," Jewel whined.

"Yes, but now you're having ice cream, so you'll need to brush them again," Bryce told her.

"Okay," Jewel replied, taking a spoonful of her ice cream.

Once their bowls were rinsed and put in the dishwasher and their teeth brushed, Bryce followed Jewel to her room first. "I'll come say goodnight to you after I've tucked Jewel in," he told Savannah as she walked towards her room.

Bryce followed Jewel as she skipped along the hallway and waited for her to open the door to her bedroom. He immediately noticed the vast difference in decor from the room here compared to her room at his farmhouse.

Her room at the apartment could have been any of the guest rooms; white walls, white furniture, and bedding. The pictures hanging on the walls in glass frames were obviously picked by Patricia, consisting of young ballet girls posing, dressed in tutus. Patricia never allowed thumbtacks or tape on any of the walls, and he assumed that was still the case. The room didn't represent any of Jewel's tastes nor have any toys on display or on her bed. He did notice a white bench across the room where under the seat was probably storage. Bryce was guessing it held all her toys. Hidden and no clutter, just how Patricia liked it.

At the farmhouse he allowed the girls to decorate their rooms however they wanted. It was their space and he wanted them to know that. Thumbtacks and tape were okay.

Jewel collects stuffed animals, so each time she visits, Bryce would always buy her a new one to add to her collection where she would proudly display it on her bed with the many other ones. Her walls are adorned with Taylor Swift and The Little Mermaid Posters. Toys are always scattered across her bed, and a variety of books line the pine bookshelf against the wall.

Savannah's room at the farm is cozy, with a brown faux fur bedspread and a CD player where she blasts Taylor Swift's music. A beanbag, posters of her idols and photos of her pony, Cleo, are taped to the walls, and CDs and books line the pine shelves.

Bryce kissed Jewel on the forehead as she lay in bed looking up at him. "I'll see you in the morning, Munchkin. We'll make pancakes and eggs for breakfast, okay?"

"Okay, Daddy. I love you," she said with a sweet smile from beneath the covers.

"I love you, too. Sweet dreams."

After turning off the light and closing the door, he walked over to Savannah's room at the end of the hallway and found Savannah already in bed. Her room looked exactly like Jewel's; white walls, white furniture, no clutter, and pictures of a young girl playing the piano. He smiled at his daughter, walked over to her bed, and kissed her on the forehead. "Sweet dreams. I'll see you in the morning."

Savannah nodded and smiled. "Goodnight, Dad."

After closing the door to Savannah's room, Bryce's curiosity crept in, and he walked over to the double-doors of the master suite. A room he once shared with Patricia, where they'd made love and took showers together. There was a time when they were happy before the demons of the city swallowed them up and their priorities and values were pushed to the back burner.

Bryce took a deep breath before opening the door to what was now Patricia's room. Slowly he entered the room and took another deep breath. It was white from floor-to-ceiling just like the rest of the apartment. The King size bed was different from what he remembered. The headboard was white metal and more ornate. He also noticed the lamps on the end tables were different, too. As he stood in the room feeling alienated, he stared at the bed and couldn't help himself from wondering if other men had shared her bed since he'd left. He quickly erased the thought, asking himself, *why does it matter? They're divorced.* He reminded himself that he'd had a couple of flings since moving out, so why shouldn't Patricia? But he couldn't lie to himself, he did feel a twinge of jealousy at the mere possibility that Patricia may have had romantic rendezvous with other men within this room and in that bed.

Bryce didn't like where his head was taking him and quickly turned around to exit the room. After closing the door behind him, he headed back downstairs to turn off all the lights, deciding to call it a night. Even though he wasn't on the farm, he knew his inner clock would kick in and he'd be awake at 4:00 am, just like every other day.

Tomorrow he'd call Darren to check in and see how things were going on the farm.

During his next visit with Patricia, he intended to find out more about her parents and what the letter involved.

CHAPTER 18

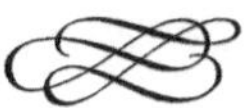

*J*ust as he'd predicted, Bryce woke up at 4:30, just before the sun rose. After making a pot of coffee, he took a seat at the table in the kitchen and called Darren, knowing he'd already be up and probably getting ready to do the first milking of the cows. Bryce wanted to catch him before he started.

Darren answered on the second ring and sounded his usual cheerful self. "Hey mate, how's the big city treating you? And how's that ex-wife of yours?"

"I can't wait to get out of here," Bryce joked. "I can't believe I stuck it out so long, living here. Patricia is doing okay. She broke her arm and wrist and has a concussion. She'll be home from the hospital in a day or so. Will you be okay running things until I get back? And how are Goldie and Jack?"

"Yeah, everything is okay. Like I said, we have extra help. No worries here mate, all is good. The dogs are sleeping with me in the cottage. Don't you worry about them, they're fine."

"Okay, that's good to know. I just wanted to call and check in. If you need me, you know how to get in touch. I'll be staying here at Patricia's apartment with the girls until she gets out of the hospital."

"You're at your old place?" Darren laughed. "That's gotta feel weird, mate."

"It does, but it's just for a couple of days. I think I'll be able to handle it. It's a good reminder of why I left this place. I gave Patricia the option to come with me, but she's molded her life around the elites of this crazy city. Sadly, I don't think she'll ever change."

"Yeah, I think you're right there. Anyway mate, chores are calling. I'll see you when you get back. Tell Savannah and Jewel that Uncle Darren says hi."

"Will do. Cheers, mate."

After ending the call, Bryce poured himself another cup of coffee and headed out onto the veranda of the kitchen to watch the sun rise over the city. It was almost 5:00 and cars and taxis were already filling up the streets as well as pedestrians, most carrying briefcases and wearing office attire, making their way to their offices, where they'd spend their days prisoners of the corporate world. Something Bryce didn't miss.

He was surprised to see all new furniture on the veranda. He remembered he had personally picked out the black cast iron set with the luxurious grey cushions and matching round end tables. Patricia had told him it was too masculine. She had since replaced it with new furniture that was more modern and, of course, all white. Bryce took a seat on one of the oversized lounge chairs, setting his cup next to him on the square fiberglass table and looking at the New York skyline before him. The sun was beginning to make its appearance and the sky was brilliant shades of red, orange, and yellow.

"Well, good morning, New York," he said, picking up his cup and raising it to the sky. "What do you have in store for me today?"

Bryce remained on the veranda for the next half hour, reminiscing about the many mornings he'd spent out here with his morning coffee. It used to be his quietest moments, and his favorite place to start the day as Patricia made her phone calls, checked her emails and whatever else she did every morning. They never spent their mornings together or chatted over coffee. Patricia was too busy for that and spent most of her mornings on the phone, while Letti tended to the girls. He realized by the time he moved out they'd become strangers living under the same roof.

His thoughts were interrupted by the sound of Savannah calling him.

"Dad are you in here?" she called.

Bryce stood and returned to the kitchen and found Savannah standing in the middle of the room, still dressed in her white silk pajamas.

He approached her and gave her a loving hug. "Hey, how are you doing this morning, sweetheart? Is your sister awake?"

"I'm good. I don't know if she is. I didn't go in her room."

"No worries, she'll come down when she wakes up. Do you want some orange juice?"

"Yes, please," Savannah replied, taking a seat at the table.

Bryce grabbed two glasses from a cupboard and set them on the table. "We can start making the pancake batter if you'd like. I'm sure Jewel will be up soon," he told her, grabbing the carton of orange juice out of the fridge.

Jewel joined them in the kitchen fifteen minutes later, also in her pajamas, clutching a white teddy bear in her arms.

"Hey Munchkin, how did you sleep?" Bryce asked, watching Savannah stir the pancake batter.

"Good," Jewel replied, rubbing her eyes. "Can I help?"

"Of course you can, love. After breakfast, I'm going to jump in the shower, and I want you two to go upstairs and get dressed. Letti will be here at 10:00 to watch you both while I go to the hospital to see your mom," Bryce said, taking the batter from Savannah and walking over to the stove where the griddle was heating up.

Just as Bryce remembered, Letti was her punctual self and arrived at 10:00 on the dot, ready to take over the household and tend to the girls.

"Morning, Letti," Bryce called from the couch where he sat with Savannah and Jewel, reading one of Jewel's books with them.

"Good morning, Mr. Levenick," Letti replied, taking off her coat. "What time are you leaving?"

"I'm going to take the girls for a walk in Central Park in a few minutes, and then I'll leave around 11:00 and let you fix them some lunch."

Letti nodded and headed to the kitchen.

Bryce didn't leave the apartment until 11:30. He hadn't been to Central Park since he'd left New York, and once again found himself reminiscing on the times he'd spent there. The last time he strolled through the park Jewel was three, and he'd pushed her in a stroller. Being close to where they lived, it had been a frequent activity that he'd do with the girls on weekends; on rare occasions Patricia joined them.

"Can we go on the Carousel?" Jewel begged as they left the pond after watching and feeding the ducks.

It had always been a favorite place for the girls, located in the part of the park called Sheep's Meadow.

"Does Letti still bring you here and take you there?" Bryce asked, taking Jewel's hand.

"Not as often as she used to," Savannah replied. "But when she does, we always go to the Carousel."

"Okay, we have time for one ride, then we have to get back."

"Yay!" Jewel squealed, skipping ahead.

Bryce finally arrived at the hospital later than expected, around 1:00 due to heavy traffic. He had texted Patricia, letting her know he was running late. She never replied and he assumed she was resting.

When he entered her room, he found her awake, sitting up and on her laptop, her briefcase next to her on the bed. She looked up and gave him a weak smile.

"Sorry I'm late," Bryce said, approaching the bed. "Is there ever a time in New York when there's no traffic? I've forgotten how long it takes to get around in this city. I could have walked here faster," he groaned.

"Most people do walk," Patricia said, keeping her eyes focused on the screen of her laptop. "How are the girls? I miss them."

"They're good. We watched a movie last night, had a pancake breakfast this morning and then went for a walk in Central Park."

"Happy to hear you have time to do such things," Patricia said in a sharp tone, still focusing on her laptop.

"It's a matter of making time. If you don't, they'll both be grown up and will no longer want to do things with us. You're missing out Patricia, I keep telling you that."

Patricia finally looked up and gave him a hard stare. "And I keep telling you that I have to work!" she snapped.

Bryce stood by the bed, his hands in the front pockets of his jeans. "I'm not going to stand here and argue with you. Let's do what I came here for. Let's make the phone call to the attorney in Alaska, and I want you to put the call on speaker so I can hear everything he says."

Patricia leaned back against the pillows and smirked. "I've already called them. Everything has been taken care of."

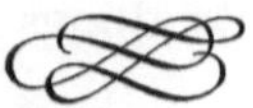

CHAPTER 19

Bryce felt his cheeks flush, his heart race with anger and his lips narrow when he spoke. "You did *what?*"

Patricia folded her arms and gave him another condescending smirk. "I called him first thing this morning. I wanted to be done with all of it, and I am. I didn't have time to wait around for you."

Bryce raised his voice, pulling his hands out of his pockets and raising them in the air as he spoke. "You're lying in a friggin' hospital bed for Christ's sake! What do you mean you don't have time?" Fueled with anger, his heart raced as he approached her bed, pointing his finger at her, his eyes narrowed. "You're full of shit Patricia, fourteen bloody years you've been hiding your past from me and your daughters and I'm sick of it."

Patricia waved a hand in the air. "Ssh. Keep your voice down."

"I will not keep my bloody voice down. You owe it to us. You made that damn call before I got here because there's something you don't want me to know, now what the hell is it?"

Patricia raised her voice a notch. "I just don't want you listening to my personal business, okay! I'm not your wife anymore, and I don't owe you an explanation."

Bryce snarled his words. He couldn't remember the last time he felt such anger toward a person. "Wrong Patricia, you owe it to your daughters, and yes, I do have a right to know, because I would like to know the heritage of my girls."

"Then I will have a talk with our daughters when the timing is right, if that's your concern."

Bryce rolled his eyes as he threw back his head and let out a loud sarcastic laugh. "Yeah, right! Savannah is eleven years old, and you've told her nothing. It will never be the right time for you. Patricia, whatever it is that you've put off all these years not telling them is not going to go on any longer, and I'm telling you now, I'm going to be there when you do."

Patricia's smirk disappeared from her face and was replaced with worry. "What do you mean? I told you I would talk to them."

Bryce shook his head. "Nope, it's not going to work this time, Patricia. You've had eleven years to tell Savannah." Bryce sat on the edge of the bed and picked up her phone that was next to her. "Now, I'm going to tell you what you're going to do and I'm not leaving this room until you do it. Letti is with the girls, so I have all day if you want to be stubborn about it. Shit I have all night, I'll just call Letti and ask her to stay later. First, you're going to tell me what business was taken care of with the attorney when you called them, and I conveniently wasn't here!"

Patricia shrugged her shoulders. "We discussed everything. It's all done, there's no need to call them back. They are going to send me the papers to sign, and they'll take care of selling everything. It was all completed in a matter of minutes."

"Not so fast," Bryce said, raising his hand. "What will they be selling?"

"His property, of course," Patricia told him.

"Where he lived?"

"Well, yes, of course. He only had one house."

"How would I know that? I know nothing about him, remember? Well, that's about to change." Bryce shook his head. "You're going to call him back and tell him not to send the papers."

"What?" Patricia shrieked. "It can't be sold unless I sign the papers!"

"Oh, you're going to sign them, but in person."

Patricia sat up straight, her body stiffened. "I'm not flying all the way to Alaska to sign some papers when I can sign them here for the cost of a stamp. You're insane. I'm not doing it Bryce."

"Oh yes you are. In fact, are all his personal belongings still in the house?"

"Yes, as far as I know, nothing's been touched."

"Even more reason to go. The girls may want to have something that belonged to the grandfather that *they never met.*" He spat out the last three words. He paused and looked down at her, his hand resting on the wall next to the bed. "Tell me something - is it the same house that you grew up in?"

Patricia didn't answer right away, avoiding eye contact with him. When she spoke, it was barely a whisper, "yes, it is."

Bryce leaned in. "Did you say it was?"

Patricia nodded without speaking.

"Then we're all definitely going. I want to see where the grandparents of my daughters grew up, too."

Patricia looked up. "You? You never mentioned you wanted to go. First you insist I go, and now you want to drag the girls and yourself into this. No, Bryce. I'm not doing it. You can't make me."

"What's the big mystery around your parents? Why have you refused to tell me anything about them? Were they that bad?" Bryce paused. He had a terrible thought. "Wait. Did your father hurt you in some way? Is that why you left?" Guilt swept over him. Had he pushed too hard? "Did he, Patricia? If so, all the secrecy would make sense."

Patricia shook her head; she immediately saw an opportunity to end Bryce's questions and stop him from probing into her past, but she couldn't do that to her father's memory. She may have done some dreadful things in her life, but she couldn't stoop that low. "No, he didn't hurt me."

Bryce's guilt quickly left as fast as it had appeared. "Then why,

Patricia? I just don't get it. Like it or not, I'm getting to the bottom of this. Now, we can do this the easy way or the hard way. Your choice."

Patricia arched her brow. "What do you mean?"

Bryce picked up her phone again. "Well, you can call the attorney like I asked, or I can go home tonight and tell the girls that their grandfather just passed away and that he was alive all these years. Then it will be up to you to explain to them why you've never allowed them to meet him. At least with the first option we can discuss it together, the best way to tell them before we go to Alaska."

Patricia's jaw dropped. "You wouldn't!" She smacked the sheet of the bed with her good arm in frustration. "Why are you doing this?"

"Why have you held secrets the whole time I've known you?" He folded his arms. "So, what's it going to be?"

Patricia closed her eyes. She needed a moment. Everything was happening so fast, and her world was about to come crashing down. She opened her eyes and looked at Bryce, her face pale. "Fine. I'll call the attorney. Hand me my phone."

Bryce handed it to her and smiled. "Good choice and put your phone on speaker."

After a few rings, a male voice came on the line. "Edwards Law Firm Alaska."

Patricia spoke in a friendly tone. "Mr. Edwards, this is Patricia Levenick. We spoke earlier today."

"Yes. You just caught me. I was just about to close up the office for the day. My assistant has already left. How can I help you?"

She looked at Bryce before speaking and he gave her a slight nod. "I've changed my mind. I'd like to sign the papers in person."

"You're going to come to Alaska?" Mr. Edwards asked, unable to hide the surprise in his voice.

"Yes, that's correct. Please hold onto the documents until I get back to you. I need to make some travel arrangements."

"Yes, of course. Not a problem at all. They're safe here. I'll wait for your call. Have a good evening."

"Thank you, you too," Patricia replied before ending the call.

Bryce smiled at her. "See? That wasn't so hard now, was it?" He turned and walked to the other side of the room, dragged a chair to the side of her bed and took a seat. He folded his arms and smirked. "Now it's time for a little chat."

Patricia didn't smile, afraid of what was coming next. "A chat about what?"

"Your dad. I know a little about your mom. Now it's time for you to tell me about your dad."

CHAPTER 20

*P*atricia squirmed beneath the sheets, her discomfort on full display. Bryce had her cornered and there was no escape. What she'd feared since leaving Alaska 20 years ago had finally emerged. Her past had finally caught up with her.

Bryce leaned back in his seat, his hands resting on the arms of his chair. "You can begin by telling me your father's name."

Patricia spoke without looking at him, "Billy Matts, but everyone called him One Eye."

Bryce creased his brow, "One Eye? That's a weird name. Did he actually have one eye?"

Patricia nodded. "A few years before my mother died, walking up to the house in the snow, he fell and hit his face on a rock buried beneath the snow. His eye socket was shattered, and he lost his eye. Since then, everyone called him One Eye."

"Did he wear an eye patch? "Bryce asked.

"Yes, he did." She paused. "Now that you mention his patch, I never saw him without it."

"When was the last time you saw him?" Bryce asked.

"When I left home at eighteen," she replied, looking up at the ceiling.

"And you've never been back?"

"No," Patricia said, her tone flat. "There was no need to."

Bryce moved his hand up to his chin, puzzled by her confession. "But why? He was your dad, Patricia. Didn't you ever pick up the phone and call him? Or wonder how he was doing?"

"No," Patricia said in a cold voice.

"So, what did he do for a living; was he a lawyer like you?"

Patricia let out a loud laugh. "No. Do you think my mother would have been a waitress if he was?"

"So, what did he do?"

Patricia paused and closed her eyes, taking a deep breath. It was painful for her to say the words and her tightened skin showed it. "He was a fisherman."

"A fisherman!" Bryce bellowed in surprise. "Crikey! I wasn't expecting that." Bryce rubbed his chin in deep thought. "So, you and I had similar backgrounds."

Patricia turned and looked at him. "What do you mean? No, we didn't. You grew up in England; how is that like Alaska?"

"Both our parents made a living off the land and worked damn hard," he chuckled. "And all these bloody years I thought you came from a rich family. Bloody hell Patricia, you certainly played me. I don't know you at all."

"Stop saying that!" Patricia snapped. "I'm sure there are things about you that I don't know."

Bryce shook his head. "Nope, can't think of anything. I'm an open book. I've told you everything. So why did you leave Alaska and not tell anyone about your parents or where you're from?"

Patricia raised her voice, her cheeks now flushed with frustration. She wanted this conversation to end. "Because I never wanted to go back. I didn't want to give him the chance to make me feel guilty. If I did, he would have talked me into staying. I couldn't let that happen under any circumstances. I wanted more than what he could give me, and if anyone knew that my father was a fisherman, it would have spoilt my image with the people I was getting acquainted with in New York."

Bryce corrected her. "You mean the elites." He leaned forward and gave her a stare, his brow creased. "So, in other words, you were ashamed of your father?"

"I don't know. I just knew I didn't want to be there, so I left. Can we stop now? I'm getting tired."

Bryce didn't push her this time. He'd heard enough. He was looking at a stranger. He didn't know Patricia at all. Something wasn't adding up, though. What young girl leaves the only home she knew, never to look back, only to abandon everything related to her real self? He was determined to get to the bottom of her story and her past.

"I'll stop, but I'd like to book a trip to Alaska soon. You, me, and the girls are going on a trip." He paused and gave her a hard stare. "You do realize we have to tell the girls about all of this?"

"Bryce, I can't just pack up and take off to Alaska. It's going to have to wait." She didn't acknowledge his comment about telling the girls.

"Yes, you can, Patricia. Stop making excuses; it's what you've been doing since I've known you. Now is the perfect time to go. You are going to be laid up for a while with your broken arm. I don't think you'll have a problem having one or a few of your associates fill in for you."

"And where are we supposed to stay, Bryce?" she hollered. "My parents lived in the middle of nowhere!" she hissed, continuing with her outburst. "Do you honestly think we can stay together under the same roof? May I remind you that we're divorced. How do you think that's going to work out?"

Bryce chuckled at her remarks, always looking for excuses. "We may be divorced Patricia, but I still consider you a friend. You're the mother of my daughters for god's sake. We were no longer compatible which is why I left, not because I didn't love you, you know that. It was one of the hardest things I had to do, but I did it for my sanity, and as much as I miss having my girls with me 24 hours a day, I know in my heart it was the right decision. The girls are getting to experience life outside of the corporate world once a month. Which quite frankly was choking me and my morals, and whether you see it or not, it's doing the same to you."

Patricia waved his remarks off with a gesture of her good arm. "You're being ridiculous. I have morals, and we had an incredibly good life together. I'll admit that my life can be hectic at times, but it's a rich fulfilling one with amazing opportunities for Savannah and Jewel. They could never get that on your damn farm, Bryce. Be honest with me - could they really?"

"Life is what makes you happy Patricia, not what you have or what you think others expect from you. I can honestly say I've never been happier. Can you say the same thing? Are you happy, Patricia?"

"Of course I'm happy. What a stupid question."

Bryce shrugged his shoulders. "I don't think it is. I'd never asked myself that question before, I just assumed I was, but when I did, I had to think about it. I mean, I *really* had to think about it and dig deep inside of myself for an honest answer. You didn't do that when I just asked you. You answered right away, not giving it any thought. One day you should take the time and ask yourself the same question and take the time to answer it *honestly*. You may be surprised."

"Enough of this nonsense, Bryce!" Patricia snapped. "I know I'm happy, I don't have to question myself." She quickly changed the subject. "So, you believe we can stay together for a period of time while we go on this silly adventure you insist upon? I doubt there are any hotels nearby, so what do you suggest?"

"We can stay at your father's house. If your dad lived there up until his death, then I'm sure it's still livable. I want to experience where you lived as a child, and I'd like our daughters to as well."

Patricia gasped. "You can't be serious! It was a shack. There's not enough room for all of us, and I don't want to subject our daughters to such conditions. Don't you understand that that's one of the reasons I left?"

"I'm not going to argue with you, Patricia. We're doing this, and you might be surprised when the girls actually end up loving it. Our daughters love being outdoors and in touch with nature. I see it on their faces every time they stay with me on the farm. Here in this ugly city, they are living a bloody image that you've portrayed, and it's not real. When will you understand that?" He rested his palms on the edge of the bed, leaned in and spoke in a serious tone, giving Patricia a hard stare. "Now, tomorrow when they release you, we will book this trip together and tell the girls. Do you understand?"

Patricia knew she'd lost the battle; his body language told her he was going to stand his ground. There was no escape, she'd have to go through with this. "Okay Bryce, you win, but I'd like to request one thing."

"And what would that be?"

"*I'd* like to tell the girls once we're in Alaska. It would be easier for me to tell them when we're at the cabin, surrounded by my father's things."

Bryce understood her logic and also thought she'd tell them more once they were there. "Okay, I like your idea and I'll go along with it. But you do know that the girls will want to know why we're suddenly going to Alaska, and together, something we've never done since our divorce, and I'll tell you right now, I won't lie to them."

"I don't want to lie to them either." She thought for a moment. "How about we tell them that I have business in Alaska to tend to, and I need your help with it, so we've decided to make it an adventure and stay in a cabin. That wouldn't be lying. It's *sort* of a business trip and I *do* need your help, I guess, by giving me support when I tell the girls."

Bryce entertained her idea in his head for a few moments. "Okay, I'll go with that. So tomorrow while Savannah and Jewel are in school, I'll come pick you up and we'll book the trip. We'll tell the girls when they get out of school, and then I'll head back to the farm. I've left Darren alone long enough, and I need to get back. This city is choking me."

Patricia nodded nervously. "Okay. Sounds good." She was not looking forward to the thought of returning to a world she'd left behind so long ago.

CHAPTER 21

After Bryce had left, Patricia immediately reached for her phone, her body trembling, her heart racing, and called Cassie. She slammed the phone down on the bed in frustration when the call went to voicemail. Too upset to leave a message and not knowing what to say, she closed her eyes tightly and wished she'd just torn up the letter and ignored it. Whatever was left behind by her father she had absolutely no use for. The few dollars she would inherit from whatever needed to be sold were not worth this turmoil in her life. If she'd just tossed the letter in the trash, none of this would be happening, and Bryce would never have known about it.

"God, how could I have been so stupid!" she yelled aloud, slamming her good hand down on the bed. "I don't want to do this, and I sure as *hell* don't want to go to Alaska," she yelled. "But Bryce has me cornered and won't take no for answer. Damn him!"

With her eyes still closed, she thought about Savannah and Jewel. How was she going to explain this to them? Being older and wiser, Savannah's reaction feared her the most. Would this destroy their relationship? She was only trying to protect them. Would Savannah understand that and forgive her?

She didn't know if she could handle going back to the cabin - the thought terrified her. Did Bryce realize what he was asking of her? She could barely picture it in her mind it'd been so long since she was last there. She did remember that it only had two bedrooms, and the entire house was probably smaller than the opulent kitchen at her apartment. How were they all going to stay in that tiny rundown shack of a cabin? Patricia wondered. She didn't know if she could live in such conditions, especially with Bryce, whom she hadn't spent any length of time with since he'd left. This was all too much to deal with; how was she ever going to get through it?

The ringing of her phone disrupted her thoughts, and after looking at the screen and seeing it was Cassie, she quickly picked it up.

"Cassie! Thank goodness you called back."

"Yes, I saw that you called. You sound terrible. Are you okay?"

"No! I'm not okay!" Patricia cried. "Bryce knows about One Eye, and he wants to go to Alaska. And, get this, he wants to see where I grew up, and not only that, he insists on taking the girls! What am I going to do? I can't do this, Cassie!"

Cassie released a loud gasp, shocked by her words. "You can't go to Alaska! What if you never come back?" Cassie screamed into the phone.

Patricia creased her brow, confused by what Cassie had said. "Of course I'm coming back. What makes you think I wouldn't?"

"My sister Louise never did. You can't go, Patricia. Please tell me you won't do this."

Patricia was stunned by her outburst. "Cassie, I think you're over-reacting. Do you honestly think I'd give up my luxurious lifestyle in New York for a shack in Alaska? Come on now, be reasonable."

"Louise had a good life; me, a sister that loved her, and a loving family. She gave it all up for that man. You may do the same. I can't lose you, too. I've raised you like you were my own daughter after Louise passed away."

"I can reassure you, Cassie, I have no intention of staying in Alaska, and trust me, Savannah and Jewel would think their mother had lost her mind if I even suggested such a thing. I would never subject my daughters to a life of such terrible conditions, but the thought of Bryce accompanying us is going to be the hardest part. We're divorced, and he's expecting me to spend time with him like this is some sort of family vacation. He's insane! Trust me, I can't wait for this to be over and I'm sitting on a plane on my way back to New York."

"You promise me that, Patricia?" Cassie said, her voice shaking.

"Yes, I promise you. I honestly don't want to go, but Bryce is insisting. I have no choice. He's adamant about going."

"But why take Savannah and Jewel?" Cassie interrupted. "Why subject them to Bryce's ridiculous demands?"

"Because he believes that the girls have a right to know about their family background."

"So, the girls also know about One Eye?" Cassie asked.

"No, not yet. I was able to convince Bryce to wait until we're in Alaska before telling them. I don't know why, but I think it will be easier if I tell them at the cabin." She paused. "I have to say, as much as I'm dreading this trip and spending time with Bryce, I'm thankful that he'll be there when I tell them. I'm fearing their reaction, especially Savannah's."

"Well, it's like I've always told you since you came to New York. When you first arrived, I said that your life begins *now*, there's no need to dwell in the past. It's irrelevant to what lies ahead of you and what you can achieve. Your past would only be detrimental regarding the opinions of those you want to impress. You can tell Savannah the same thing; you know it's true."

"Yes, you did, Cassie."

"Everything you've done, Patricia, is for your girls and to protect them. There's nothing wrong with that. You must realize that."

"I do, but will the girls?"

CHAPTER 22

$\mathcal{B}$ryce spent the ride back to Patricia's apartment deep in thought, still finding it hard to believe that Patricia grew up in a small cabin in Alaska. It suddenly dawned on him that he'd no idea even what town she had been - he'd forgotten to ask. All of that would be revealed when they booked their trip, he reminded himself. The fact that her parents were poor like his, struggling to make ends meet, and that her mother had to work as a waitress blew him away. She had hidden it well all these years, and he couldn't wait to see what else she'd been hiding. He was determined not to leave any stone unturned.

By the time they'd return from Alaska, he wanted to know every-thing there was to know about his ex-wife, and his gut was telling him that he'd just skimmed the surface.

When he returned to the apartment, he found Jewel in the kitchen helping Letti make homemade pepperoni pizza. Jewel looked over her shoulder, holding a handful of grated cheese.

"Hi Daddy, we're making pizza for dinner."

Bryce approached her, knees bent, and hugged her. "Hey Munchkin, that looks delicious. I can't wait to try some." He scanned the kitchen. "Where's Savannah?"

"She's in her room," Jewel replied. "How's Mommy?"

"She's doing well, sweetheart. She'll be coming home tomorrow."

"Yay!" Jewel screamed with joy, sprinkling cheese on the pizza "What time is she coming home? We have to go to school tomorrow," she asked.

"I'm going to pick her up in the morning and she'll be here by the time you get home. Why don't you go get your sister? I'm going to take you to the park before dinner."

Jewel got down off the stool she was kneeling on. "Okay, Daddy," and skipped out of the kitchen.

Bryce smiled at Letti as she picked up the pizza and slid it into the custom-made pizza oven. "Thank you, Letti, for being here. When will dinner be ready?"

"In about 45 minutes. I'm going to make a green salad as well as a fruit salad with melons, grapes, and strawberries."

"Great, that's enough time to take the girls to the park. We'll be back soon."

After the girls had left for school the next morning, Bryce spent the next hour on the phone with Darren, getting updates on how the running of the farm was going before going to pick up Patricia from the hospital. He wasn't surprised when Darren told him there'd been no issues, and everything was running like clockwork. Bryce had full confidence in him.

"I knew I had no worries about leaving you in charge for a few days," Bryce said. "How would you feel about running the farm for a few weeks, with help of course, while I take a trip?" he asked.

"A trip? This is all very sudden. Where are you going, mate?"

"I'm going to Alaska with Patricia and the girls; not sure when yet. We're going to book it after I've picked up Patricia from the hospital. She's coming home today."

Darren couldn't hide the surprise in his voice. "Wait, you're going to bloody Alaska with your ex-wife? What the hell is going on Bryce?" He paused. "Wait, don't tell me you and her are getting back together? This sounds like a family vacation to me. Did she cast some sort of spell on you, mate?"

Bryce laughed. "No, it's nothing like that, trust me. Call it family business. I'll tell you all about it when I get home, and by then I'll have some dates for you too, if you're okay with running the farm that is?"

"Sure. I've got no problem with that. But why Bloody Alaska?"

"I'll just say that we're going back to Patricia's roots. You won't believe what I've found out since I've been here, and I can't wait to learn more."

"Wow! I can't wait either," Darren laughed. "So, when will I see you? I think Goldie and Jack are missing you, mate. Goldie has been sleeping on your bed and Jack at the foot of it."

"I thought the dogs were sleeping in the cottage with you?" Bryce asked.

"So did I, but the second night, they wouldn't have it. Both of them scratched at the front door, whining like crazy. I finally gave in, grabbed their dog beds, and took them back to your house. In the morning, they came back to my cottage barking at the front door," he laughed.

Bryce matched his laughter. "They know how to get their way. Anyway, I'll be leaving this awful city late this afternoon after we've booked the tickets. I can't wait to get back to the farm."

"Sounds good. I look forward to seeing you, and anxious to hear more about this sudden trip of yours with the ex."

After saying goodbye to Darren, Bryce checked the time and called the hospital to make sure Patricia was still being released today. She was and would be ready in an hour, the nurse told him.

Bryce wasted no time; it was close to 10:00 and he feared the city traffic at *any* time of the day. What would be a fifteen-minute drive in Connecticut could easily take close to an hour in New York. He looked out one of the large windows in the living room and saw that it was still cloudy and raining. Typical April showers he thought to himself, heading upstairs to grab Patricia's clean clothes that Savannah and Jewel had picked out for her as well as a jacket for himself from his suitcase.

~

Bryce made it to the hospital in under an hour with moderate traffic and found Patricia sitting up in bed, anxious to leave.

"Finally, you're here," Patricia said in a sharp tone. "I can't wait to get out of this place. Did you bring me some clean clothes? This gown makes me itch."

"Yes, the girls packed a bag for you," he replied, handing her a white Gucci leather tote.

"Great! And my makeup bag?" she asked, taking the tote.

Bryce shrugged his shoulders. "I have no idea. I didn't pack it and I'm not going through your things."

Patricia hastily rummaged through the tote with one hand and smiled when she pulled out a matching white leather makeup bag. "They did!" she cheered, pulling the blankets aways from her body and swinging her legs over the side of the bed.

"Where are you going?" Bryce asked.

"To the bathroom to get dressed."

Bryce nodded, amused that she was now hiding her body from him after years of making love to each other and parenting two daughters.

Ten minutes later she reappeared from the bathroom carrying the tote wearing black flared dress pants, black heels and a black blouse with sleeves which luckily went over the cast on her arm.

Bryce had no idea how she managed to do her makeup with one hand, but he couldn't help noticing how perfect it looked, along with her perfectly groomed hair.

"You look great," he said, smiling as he got up from his chair.

"Oh, *now* you're being nice to me. Is it because you're getting your way and making me go to Alaksa? Something you know I don't want to do?" she snapped.

. . .

Bryce smirked. "Oh, come on. It won't be that bad. I'll even pay for everything. My treat."

"Some treat," Patricia snarled. "I spent all of last night and this morning begging my associates to take over my cases and run the office. I informed them I have to take a month off due to my accident. That's all I can give you, Bryce, then I want to get on with my life," she said, her voice loud and harsh. "Now, can we get out of here? I want to go home."

"A month should be plenty of time. The girls get out of school next week for spring break. We'll book the tickets as soon as we get back to your apartment," he told her, taking her tote from her so she could pick up her purse from the bed.

~

"Why in heaven's name do you drive a truck?" Patricia hollered, holding Bryce's hand for balance as she climbed into the cab.

"Because a Lexus is not too practical on a farm."

Once she was buckled in, Bryce fired up the truck and backed out of their parking space to head to the apartment. When he came to the first red light of many, he turned and looked at Patricia. "You know, the doctor at the hospital told me they found alcohol in your system. Were you drunk when you fell?"

Patricia looked out of the window avoiding his stare. "I may have had a drink or two. It's not a crime, you know."

"That not what I asked. I asked if you were drunk?"

"I may have had one too many," Patricia confessed, still looking out the window.

"Patricia, look at me," Bryce demanded.

She ignored him.

"Patricia, did you hear me? Look at me."

Patricia turned her head and looked at him. "What?"

"Do you have a drinking problem? How often do you get drunk?"

"No, I don't have a drinking problem. I may have had a little too much to drink that night, but I was lonely. The girls were with you, and I didn't want to go home to an empty apartment. It doesn't mean I have a drinking problem; I was just feeling sorry for myself."

"Is that what you always do when I have the girls? Drink your sorrows away?"

"It's only once a month, Bryce. When the girls are with me, I'm fine. It's no big deal."

"Well, I disagree with you," Bryce told her. His tone softened. "You're not happy. When are you going to be honest with yourself and realize that?"

"You have no idea how I feel. Just because I had a little too much to drink one night doesn't mean I'm not happy. Look at the life I'm living, Bryce. I'm rich and I can buy anything I want."

"But are you happy, Patricia? Do all the things you own provide happiness and fulfillment? Be honest with yourself - do they?"

"That's such a stupid question," Patricia barked, waving him off with her good arm. "I'm not going to even waste my time answering it."

"Fine. You don't have to. But I think you will want to one day, and like I've said before, you'll probably be surprised at the answer," he replied, staring straight ahead.

When they arrived at the apartment Letti greeted them, welcoming Patricia home and offering to bring them some coffee, which they gladly accepted.

Bryce glanced at his phone he'd set on the coffee table. "It's almost 1:00. What time will the girls be back from school?" he asked Patricia, who took a seat next to him on the couch.

"Around 4:00," she replied.

Bryce leaned over the arm of the couch and picked up his computer case which held his laptop and set it on the table. "Okay, that gives us enough time to plan the trip, and I'll stay for a bit after they get home so we can tell them about it together."

"Fine," Patricia snapped, taking a sip of her coffee. "I still can't believe you're making me do this, Bryce."

Bryce smirked. "I think you'll thank me later," he said, opening his laptop and powering it up.

"Thank you for what?" Patricia shrieked. "I honestly think this is such a waste of our time!"

"Enough with the attitude. Let's just get this done. Now, when is spring break?"

"They have two weeks off in April, let me check the calendar," Patricia said, looking at her laptop. "April 7th through April 21st."

"That's two weeks away, and where in Alaska are we going?"

"Hope, Alaska," Patricia replied, taking another sip of her coffee.

Bryce looked at her with a creased brow. "Hope? I've never heard of it."

"I told you, my father lived in a small town. The nearest city is Anchorage. It's about two hours away by car, if I remember correctly," she told him.

"Then we'll fly into Anchorage and rent a car. What's the weather like there this time of year?"

"I have no idea. I'm sure it's pretty mild."

"I'll look it up when I'm home. I just want to get these tickets booked."

"You know I have an assistant that can do all of this for us."

Bryce shook his head. "Nope, I prefer to do things myself now. It's much more rewarding, plus there are no surprises. You should try it sometime."

Patricia rolled her eyes. "Whatever. Having an assistant saves me a lot of time."

Within the hour Bryce leaned back smiling. "There, we're all set. I've booked four 1st class tickets for April 8th. We leave from JFK Airport at 8:00 am with a layover in Dallas, Texas. From there we fly to Anchorage, Alaska, and arrive at 7:00 pm. I've booked us a car rental which we can pick up at the airport, then from there we can drive to Hope."

"And when do we come home?" Patricia asked anxiously.

Bryce looked at the screen on the laptop. "We return home on April 18th. We'll have ten days in Alaska."

"Ten days?" Patricia squealed. "And what the hell are we supposed to do in Alaska for ten days?"

"Learn about your family," Bryce said with a smile.

CHAPTER 23

*P*atricia couldn't wait for this to be over; not only was she dreading the thought of revealing her awful childhood that she'd tried to disconnect from in every conceivable way since arriving in New York, but also her daughters' reactions. She wasn't sure which one she feared the most. This could destroy her relationship with her daughters, and she vowed she'd never forgive Bryce if that were the consequences of his ridiculous idea. Because of his selfish needs he claimed would also benefit Savannah and Jewel, he was willing to risk everything. She suddenly had a terrifying thought and found herself thinking about the return flight home - *would any of us be speaking to each other?*

Bryce interrupted her thoughts. "Hey, how are we supposed to get into your dad's house?"

Patricia paused for a moment. It felt strange hearing the word dad. "I'm assuming that the attorney will have the keys."

"Well, we don't land in Anchorage until 7:00 pm. You'll need to call him and make arrangements to pick them up. We may have to book a hotel near the airport for the first night and pick up the keys the next day," Bryce informed her.

"Fine," Patricia replied, folding her arms and rolling her eyes.

"Call them first thing in the morning and let me know so I can book the hotel, if needed, which I'm sure we'll have to do."

"I'll call them when I get to my office."

"You're supposed to be taking a month off? Why are you going into the office?" Bryce asked, raising his voice.

"I can't just take a month off without holding a meeting with my staff, Bryce. I need to tell them firsthand what's going on and go over the schedule and assignments for the month while I'm not there. There's a lot at stake while I'm out with this stupid arm, and I want to make sure everything runs smoothly. I said I'd call them first thing before the meeting, then I'll call you."

Bryce shook his head. "You just can't stay away, can you? You think the place is going to fall apart without you. It'll be fine." He raised his hands in defeat. "But, do what you must do. It's your business. Just make sure to call me, okay? "

"I said I will. How many times do I have to tell you!"

"Oh, and another thing, you need to make time to buy a new wardrobe. Do you even own a pair of jeans?" Bryce joked.

"I haven't worn a pair of jeans in decades," she confessed. "I guess I'll have to buy some."

"And don't forget, sweaters, t-shirts, tennis shoes and hiking boots. I'm sure you don't own any of those things either," he chuckled. "It's going to be something to see you in casual clothes, and, I might add, comfortable clothes which I don't think I ever have."

Patricia picked up a notepad from the table and quickly wrote down the items Bryce was reeling off.

"And what about the girls? They have plenty of that stuff on the farm, but I'm sure you'll want Letti to pack their bags here. Make sure you get them appropriate wardrobes, too," Bryce told her.

Patricia added his comments to her list. "Anything else?" she snarled.

Bryce leaned back on the couch, clasping his hands behind his head. "Nope," he said, grinning.

"Good. I need some fresh air. I'm going out on the balcony to call my office and have Leslie schedule a meeting for the morning. Savannah and Jewel will be home shortly."

"Great, we can tell them about our trip, then I gotta get on the road and head back to the farm."

~

Just as Patricia had predicted, Savannah and Jewel arrived home a little before 4:00 after being dropped off by the chauffeur.

Jewel entered the living room first where she found her dad sitting on the couch with his computer in his lap. "Daddy! You're still here!" she squealed. "Is Mommy here?" she asked, looking around the room.

"Hey, Munchkin," he said, placing his laptop on the table and opening his arms to greet her in a hug. "Yes, she's out on the balcony. Go tell her you're home - we have something to tell you."

"Ooh, is it a surprise?" Jewel asked, her eyes wide.

Bryce laughed. "Just go get your mom."

Savannah entered the room and sat next to her dad. "Hey Dad, I wasn't expecting to see you still here. I thought you'd be back at the farm by now."

"I'm leaving soon. Your mom and I want to talk to you first."

"Mom's home? Is everything okay?" Savannah asked, looking worried.

Bryce rubbed her shoulder. "Yes, everything's fine. Your mom's doing well." Hearing footsteps, he looked up and saw Patricia and Jewel enter the room.

"Look Savannah, Mommy's home and she has a broken arm," Jewel squealed, taking a seat next to her sister as Patricia sat in the chair across from them with her hands resting on her lap.

Bryce hugged Jewel. "Your mom and I wanted to tell you that we're all going to take a trip together to Alaska during Spring Break."

Savannah creased her brow, "All of us? You and Mom together?"

Patricia nodded. "That's correct, Savannah. I have a business trip in Alaska, and I need your father's help, so he suggested we all go together. You've never seen Alaska, and your father thought it would be a wonderful opportunity for you, so I agreed."

"Where's Alaska? "Jewel asked.

"It's a long way away," Bryce told her, tickling her side. "We'll be taking a plane there."

"Oh, cool!" Jewel cheered. "I love flying in airplanes."

"Wow! You and Mom on a trip together - when was the last time you did that?" Savannah asked. "I must have been really little, 'cause I don't remember."

"It's a business trip, Savannah. I really need your father's help."

"So, you're going to be working the whole time?" Savannah moaned. "And what are me and Jewel supposed to do?"

Bryce wrapped his arm over Savannah's shoulder, pulling her in with a hug. "No, it won't be all work, I promise. We'll go exploring, hiking, and Alaska is famous for fishing, too."

"It is?" Jewel screamed. "Can I bring my fishing pole?"

Bryce laughed. "No, it will be awkward to take it on the plane. I'm sure we can find you one there."

Patricia gave him a hard stare. "You didn't tell me you wanted to do all of those things on the trip."

"It's Alaska! Of course we're going to have some adventures. I think it will do us all some good."

"I'm not sure if we'll have the time. There's going to be so much to do on the business side," Patricia remarked, not liking his ideas.

Bryce waved his hand. "Oh, stop making excuses. We'll make time." He squeezed Savannah again and leaned in, pressing his cheek against hers. "Right, Savannah?"

Savannah nodded and smiled, looking at her mom. "Right!"

Releasing his hold on his daughter, he patted his knee. "Okay, I need to get on the road," he said as he stood up. "Call me in the morning, Patricia." He looked at his girls. "Come give your daddy a kiss." He turned and looked at Patricia. "Oh, and your car is being driven here from your office around 6:00 tonight. Your parking space will be free by then."

"Thank you," Patricia said as she stood up. "I need to get some work done. Girls, go change and be ready for dinner in 30 minutes."

Bryce arrived at his farm a few hours later, thankful the traffic was light once he got out of New York. He could hear Goldie and Jack barking the minute he turned onto the long driveway leading up to the house, spotting them halfway down, running towards his truck, their tails wagging and their barks growing louder.

Winding down the window of his truck, Bryce shouted, "I'm home," greeting his dogs who were running alongside as he pulled up to the house. Stepping out of the truck and remembering he could just leave his bags and laptop in the cab, and they'd be safe (unlike in New York), he filled his lungs with the fresh air and took in the magnificent view of the wide-open land, green pastures and rolling hills. "God, I've missed this place," he said, smiling as he kneeled and pet his dogs vigorously. "Come on, let's go inside," he told them, standing up and heading for the front door.

Once inside he immediately put the kettle on, not having had a decent cup of tea since being in New York. He then called Darren's cell phone as Goldie and Jack circled his legs. Darren didn't answer, so he figured he was out on the farm somewhere doing chores and left a message. "Hey Darren, I'm home. I'm going up to the barn to check on Cleo. I'll be back at the house in about an hour."

Bryce spent the next hour walking the farm, checking on the pony, chickens, and baby chicks, the two dogs following closely behind. It seemed they weren't going to let him out of their sight again.

By 8:00 with the sun almost set on the horizon, Bryce returned to the farmhouse, grabbing his things from the truck. When he entered the house, he found Darren in the kitchen peeling an orange and drinking tea. He looked up and smiled. "Hey mate, welcome home. Kettle's hot."

"Hey Darren, the place looks great. All good on the dairy side?" he asked, grabbing his cup off the table.

"Yep, running like clockwork. No worries there, mate. I'm going to hand over tomorrow's morning shift to you, though. I want a lie in. The help will be here at 4:00 am," Darren said.

"Not a problem, mate. Thanks for holding down the fort while I was gone. Me and you will team up on the second shift."

"Sounds good. So, enough farm talk. Tell me about this sudden trip of yours to Alaska."

Bryce poured his tea and joined Darren at the table, Goldie and Jack resting on top of his feet. He went on to tell him everything he'd learned about Patricia over the past few days and the reason for the trip.

"Bloody hell, mate. Why did she hide all that stuff?"

"I'm not sure yet, but I think a lot of it was because she was afraid of tainting the image she wanted to portray when she came to New York. She wanted to be part of the elites, and I figure she thought she wouldn't be accepted if they knew where she was from and what her parents did for a living. It's as if she was ashamed."

"But you've never hidden where you were from. We were poor and raised on a farm; that never stopped you. You've always been honest about your background, and you went on and became a multi-millionaire."

"Yeah, I know, but she's a woman. Maybe they overthink things." Bryce shrugged his shoulders. "I dunno," he laughed. "I think there's more to her story – I'm not sure what it is yet - but I'll get it out of her. Another reason for this trip," he winked, refilling his cup.

CHAPTER 24

Over the next two weeks before he and Patricia left for Alaska, Bryce spent his evenings researching everything he could about the small town of Hope where Patricia grew up, and from what he discovered, he couldn't in his wildest dreams imagine Patricia living in such a place. It was everything she wasn't. Boy, he loved the internet - everything he needed to know was at his fingertips.

If you wanted a simple life it seemed like Hope would be the ideal place. A small, rural historic mining town with only 200 residents, and only half of them living there full-time. Bryce assumed Patricia and her family were one of those full-time residents, and her father continued to live there full-time until he passed.

He also learned the town had one school building with only two classes. One for Kindergarten through 5th grade, and the other for 6th through 12th grade. Bryce assumed Patricia attended that school. Her education, like his, was pretty basic. How in heaven's name did she afford not only to leave Alaska, but pay for an education in law school?

Bryce was happy to see that there were a few restaurants in the town which he planned to check out with the girls and Patricia. He was also excited to read that Hope was a huge fishing spot during the pink salmon run in the summer months. He made a note to check out what fishing was available in April; he was excited to take Jewel. He chuckled when he thought of Jewel and how much she loved to fish. *It makes bloody sense now*, Bryce laughed aloud to himself. *Her grandfather was a fisherman. It's in her blood,"* he realized.

Bryce also researched the average weather for Hope in April and was pleased to see it averaged around 45 degrees, but the nights would be chilly, dropping below freezing. "God, I hope the cabin has heating," he said, taking notes and adding that the daylight length was around fourteen hours.

He was happy to sense the excitement in his daughter's voices when he talked to them on the phone a week before their departure - especially Jewel - who squealed when Bryce told them about the fishing in town. Up until now she'd only fished in his pond on the farm and a few times at the reservoir. Savannah was excited about the plane ride and going for hikes and a picnic, but one of her questions surprised him.

"What's Mom going to do when we go for a hike?" Savannah asked.

"Well, she's going with us," Bryce told her.

Savannah replied with a loud laugh. "Mom doesn't hike, Dad. I've never known her to hike, *ever*," she confirmed.

"Well, there's a first time for everything."

"I bet you anything she doesn't go, Dad. It'll be too dirty for her, walking on a muddy trail," Savannah joked.

"I may just have to prove you wrong, young lady," Bryce chuckled before saying goodnight.

Bryce talked to the girls one last time the night before they were set to depart, and he could hear the excitement in their voices that had tripled from a week ago.

"We're all packed, Daddy," Jewel said excitedly. "I have new jeans, sweaters, some warm socks, shoes and boots, a bright red beanie and scarf, a warm jacket and a backpack."

"I do too," Savannah hollered into the phone.

"That's fantastic. Did your mom get new clothes too?"

"Yes, she even got some jeans and sweaters, Dad," Savannah told him.

"I can't wait to see you, Daddy," Jewel said.

"Me too, Munchkin. Now, you two need to get to bed soon. We all have to be up early. I love you both. Let me talk to your mom really quick."

"Okay, Daddy. Love you too. See you tomorrow," Jewel said, and then hollered, "Mom, Daddy wants to talk to you."

A few minutes later Patricia came to the phone. "Hello, Bryce."

"The girls sound excited for the trip. Are you?"

"I think you already know the answer to that, Bryce. You're forcing me to go, and I think it's cruel of you. I talked to Cassie last night, and she's terribly upset about this trip. She said you have no right digging up the past and making me do this."

Bryce bit his tongue and was cautious with his words. The last thing he wanted was to have a fight with Patricia on the eve of their trip. "I honestly don't care what Cassie thinks. It's really none of her business. Like I said before, you may have a grudge against me right now, but I honestly think you'll be thanking me by the end of the trip."

"I honestly doubt *that*," Patricia snarled.

"Look, can we at least try to have an enjoyable time for the girls' sake? I want this to be a trip they'll remember. It's why I'm doing this - for them. I want them to know their family history on your side. Is that such a terrible thing?"

"Oh, they'll remember this trip, trust me," Patricia said with a hint of sarcasm. "I've protected them from my past their entire life for good reason and you'll soon see why."

"I think you're overreacting. Look where I came from, and the girls are fine with it. Anyway, lets discuss the plan for the morning before I hit the sack."

They spent the next fifteen minutes discussing details. Bryce had hired a car to take him to the airport in the morning, and Patricia was doing the same. They arranged to meet outside the terminal at 6:30 am.

After saying goodnight, Bryce called Darren, now settled in his cottage for the night, and went over a few things with him.

Once in bed with both dogs at his feet, Bryce couldn't help but look at the trip as a family trip, even though he and Patricia were no longer married. It would be the first time they'd be taking a trip together since their divorce. They may not be married, but he still considered themselves a family. He wondered if Patricia thought the same.

CHAPTER 25

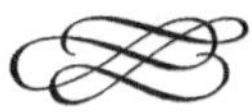

*P*atricia woke up wishing the day hadn't arrived. After having spent a sleepless night stressing over the trip she was being forced to take, she wanted nothing more but to remain in bed and bury her head in her pillow and be anywhere but in the present moment.

She glanced at the clock on the nightstand and saw that it was almost 4:00 am. The car would be arriving at 5:30 to take her and the girls to the airport. Thankful that Letti had spent the night to help get Savannah and Jewel ready and fix them breakfast, Patricia reluctantly pulled the covers away from her body and dragged herself to the master bath to take a shower, a task that had become a challenge with her arm in a cast. "God I'll be glad when this damn thing comes off," she yelled from in the shower, struggling to rinse her hair.

Fifteen minutes later, her body and hair wrapped in white towels, feeling irritated about everything going on in her life, she laid her chosen wardrobe for the trip on her bed, including a pair of black slacks - she had no intention of wearing jeans until they were in Alaska. She pulled a folded black sweater from one of the shelves in the closet and set it on the bed next to the pants, then finally found a pair or flat black slip-on shoes.

In the midst of removing the towel covering her body, the bedroom door suddenly flung open, and Jewel came barging in.

Patricia quickly wrapped her body back in the towel. "Jewel! You're supposed to knock before entering my room."

Jewel skipped around the room. "I'm sorry, Mommy. I'm just so excited. We're flying on a plane today and going to Alaska!" she squealed, spinning in circles around the room.

Patricia held onto her towel. "Yes, we are, dear. Did you have your breakfast?"

"No, not yet. I just got dressed and I'm going down to eat now. Are you coming?"

"Well, Mommy isn't dressed yet. Why don't you go downstairs, and I'll be there soon. Tell Letti I only want coffee. I'm not in the mood to eat."

"Are you not feeling well, Mommy? I hope not."

Patricia forced a smile. "I'm fine, I'm just not hungry. Now, go on down," Patricia urged, opening the door. "Is Savannah dressed?" she asked as Jewel left the room. Jewel turned and looked at her. "Yes, she's already downstairs."

Relieved to be alone again, Patricia removed her towel and proceeded to get dressed, thankful that the sleeves of the sweater fit over her cast. Sitting at her dresser in front of the mirror applying her makeup, she paused and looked at her reflection. What she saw depressed her. She looked and felt that she'd aged ten years in the last two weeks, certain that the stress of the trip was the cause. Leaning closer to the mirror, she gasped when she saw a few grey hairs on her crown. "See what you're doing to me, Bryce," she moaned, attempting to hide the hairs but failing.

Slamming down her brush in despair, not wanting to look at her aged face, Patricia quickly stood up, packed her laptop in its case and set it by her already packed suitcase before heading downstairs to grab a much-needed large cup of coffee.

Seeing how excited the girls were about the trip, Patricia forced herself to change her demeanor and smiled at the girls as they pranced around the kitchen chatting excitedly about the trip.

"Daddy says there's lots of places to go fishing," Jewel grinned. "I hope we get to go."

"And he also said that we're *all* going for a picnic and a hike." Savannah made sure to emphasize the word *all* while looking at her mother.

"Oh, he did, did he?" Patricia said, sitting at the table, looking over her coffee cup that she held. "Well, he didn't ask me."

Savannah approached her mom, resting her hand on Patricia's shoulder. "But you'll go, right?"

Patricia gave a subtle smile, reaching up and patting Savannah's hand. "We'll see, dear."

Letti entered the kitchen, interrupting their conversation. "The car is here, ma'am. Shall I have the driver take your bags down?"

Patricia took a deep breath - the moment she had been dreading had arrived. "Yes please, Letti, we'll be down in a few minutes."

"Okay girls, go get your coats. It's time to go."

"Yay!" Jewel screamed, before racing up the stairs to her room.

Bryce arrived at the airport fifteen minutes late due to an accident. He texted Patricia to let her know, but she hadn't replied. He spotted her from his car, standing outside the terminal as his driver pulled up to the curb.

When Patricia saw him step out of the car she gave him a hard stare. "You're late!" she barked. "We've been standing here for ages and we're freezing."

"There was an accident. Not my fault," Bryce said, waiting for the driver to unload his bags. "Didn't you get my text?"

"My phone is in my purse, and I didn't hear it. Will you hurry up? The girls and I need to go inside where it's warm," Patricia snapped, stomping her feet trying to stay warm.

"I'm fine, Mommy," Jewel told her, walking circles around her mother as she hummed a tune.

"Well, your sister and I are cold," she snapped.

Bryce chuckled, taking a bag from the driver and thanked him as he gave him a tip. "Well, look what you're wearing. Those pants must be made from the thinnest material ever. I thought you bought some jeans."

"I did, but I'm not traveling in public wearing those. It's not appropriate."

Bryce smirked. "Then be cold. For me, comfort and practicality come first."

The flight left on time and Jewel was excited to have the window seat. Bryce had so many questions for Patricia about the things he'd discovered about the town of Hope but chose to keep the conversation to a minimum, knowing the girls had no idea they were returning to where their mother grew up.

Patricia made it easy by spending most of the flight reading - buried in magazines and a book - leaving Bryce to entertain the girls by playing card games, thankful he had packed a deck. For over an hour of the flight they also played one of Jewel's favorite games; paper, rock, scissors, and for the last two hours of the flight he watched a movie with them.

The connecting flight from Dallas to Anchorage was on time and thankfully flawless. They finally touched down in Alaska at 7:00 pm.

Stepping off the plane and walking to the terminal with the girls skipping and chatting in front of them, Bryce leaned into Patricia and whispered.

"How does it feel to be back in Alaska?"

"Awful," Patricia hissed, increasing her pace to catch up with Savannah and Jewel.

Bryce rolled his eyes, watching her escape his questioning, but believed she'd eventually come around and soften her tone.

After Bryce grabbed their luggage with Savannah and Jewel's help, they headed over to the rental area inside the airport to pick up their car. Bryce couldn't resist laughing at Patricia when they stepped outside to wait for it.

"My god! It's freezing out here!" Patricia shrieked, hugging her waist.

"Welcome to Alaska," Bryce said with a large grin.

CHAPTER 26

*P*atricia blew into her hands as they stood outside waiting for their car to arrive, her body trembling from the cold that reached into her bones. She didn't want to mention to Bryce how cold her legs were, he was right about wearing pants made from a light material that gave no insulation to her skin. She didn't want to see the satisfaction on his face knowing he'd been correct. She was thankful she had packed a fleece-lined jacket in her carry-on luggage and had put it on before stepping outside.

It was almost 8:00 pm and still light outside. They had a couple hours of daylight left with the sun setting around 9:00, and the temperatures would be dropping into the low 20's. There was no wind, which made the colder temperatures more forgiving, but it still felt brutal.

Savannah and Jewel, now bundled in puffy jackets, gloves and beanies that Bryce had pulled out of their luggage, stood next to their parents.

Jewel raised her hand and pointed. "Look, there's snow on those mountains," she exclaimed. "Can we go play in the snow?"

Bryce laughed. "They're very far away, Munchkin. I wonder what those mountains are called?"

"The Chugach Mountains," Patricia replied, her tone flat.

"How do you know that, Mom?" Savannah asked.

"Geography class," Patricia quickly answered, looking at the tall mountain range, realizing the last time she was at this airport was when she left Alaska at the early age of eighteen with no intentions of returning. She couldn't believe she was back, but it wasn't by choice.

Within a few minutes their car rental pulled up to the curb, a white GMC Yukon, recommended by the rental company when Bryce made the reservation. Patricia quickly rounded up the girls and shuffled them into the back seat, welcoming the warmth when she took her seat in the front.

After Bryce had loaded their luggage in the cargo area, he joined them in the car, rubbing his hands together to warm them before bringing up the address of their hotel on his phone.

"Damn, I should have packed my gloves in my carry-on bags, my hands are freezing," he said, looking at Patricia who was rubbing her legs with her good hand. "How are you holding up? I bet your legs are freezing in those pants?"

Patricia removed her hand from her legs and lied, "they're fine."

"It looks like the hotel is only about two miles from here." He turned and looked at Savannah and Jewel sitting in the back seat. "How about after we're settled in our hotel room, we order some pizza?"

"Yay!" Both girls screamed at the same time.

Patricia remained quiet.

"Does that sound good to you?" Bryce asked, looking at Patricia.

"Sure. Whatever the girls want is fine with me."

After checking in at the Courtyard Marriott Hotel, they were escorted up to their suite with the help of a porter. It was a spacious suite with three separate rooms; one for Patricia, one for Savannah and Jewel, and one for Bryce, each with their own bath. There was also a central living area with comfortable beige couches and two oversized armchairs, a large-screen TV, a wet bar, and a teak coffee table.

"Wow! This is nice," Bryce said, admiring the view of the mountain from the large picture window on the left of the central room.

"Which is our room?" Jewel yelled excitedly, racing behind the couch to the three bedrooms on the right.

"You and your sister get the one with the two twin beds," Bryce called, as Savannah and Jewel left to go explore the rest of the suite.

"I'm going to go change," Patricia said, approaching one of the other rooms. "I'll take this room, if that's okay?"

"Sure, that's fine. I'm going to call Darren and let him know we've arrived, then I'll order pizza."

Patricia nodded before entering the room and closing the door, leaving Bryce alone to make his calls.

As he was talking to Darren and checking on the farm, the girls returned. "Dad, can we put our PJ's on?" Savannah asked. "We want to go to bed after we eat. We're tired," not realizing he was on the phone.

Bryce turned and nodded. "Yes, that's a good idea. I'll be off the phone in a minute," he told her. "The pizza will be here in 20 minutes," he added, resuming his conversation with Darren.

Ending the call and feeling confident about leaving Darren in charge, Bryce was surprised when Patricia joined him in the room wearing a white terry bathrobe and slippers. He smiled. "Well, you look cozy and comfortable. I can't remember the last time I saw you in a bathrobe."

She took a seat in one of the oversized chairs across from him. "I'm so tired. Why change into other clothes? I plan to go to bed after we eat."

"The girls said the same thing. They're putting on their PJ's too." He turned when he heard footsteps entering the room and saw Savannah and Jewel, also dressed in white bathrobes and slippers. "Here they come now." He patted his knees and laughed. "It looks like we're having a pajama party."

Jewel laughed with her father, taking a seat next to him and hugging his waist. "We are, Daddy. You need to change and put your pajamas on too."

Bryce stood and smiled at his daughters. "Okay, I'll be right back. The pizza should be here any minute."

When he returned from his room dressed like everyone else (except for his robe which was navy blue), he found Patricia sitting on the couch, serving the girls pizza on paper plates.

"That smells delicious," he said. "And we have chocolate milk," he added, handing Savanah and Jewel each a carton before grabbing a plate of pizza and taking a seat in one of the chairs. "I could get used to these parties," Bryce said, taking a bite. "This is so cozy."

"This is fun!" Jewel said. "I hope we do more of these while we're here."

"I'm sure we will, Munchkin." He looked over at Patricia, sitting across from him. "Right, Mom?"

Patricia looked up. It had been a long time since he had called her mom, and it took her by surprise. When they were married, he'd always call her mom when with the girls, never by her name.

She wasn't sure how to take it but resisted acknowledging it. She gave him a subtle smile. She wouldn't deny it, she *was* enjoying the cozy atmosphere sitting in her bathrobe eating pizza, something she hadn't done in a long time, well before their divorce at least. "Yes, I'm sure we'll be having more of these parties," she said, looking at Bryce then at the girls.

"Yay!" Jewel squealed, taking another bite of pizza. "I love pizza and pajama parties."

Bryce leaned back in his chair, his belly full after eating three slices and smiled at Patricia, who was delicately wiping her lips with a napkin. They'd just said goodnight to Savannah and Jewel and were now alone.

"Do you realize this is the first family meal we've had since our divorce? I'm looking forward to many more of these on this trip."

"Family meals?" Patricia said, her brow creased. "Bryce, we're divorced."

"Yes, we are, but we're still a family. We had two daughters together and that is a family. Don't you agree?"

"Yes, I guess so. It just sounds strange when we're divorced and no longer living together."

"But for the next two weeks we *will* be together, like a family," Bryce said, smiling.

"If you say so," Patricia agreed, not wanting to admit she enjoyed the cozy feeling she'd experienced during their pizza party.

Bryce changed the subject. "So, after we've picked up the keys from the attorney's office, I'm assuming we'll drive straight to your father's cabin, correct? According to my phone, the attorney's office is just fifteen minutes from here in Anchorage."

"Yes, that sounds good," Patricia said nervously, her anxiety rising.

Bryce gave her a piercing stare. "And then we're going to tell the girls once we're at the cabin, right?"

"That's what we agreed on. That is why we're here, isn't it? This would have all been taken care of by now if it wasn't for this stupid idea of yours."

"I'm not getting into it again, Patricia. I just wanted to make sure we're on the same page." He patted the arms of the chair with his palms. "Well, we have a big day tomorrow. I'm off to bed, so I'll see you in the morning," he said as he got up.

Patricia nodded. "Goodnight," she replied, watching Bryce walk to his room and close the door, wishing tomorrow would never come.

CHAPTER 27

Savannah and Jewel were anxious to leave the comforts of the hotel suite and explore Alaska. They let their excitement be known by barging into Bryce's room at sunrise.

"Daddy, get up!" Jewel screamed; her voice peaked with enthusiasm, excited to start the day. "It's light out and I can't sleep," she exclaimed, jumping on the bed as Savannah went to open the drapes.

"Look Dad, you can see the mountains from here. They look so pretty with the snow on top," Savannah said, smiling, "and the sky is a brilliant blue."

Bryce squinted his eyes at the sudden burst of natural light beaming into the room from the now exposed window and reached for his phone on the nightstand. It was only 6:30 am. "Girls, it's not even 7:00 yet. What's your hurry?"

"We want to see Alaska. Come on Daddy, get up," Jewel said again, kneeling on the bed and shaking his body.

Bryce rubbed his eyes and raised his hands. "Okay, okay, I'm up. Did you wake your mother the same way?" he said, followed by a laugh.

"No, Mom doesn't like to be woken up. She'll come out when she's ready," Savannah told him.

"How come she gets a break?" Bryce smirked.

"Because she's Mom," Savannah said, folding her arms and standing in front of the window.

Bryce pulled back the sheets and left the bed. "Let me get dressed and freshen up. By then your mom should be awake. As soon as we're all dressed and packed, we'll go down to the courtyard here in the hotel and have some breakfast before we check out."

"Yay!" Jewel said, jumping off the bed. "Can we watch TV after we get dressed?" she asked.

"Yes, turn up the volume when you do. Maybe it will wake your mother up," he said, heading to the bathroom.

Bryce's suggestion worked; within ten minutes of the TV on high volume, the door to Patricia's room opened. "Girls! Can you turn that down a little? It's awfully loud."

"Sorry Mommy," Jewel said with a giggle.

"Good morning, Patricia," Bryce said from the nearby table where he sat answering texts. "Did you sleep well?"

"Not bad, thank you."

"Well, as soon as you're dressed and packed, we thought we'd get some breakfast before checking out."

"I just need coffee," Patricia replied, rubbing her brow. "Give me half an hour," she added, returning to her room and closing the door.

When she reappeared dressed in blue jeans, a white wool sweater, black suede ankle-laced boots and a jacket flung over her arm, Bryce was taken aback by her appearance. Stripped of her Gucci wardrobe, stilettoed heels and a face hidden behind mascara, lipstick and rouge, she looked quite attractive. Her complexion looked natural, wearing no eye makeup, and her lips had just a hint of color. "Well, I never thought I'd see the day with you in a pair of jeans and looking all natural. You look great!" he said, smiling.

Savannah and Jewel both looked over the back of the couch and gasped.

"Wow, Mom is wearing jeans!" Jewel cried.

Patricia gave a subtle smile, not liking the stiffness of the denim against her skin. "Don't get used to it. It's just while we're here. Now, come on, I'm ready. Let's go."

~

After a scrumptious breakfast of pancakes, eggs and bacon, (Patricia sticking to just coffee), they still had an hour before their meeting with the attorney a few miles away.

Bryce loaded up the car with their luggage, and with everyone buckled up started the car and headed out on to Spenard Road. Within a few minutes they were looking at the spectacular view of Spenard Lake.

"Wow, Dad! Look, a plane is landing on the water," Savannah hollered from the back seat. "That's so cool."

Bryce looked out of his window at the vast area of water. "That's one of the largest seaplane bases in America. Floatplanes take off and land all day from here." He looked at the girls through his rearview mirror while keeping his eyes on the road. "We have some time to kill. Do you want to stop and watch the planes for a while?"

"Yes!" Savannah and Jewel cheered, raising their arms.

Bryce smiled as he slowed the car down and pulled off into a designated parking lot looking out over the water. The view was breathtaking. Once the car came to a complete stop and Bryce had turned off the engine, Savannah and Jewel quickly unbuckled their seatbelts, opened their doors, and jumped out.

Bryce quickly followed with Patricia close behind.

"This is amazing," Bryce said, taking a seat on one of the wooden benches overlooking the lake.

He breathed in the fresh air, admiring the many trees surrounding the lake and the spectacular snow-capped mountains in the distance. Jewel jumped up and down in front of him, squealing and pointing to a plane taking off over the water. They made it look so easy, Bryce thought, but knew it took months of training to master the task. He scanned the lake and was surprised to see so many floatplanes tied to the shores.

"Did you ever come here when you lived here?" Bryce asked Patricia in a whisper as she sat next to him on the bench, making sure the girls didn't hear him.

Patricia knew this would be the first of many questions on the trip; avoiding them would no longer be an option. She nodded. "A few times, yes," she said, keeping her answer short.

"Did you ever fly in one of those planes?" Bryce asked, wanting to know more.

"Patricia nodded again. "Yes, with my father. I don't remember much about it; I was incredibly young."

Bryce leaned back on the bench. "Wow! What an experience. We should see if we can rent a plane while we're here. I'd love to take the girls up in one. The views would definitely be amazing, and they'd remember it for the rest of their lives."

"Let's take care of business first and see how much time we have left," Patricia replied, not fond of Bryce's idea. She wanted nothing more than to tend to business and leave Alaska as soon as possible and not play tourist.

"Oh, we're going to make time," Bryce told her. "We can't come all this way and pass up such an opportunity. Who knows when or if we'll ever have the chance again."

Patricia tried to defend herself. "I'm just being realistic Bryce, that's all. We have a lot to do while we're here."

"Look at the smiles on Savannah and Jewel's faces," Bryce said, sporting a large grin. "They've never experienced anything like this. The memories that will be made on this trip are going to be priceless."

Patricia wasn't sure how to react to his comment. She still feared her daughters' reaction when they'd tell them the real reason they were in Alaska. It might ruin the entire trip for all of them and leave nothing but bitter memories. She quickly erased her negative thoughts. "They're certainly enjoying watching the planes," she said, managing a smile at Savannah who was pointing at a floatplane coming into land.

"I envy you growing up here, Patricia. I don't understand why you've kept it a secret all these years." Bryce said, memorized by the view before him.

Patricia's skin crawled with nerves. "Please Bryce, not now. It's not easy for me to be here. I'm not sure how to react to all of this," she said, closing her eyes. "You have no idea how hard this is for me," she added, tears pooling in her eyes. "I'm an emotional wreck right now. I need to transition slowly and not be bombarded with a bunch of questions."

Bryce was taken aback by her raw honesty. For the first time he felt a twinge of guilt seeing Patricia exposing her emotions to him, something she'd never done before. He gently patted her shoulder. "Hey, I'm sorry. For whatever reason, I understand this trip might be hard for you, but in all honesty, and when you're ready, I think talking about it will help you." He gave her a caring glance. "I honestly believe that. We all need to talk about things and not keep them bottled up inside. It's the reason you're so emotional right now because you've never talked about growing up here."

Patricia wiped her damp cheeks and eyes, ignoring what Bryce had said. "I don't want the girls to see me crying. Are you ready to go in a few minutes?"

"Sure, we'll give the girls a few more minutes to watch the planes, and you some time to compose yourself," Bryce said in a tender voice, concerned how she'd react returning to her father's cabin. Even though he didn't like to see Patricia upset, he was certain he was doing the right thing bringing her here. He knew in his heart it needed to be done and that they'd all benefit, especially Patricia.

CHAPTER 28

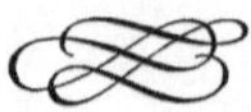

It was just a ten-minute drive to the attorney's office on 6th Street in Anchorage, and Bryce smiled when he pulled up in front of the building and saw that it was made of logs.

"Now that just screams Alaska," he said, undoing his seatbelt and opening the car door to admire the one-story log building from the sidewalk.

Patricia took her time getting out of the car. She'd been dreading this appointment ever since it was made, and now there was no turning back. She hoped to make the meeting with the attorney as short as possible. She had no desire to get into a long, drawn-out conversation with him, especially with the girls present. The less said the better.

Bryce led the way up the four steps to the double doors and held one open as the others walked in. They found a young woman on the phone sitting at the reception desk. She talked in a professional tone, smiling as she tapped away on the computer keyboard. She looked up, held her hand over the mouthpiece of the phone and whispered, "I'll be with you in just a moment."

Bryce raised his hand. "No worries, take your time."

The woman returned to her call, tossing back her head of red hair before typing again.

After a few minutes, the receptionist ended the call and gave Bryce and Patricia another smile as the girls sat on the wooden bench by a table with a bucket of crayons and coloring books.

"I'm sorry to keep you waiting," the receptionist said, showing off her pearly whites. "How can I help you?" She looked down at Patricia's arm in a cast. "What happened to you?"

Patricia approached the desk, her nerves on edge, and looked down at her injured arm, "Oh, I took a fall. No biggie," she said quickly, not wanting to be reminded of her stupidity. "My name is Patricia Levenick and I have an appointment with Neil Edwards at 10:00.

"Hi Patricia, I'm Melanie," the receptionist said as she stood up. "I'll let him know you're here," she added, walking to a door down the hallway.

As she was standing in the middle of the room waiting for Melanie to return, Patricia looked over her shoulder and saw that the girls were happily occupied with the coloring books. She had a thought that pleased her and immediately suggested it to Melanie when she returned took her seat behind the desk again a few minutes later.

"He's ready to see you, let me take you to his office," Melanie said, before tapping a few more keys on her keyboard.

Patricia approached her desk. "You know, our daughters seem to be enjoying coloring, would it be okay if we left them out here? I don't think our meeting will take too long."

Melanie nodded and expressed a friendly smile. "Of course, that's fine. I can keep an eye on them."

Bryce understood and remained quiet. It was a good plan; he'd been concerned about Savannah and Jewel being present while they talked to the attorney, especially since they still didn't know the real reason why they were in Alaska. It didn't surprise him that Patricia had a solution. She had become a pro at hiding things from people for decades, including their daughters. He walked over to his girls and sat down next to Jewel. Tapping her knee, he glanced at the picture of the fishes she was coloring. "That's really good, Munchkin. Your mom and I are going to talk to somebody here for a few minutes. Do you have enough to keep you busy for a bit?"

Jewel nodded, not taking her eyes off her coloring book. "Sure, Daddy. There are a lot of fish to color in this book."

Bryce stood up and smiled at Savannah." Okay, we won't be long. Melanie, the lady behind the desk, will be keeping an eye on you."

Patricia was quiet as they were led to the lawyer's office - her palms sweaty - and she soon felt a headache coming on. Unable to rub her palms together due to the cast on her arm, she wiped her brow with her good hand and took a deep breath before entering the office.

Neil Edwards, a tall middle-aged man with silver hair dressed in a grey suit, stood up from behind his desk wearing a friendly smile, his arm extended, ready to shake hands. "Good morning, it's a pleasure to meet you. I just wish it were under better circumstances. I'm sorry for the loss of your father." He looked at Patricia's arm. "What did you do to your arm?"

Patricia met his handshake with her left hand, which felt awkward and forced a smile. "I broke it, but it's healing fine." She quickly changed the subject. "It's okay about my father, I hardly knew him, and it's a pleasure to meet you, too. This is my ex-husband, Bryce. He accompanied me on this trip with our daughters," Patricia told him, nervously.

Bryce shook his hand. "Hi, nice to meet you."

The lawyer pointed to the two chairs on the other side of his desk. "Please have a seat," and then returned to his chair and picked up a file from the desk. "I have all the papers here for you to sign," he said, scanning through the documents.

Bryce interrupted. "We've decided to take the papers back to the cabin with us and read them over if you don't mind. We're going to be here for a couple of weeks, and we'd like to go through everything in the cabin." He glanced at Patricia. "Right, Patricia?"

"Yes, that's correct. There might be things our daughters would like to have."

"That's perfectly fine. I understand. When you're ready to drop them off, give me a call first to make sure I'm here at the office." He pulled out an envelope from the file. "Now, here are the keys to the cabin and the boat."

Bryce grabbed the arms of his chair and looked at Patricia again. "He had a boat? You never told me that."

"I told you he was a fisherman," Patricia reminded him.

"Yes, you did, but I thought he was a deckhand on a boat or something. I didn't realize he had his own boat."

"Well, now you know. Can we continue this discussion later and take care of business?" Patricia persisted.

Bryce looked at the lawyer and gave an apologetic smile. "Sorry Mr. Edwards, I recently found out about her father, and this is all new to me."

"Bryce, please!" Patricia snapped.

Neil Edwards coughed before speaking, sensing the tension in the room. "Okay then. So, the boat is docked in Whittier. I believe he's had the slip for decades. His estate is currently paying the slip fees. Let me get the slip number for you."

"It's 221-B," Patricia said.

Bryce gasped. "How did you know that?"

Patricia shrugged her shoulders. "I don't know. It just popped into my head. I haven't thought about that boat since I left Alaska. It was always in that slip, though."

The lawyer looked at his notes and nodded. "Yes, that's correct. Slip 221-B."

"Wow! I guess some things never leave us no matter how hard we try to forget. Right, Patricia?" Bryce said.

"I guess so," Patricia replied, her tone flat.

Bryce smiled and rubbed his hands. "I can't wait to see this boat. Do you remember much about it?" he asked her.

Patricia hesitated. She remembered everything about it. It was her father's life and he tried to make it hers, but she left before that could happen. "It's a Salmon fishing boat. That's what my father fished for."

"Wait till Jewel finds out you own a fishing boat. I can't wait to see her face. Do you realize that she must get her love of fishing from her grandfather? Neither you nor I like to fish as much as she does."

"Oh, I don't know about that," Patricia protested.

Bryce tossed back his head and laughed. "Oh, come on, you know I'm right. Quit trying to fight with your past; accept it and be honest with yourself for once."

Patricia ignored his comment and looked at the attorney who had remained silent. "I think we're done here. Can I get the documents and keys please?" Patricia requested, her hands resting in her lap.

"Sure," he said, handing her the items. "It was a pleasure to meet you both. I'll wait to hear from you, and I hope you enjoy your stay here in Alaska."

Patricia got up first and shook his hand. Bryce followed suit and smiled at the attorney. "Thank you for everything. We'll be in touch."

"Mommy, look what I colored!" Jewel squealed when they returned to the front office. "They are chickens, just like Daddy's."

Patricia smiled and sat next to her, taking the coloring book from her. "That's beautiful, sweetie. You color very well," realizing she'd not seen many pictures Jewel had colored.

"Thanks, Mom! I'll do some for you when we go back home. Daddy has a bunch I did for him on his fridge." Jewel looked at her mother, her eyes beaming. "Hey, I can color some for the fridge at the apartment. Can I do that, Mom?" she pleaded.

Patricia nodded and patted her daughter's knee. "Of course you can."

Bryce stood in front of where they sat and looked at his two girls and Patricia. "Are we ready to go to the cabin? It's about a two-hour drive, so we should get going."

Jewel set down the coloring book and squealed. "Yes! I'm ready."

"Me too!" Savannah echoed.

Bryce looked at Patricia. "Patricia, are you ready?"

She looked up and gave him a slight nod. "As ready as I'll ever be." She got up out of her chair and was the first to reach the door. "Let's go," she said without looking back, then headed out the door.

CHAPTER 29

With everyone buckled in the car, Bryce typed in the address of the cabin which he had previously saved on his phone. He'd spent time researching the trip prior to their arrival and had discovered on Google Earth that the cabin was in a remote area, about two miles outside of town.

"According to my phone, we should arrive around 1:00 if we don't make any stops, but I want to see as much of this state as possible, so I'm sure we'll make a few," Bryce laughed.

Patricia made herself comfortable for the drive, shifting in her seat and looking out the window as Bryce pulled out of the parking lot, listening to Savannah and Jewel chatting and giggling in the backseat. A few minutes later he made his way to the Seaward Highway, which he would take for 70 miles before turning right onto Hope Highway.

Bryce tried making casual conversation during the drive, pointing to various landmarks and the spectacular view of the snow-capped Chugach Mountains ahead, but Patricia, overcome with emotion since arriving in Alaska, unsure how to handle it, only nodded or gave short answers, limiting their conversations.

Driving on the Seaward Highway along the Turnagain Arm, Patricia looked out across the bay at the mountains; she was looking directly at the town of Hope, tucked away, barely visible to the naked eye, but she knew exactly where it was. She'd ridden these roads many times with her father in his old Chevy truck when they drove to Anchorage at least twice a month. She was amazed how well she remembered everything about those trips - from the scenery, the buildings that were still standing - and then another memory was triggered when she saw fishermen standing on the rocks leading down to the water. Some were also in the water up to their waist holding nets. She'd done the same thing with her father in the spring when it was the Hooligan run, a species of smelt.

"Look, Dad! Those guys are fishing!" Jewel cried out from the back seat. "Can we stop and watch them?" she pleaded.

Bryce was thankful to see a turn-out next to where the people were fishing and quickly pulled in. "Wow! I wonder what they're fishing for? There must be a least a dozen people here and they all have nets and buckets."

"They're fishing for smelt. It's the springtime run right now," Patricia replied, stepping out of the car, not revealing she'd done it many times when she was her daughter's age.

Bryce caught up with her as Savannah and Jewel raced ahead to the edge of the rocks. "Wow! You're full of all kinds of surprising information. Did your dad fish for smelt?"

With her hands in her jacket pockets keeping warm, she nodded. "He did. He came here every year during the run."

"Did you go with him?"

Patricia nodded again, looking straight ahead, remembering those days like it was yesterday. "I did, and before you ask, yes, I fished too." She looked at a woman by the shore, dressed in grey sweats and a green wool beanie, emptying her net into a five-gallon bucket. She knew the satisfaction the woman was feeling from pulling in a full net. It reminded her of the times when she was a young girl and couldn't lift the heavy nets, always relying on her father to help her.

She looked over at her youngest daughter Jewel, wearing a huge grin, pointing to the people onshore. "Mommy, they have a whole bunch of fish! I've never seen so many!" Jewel hollered, jumping up and down with excitement.

Patricia smiled and waved back; she'd never seen her daughter so happy. She was like a younger version of herself here on the shores of Alaska dressed in jeans and sweats, just like when she'd fished with her father on these same shores. The resemblance was uncanny. She always thought Jewel took after her father; loving the farm, the outdoors, and animals, but the more she looked at her she realized she took after herself and her father, Jewel's grandfather. Patricia was astounded that she'd never seen the similarities until now. Bryce had told her many times about how Jewel loved to fish in the pond at his farm, but not actually seeing her excitement in person, Patricia was easily able to ignore it. But there was no denying it now, and it was a revelation for her. Even Savannah was enjoying the sights, pointing and laughing with her sister. Patricia found herself witnessing a side of her daughters she'd never seen before, and she was stunned.

Bryce approached her and gently nudged her arm. "Hey, are you okay?" he asked, looking at the girls playing on the rocks.

"Yes, it just feels strange to be here."

Bryce wanted to take her in his arms and offer her comfort. He understood how hard this must be for her, but he didn't know if she'd welcome his embrace and decided to restrain himself. He instead took the gentle approach. "Do you want to talk about it?"

Patricia shook her head. "I'm not sure if I can, and I honestly don't know how to describe it." She shook her head in disbelief. "I'm looking at Jewel and I see a young me, and it just feels so strange," she confessed.

"You remember it that well, eh?" Bryce asked, watching her stare at their daughters.

"I do. I didn't think I would, but it's as clear as day and it's quite haunting." She looked at Bryce and shook her head again, "I think it's time to go. We still have quite a drive."

"Sure, let me get the girls. I'll meet you at the car."

A mile from their turn onto Hope Highway, Patricia spoke in a soft voice, not wanting the girls to hear, reminding herself that they had no idea how well she knew the area. She was even surprised how well her memory served her. "The turnoff is up here about a mile on the right. It's easy to miss if you're not looking for it," she told Bryce.

"Thanks for that, I would probably would have missed it. We take Hope Highway for seventeen miles," he added.

"Yes, it will take you right into the heart of town. My father's house is about two miles out of town."

"I saw it on Google Earth. It looks pretty desolate."

Patricia turned and looked at him, checking to see if the girls were listening before speaking. She was relieved they were not and instead were busy in chatter. "You did? You never told me that."

"I didn't feel the need to. I wanted to get a feel for the town before coming here."

"Well, you could have come straight to the source. I did live here, you know."

Bryce laughed. "No, I couldn't. You've been dead set against this trip from day one, but..." he paused.

"But what?" Patricia asked.

"But I think you're starting to come around. The Alaskan air is beginning to soften you. You don't seem as tense as you always are in New York, where all you do is work around the clock and allow your life to be controlled by schedules, meetings and pompous asses." He grinned. "You have color in your cheeks, you're spending quality time with the girls, and I haven't seen you open your laptop even once."

"I've been texting and checking in with the office, if you must know." Patricia informed him, crossing her legs and looking out the window.

"Well, I've noticed a change in you, and we've only been here less than 24 hours. Like it or not, I believe this trip will be good for you," he said, turning onto Hope Highway.

It was a quiet, two-lane highway lined with tall Quaking Aspen trees and more spectacular views of the snowcapped mountains.

"You must know this road pretty well," Bryce said, keeping his voice low to prevent Savannah and Jewel from hearing.

"I do, and surprisingly, it hasn't changed at all. It looks the same as

I remember it. We'd take this road at least twice a month to Anchorage."

"Do you realize how lucky you were to have grown up in such a beautiful part of the world? I wish our daughters could have this." He looked out of his window and smiled. "They'd certainly love it. They've not stopped smiling since we arrived. It reminds me of when they're on the farm." He paused and looked at Patricia. "Now, be honest with me, do you ever see those infectious smiles on their faces in New York?"

Patricia hissed, keeping her voice low. "I had my reasons for leaving, Bryce. This place had nothing to offer me. Look what I've achieved in New York - I could never have that here."

Bryce leaned back and rolled his eyes. "There you go again with material items. I'm talking about the quality of life, and this place wins hands-down over New York when it comes to that. Surely you agree?"

"In a sense, yes, but I could never make the money here that I make in New York. You know I'm right about that."

Bryce gave a slight nod. "Yes, you're probably right, but what does money do? It buys material stuff, so we just did a bloody full circle."

Savannah interrupted their conversation. "What are you talking about?"

"Nothing important, sweetie," Bryce quickly replied. "We'll be at the cabin in about 20 minutes."

"Awesome!" Jewel hollered from the back seat. "I'm hungry."

"Do you remember if the town has any restaurants?" Bryce asked Patricia.

"There were a couple, I'm sure they're still some, and most likely a small general store, too. Every small town has one in Alaska." She turned her head and looked at Bryce. "Would you mind if we get something to make sandwiches with? The girls are hungry, and we can fix them at the cabin. There will be no food there." She then surprised Bryce with her next words, expressing her fears and anxieties. "I'm really stressing over telling them why we're really here. I want this over with as soon as possible so there aren't any more secrets. They're either going to hate me or forgive me; I hope it's the latter."

Bryce smiled and reached across, giving her shoulder a gentle pat. "I think that's a great idea. I'm sure you'll feel much better once you've told them, and you'll be able to freely share your childhood memories with them. Something I want to hear, too," he said, followed with a smile.

CHAPTER 30

The Hope Highway took them to the heart of the small town, and it was everything Bryce had imagined after studying the multitude of pictures online. He immediately recognized the Seaview Cafe at the end of the road, a white wooden building with green trim and a large sign with the word 'Cafe' on the rusty metal rooftop. Behind the restaurant he saw the vast south shore of the Turnagain Arm waters with an amazing view of the mountains behind them. A few other rustic and mostly log buildings were scattered on the quiet, two-lane road, including a schoolhouse, museum, and a general store next door to the cafe.

Bryce pulled in front of the store, put the car in park and turned off the engine, enjoying the vibes of the town.

"Wow! Look at all that water!" Jewel yelled from the backseat as she opened her door and raced towards the end of the road to see the water, Savannah jogging closely behind her.

Bryce quickly scanned both directions of the road and saw no cars coming, and felt they were safe. He turned and looked at Patricia getting out of the car. "There's no one else here," he said, shocked by the solitude he was feeling.

"During the Salmon run this town is packed to the brim with campers and fisherman. That'll be in a few months," Patricia told him. She looked at the cafe. "I can't believe this place is still here," she said. "It looks exactly the same." Patricia looked down the main road, placing her good hand in her pocket, protecting it from the chilly air and slight breeze. "The whole town looks the same. It's like time has stood still."

Bryce stood next to her as the girls played at the end of the road. He remained silent, allowing Patricia to recapture her memories, ones she'd refused to acknowledge for two-thirds of her life. She was deep in thought, holding a hand up to her forehead, looking straight ahead at the desolate road. "We'd come here every Sunday for breakfast. This is where my mother worked before she had that terrible accident. After she died, my father continued to bring me here for breakfast every weekend." She turned and looked at Bryce. "I didn't expect it all to come back to me so quickly. It's like I never left." She closed her eyes for a few seconds and looked at Bryce again. "Let's get something for lunch and go to the cabin. I'm ready to tell the girls," she said, tears in her eyes.

Bryce gave her a warmhearted smile. "Sure, that sounds good. Why don't you go join the girls, I'll be right back."

Patricia nodded and walked down the road, her hand still in her pocket as she embraced the sounds of laughter coming from her daughters, something she rarely heard at home. When she approached them, her body warmed to the familiarity of her surroundings. She knew these shores well, having caught her share of Salmon with her father. How had she so easily forgotten the quality family times she'd had growing up here, something her father had continued to try and do after her mother passed? She looked at Savannah and Jewel, immersed in nature, and asked herself; *what am I giving my daughters?* It was then she realized she had nothing. Bryce was right, the corporate world had consumed her.

"Mom! Can we go fishing here?" Jewel asked, racing to meet her.

Patricia leaned down and embraced her with one arm. "I think we can manage that. We'll talk to your dad, okay?"

Jewel jumped up and down, waving her arms in the air. "Yay! Can we come tomorrow?"

"Munchkin, we just got here. We have plenty of time."

"Will you fish too, Mommy?" Jewel asked with pleading eyes.

Patricia was taken aback by her question. She hadn't held a fishing pole since leaving Alaska. Wrapped up in her career in New York, she'd always associated it with filth and something she didn't want her daughters to take an interest in, fearing it would tarnish her image. But here, standing in the town she grew up in, she soon realized how stupid she'd been as she saw the excitement on her daughters' faces. What a fool she'd been listening to her Aunt Cassie.

Patricia smiled; her heart full of remorse. "Munchkin, I can hold the pole with my good hand, but you'll have to help me reel in the fish if I get one. Can you do that?"

Jewel's eyes lit up. "Really? You're going to go fishing with us? Yes! I can help you reel in the fish, Mommy."

Savannah heard Jewel's cries of joy. "What did you say?" She looked at her mother in disbelief. "Did Jewel say you're going to go fishing with us? I have to see this," she laughed, approaching her mom and sister.

Patricia shrugged her shoulders. "Sure, why not?"

"Mom, you hate fishing. You always complain about Jewel doing it."

"I know, and I'm sorry for that," Patricia confessed.

Savannah's jaw dropped. "Mom, what's going on with you? I've never heard you say sorry for anything. You're acting really weird."

"Savannah, please. I've never seen this side of you two before. I had no idea how much you both enjoy the outdoors and fishing."

Savannah folded her arms and gave her mother a hard stare. "Well, if you'd come to the farm once in a while when Dad invited you, you would have known that," she barked, storming off toward the store.

"Why is Savannah mad?" Jewel asked, looking at her sister marching away.

"It's my fault, Munchkin," Patricia said, taking Jewel's hand as she watched Savannah enter the store in search of her father.

Ten minutes later, Bryce and Savannah, carrying two brown bags of groceries, returned to the car where Patricia and Jewel waited. After putting the bags in the cargo area, Bryce sat in the driver's seat and typed the directions to the cabin into his phone. Patricia noticed Savannah was quiet, avoiding her stare, and said nothing to her when she got in the car and took a seat.

Patricia motioned to Bryce with her hand to put down his phone. "You don't need that; I remember the way," she told him.

"Really?" Bryce looked up at her, setting down his phone. "I'm surprised we have service out here, but my phone works great if you'd like me to use it."

She ignored his last remark and pointed ahead. "You need to go down Hope Highway and turn right on Clark Road. The cabin is at the end of the road on the left."

"Wow, you even remember the name of the street."

"I don't think it ever left me," Patricia replied as she looked out the window while Bryce put the car in drive.

After passing the few buildings in town, they drove less than a mile to Clark Road, where Bryce turned right onto a narrow, windy two-lane road surrounded by trees and a few driveways that led back to dwellings hidden by the trees.

After driving just over a mile, Patricia pointed to a driveway on the left. "That's it," she said, her heart racing, her nerves on edge.

Bryce looked at her and pointed to the same driveway. "Here?"

"Yes, that's it."

Bryce made the turn. "Okay."

Patricia stared straight ahead, knowing the driveway well, waiting for the cabin to appear after they'd made the turn through the trees lined on either side of the long driveway.

"It's way out here," Bryce said, looking ahead.

"Yes," Patricia replied, still looking ahead. Then it came into view. The small rustic log cabin, two windows in front and the log bench she'd remembered her father had built for her mother still sitting on the front porch. Three wooden steps led up to the covered porch.

Next to it was her father's old, weathered wooden stool he'd also made, and a tree stump that he used for his beer can. She looked to her left and recognized the large workshop and storage shed, both also made of logs and leading off from the driveway where they were parked, where there was another driveway leading to the large garage behind the workshop. On the outskirts of the buildings, the remainder of her father's five-acre property was adorned with tall pine trees.

"My god, it hasn't changed a bit," Patricia whispered. "It's like time's stood still here also," she added, grasping the arm of her seat, her heart pounding.

"Are you okay?" Bryce asked.

"I don't know," Patricia managed to say, frozen to her seat. "I wasn't expecting it to hit me like this." She closed her eyes tightly. "Why did we come here?" she hissed. "I need to be alone. I'm sorry. Please, can you take the girls somewhere? I'm begging you."

Bryce brought the car to a stop and turned off the engine, unsure of how to react, afraid she'd come unhinged. "Sure, er, hold on." He turned and looked at his daughters who had already opened their doors. "Hey girls, let's go for a walk around the cabin before going in. Your mother needs a minute," he said, leaving the driver's seat and ushering the girls out of the car.

"What's wrong with her?" Savannah asked as they walked away from the car. "Is the cabin too dirty for her?" Patricia heard her say, laughing as they left her in the car.

Left alone with her thoughts, Patricia let the tears fall. "My god! What is the matter with me?" She looked down at her hands, one still holding onto the arm of her seat and raised them. "My hands are shaking, and my entire body is trembling," she cried. Images of her father, sitting on his stool, drinking his beer in the evenings flooded her mind as her and her mother sat on the bench, looking at the stars.

Patricia looked over at Jewel, who had grabbed onto a branch and swung from it. Patricia noticed it was the same tree, but much bigger now, that she'd used to swing from. "My god, Jewel is me. How have I not seen this before?" she whispered, wiping tears from her cheek. The cabin seemed much smaller than she'd remembered, but then again, she'd spent the last decade living in a 5,000 square-foot luxury apartment. There was no comparison. She just couldn't believe just how tiny it was. How in heaven's name were they all going to stay in it for the next few weeks, wondering if she even could.

CHAPTER 31

Still deep in her thoughts, her good arm draped across her middle, Bryce approached her with caution, lowered his head, and rested his hand on her shoulder as he looked at her. "Are you okay? Do you need a few more minutes?"

Patricia wiped more tears away and shook her head. "I'm okay. I'm just an emotional wreck right now," she managed to say between tears. "I wasn't expecting to feel this way. I had every intention to just come here, get my business done and get back to my life in New York." She looked at Bryce, bit her lower lip, and allowed more tears to fall. "But that's not the case. I have so many mixed emotions right now - I'm not sure *how* I'm feeling."

This time Bryce embraced her, wrapping his arm around her shoulder. Patricia didn't resist, but instead found comfort, lowering her head onto his shoulder.

"Standing here in my father's driveway, New York seems so foreign - the lifestyle, the people, my career - everything about it. I feel so disconnected from it all," Patricia said between sniffles. "Maybe because it's so far away."

"Do you feel connected here?" Bryce asked.

"I don't know what I feel. I just recognize so much, and my memories being triggered are just flooding my head. It's overwhelming, and I've not even gone into the house yet."

Bryce gave her shoulder a gentle squeeze. "Are you ready to go inside now? The girls are getting hungry."

"Yes, I'm ready," Patricia said, pulling away from Bryce and composing herself. "The keys are with the files I got from the attorney which are in the car. Let me get them."

"Sure, I'll round up the girls," Bryce said, walking away.

When Patricia reached the car, she opened the door on the passenger side and reached for the files that she'd placed on the floor and pulled out a plastic bag that contained the keys. She was stunned to see the house key was the same bronze skeleton key from the time when she lived here. Then she saw the second identical key with a small red heart keychain. That used to be her key. Her father had given it to her when she became a teenager. "My god, these keys are over 20 years old."

After returning the files to the car except for the key to the house and retrieving her purse which she swung over her shoulder, Patricia waited on the front porch for Bryce and the girls. The front door was the same one; rustic planks with large, black metal hinges, and a black metal door handle and latch with a lock above it. She held the handle with her hand - the metal was cold - anticipating whether to go ahead and unlock the door before Bryce returned with the girls. She quickly pulled away, releasing her hold on the door handle, and decided against it, knowing she'd be forced to control her emotions with Savannah and Jewel present. Instead, she walked to the top of the steps and waited.

A few minutes later Jewel came racing around to the front of the house and up the stairs. "This place is really cool, Mommy. We saw a squirrel race up a tree."

Patricia forced a smile, wiping away the last of her tears. "That's wonderful, Munchkin." She smiled when she saw Bryce and Savannah walking towards her.

"Okay, we're all here," Bryce said, walking up the steps. "Let's go inside. Do you want me to unlock the door?"

Patricia nodded and handed him the keys. "If you don't mind."

Bryce took the key and held it up. "Wow, this is an old key. They don't make these anymore."

"There's a second identical key in the file envelope; it used to be mine," Patricia said, standing close to Bryce to make sure Savannah and Jewel didn't hear her.

"Wow! That's kinda of cool, don't you think?"

"More like shocking. He never put a newer, modern lock on the door."

"Doesn't seem like he needed to. Looks like the door, lock and key have held up pretty well," Bryce said, looking at the skeleton key again.

Savannah and Jewel anxiously waited behind their dad as he pushed the key into the lock and turned it as Patricia waited off to the side. Bryce looked over his shoulder and smiled at his daughters. "It works," he said, pushing the door open.

Savannah and Jewel raced past him. "Yay!" Jewel squealed.

Bryce looked over at Patricia who hadn't moved. "Ready?" he said, holding out his hand.

Patricia welcomed the support and walked slowly towards him, taking his hand.

"I'll be next to you the whole time, okay?" he whispered, leading her to the entrance of the cabin.

Patricia took a deep breath and slowly followed his lead, her heart pounding. She grabbed Bryce's hand hard, digging her nails into his flesh as she entered the cabin. "My god, he didn't change a thing. Even the couch is the same one. It must be 30-plus years old, and my mother made that quilt draped over it."

Bryce stood by her side; the girls had disappeared towards the back of the cabin. His first impression was how small it was. Patricia let go of his hand and slowly walked over to the small kitchen on the left, lined with wooden cabinets and open to the rest of the front room. He watched as she ran her hand over the wooden countertops. She turned and looked at him.

"Time has stood still here, too. It's like I never left," she said, turning to open the cabinets and look inside. "The dishes are in the same place. How do I remember such things?" She turned and placed her hand on the metal handle of a drawer. "This was the silverware drawer." She pulled it open. "It still is." She closed the drawer and walked over to the deep metal sink against the wall of the cabin and looked out of the small window. "My mom used to watch me playing outside from here when she was doing the dishes." She looked to the left and saw that the four-burner apartment-size stove was different, as was the fridge. On the other side of the kitchen was a small dining room table with four chairs. "That's the same dining room table." Patricia strode over and picked up one of the green quilted placemats. She held it in her hands as she spoke. "My mother made these, too." She held them up to her cheek and closed her eyes. "My father kept everything." When she opened her eyes, she looked over at the wooden cabinet; it was then that she saw the photographs.

Still clutching the placemat, Patricia took a few steps to the cabinet - one her father had made in his shop - and picked up one of the pictures. It was one of the three of them; her father, mother and herself sitting on the bench on the front porch. She couldn't remember who took the photo. Patricia guessed she was about six, seeing that her mother was still alive. She touched the glass of the photo, tracing her mom's face.

Bryce slowly approached her and looked over her shoulder. "Is that you with your parents?" he asked softly.

Patricia nodded, tears again streaming down her face. "Yes," she sniffled heavily. "We were a family then," she said, setting down the picture and picking up another one. "This is my father on his boat. This picture was taken when I lived here. He's younger here. I don't see any of him when he was older."

"It seems to me that he stopped putting out pictures after he lost his family," Bryce said, picking up a picture of Patricia standing on the back of his boat. "This looks to be the last one he took of you. You look much older in this picture."

Patricia took the picture and looked at it. "I was about sixteen, it was a few years before I left. You're right, that is the last picture," she said, scanning the others before picking one up of her and her mother sitting at the same table that was still in the cabin. "This is me and my mother making bread dough," Patricia said, handing it to Bryce.

"I didn't know you could bake," Bryce said, trying to lighten the mood.

"After my mother died, I learned how to cook a lot of things to help my father. I grew up quickly, cleaning this cabin, washing clothes. I refused to do anything when I left and went to New York. I was only eight when I took on all that responsibilty and it was just too much for a young child." She paused and looked at Bryce with sadness. "After my mom died, so did my childhood."

"Is that why you hated your father? Because he made you grow up too fast? "Bryce asked.

"I don't know. I was a lonely child with few friends. Most of the time it was just me and my father, and he changed after my mother died. He was always so sad."

"That makes sense," Bryce replied, thinking now was not the time to drill her with questions, but instead allow her to express and immerse herself in what he assumed was an emotional moment.

Patricia turned, put the placemat back on the table and walked to the main room of the cabin. "That was never here," she said, pointing at the small, flat-screen TV in the corner. "It looks out of place in this room. I guess they can get cable service here," she said, standing in the middle of the room and looking at the wood-burning stove surrounded by a brick hearth where more photos sat on the high wooden mantle made from a single log. She picked up one of the photos - she remembered all of them. There were pictures of her parents' wedding day. They were married at the small church in town, and the entire town had gathered at the Seaview Cafe afterwards for a feast and live music that played into the early hours of the morning.

"I was born a few years after they married," Patricia said, holding one of the pictures. "My mother told me about her wedding day so many times. She would always tell me it was the happiest day of her life." Patricia carefully returned the photo to the mantle and walked over to the couch; she lifted a corner of the quilt that was draped over it. "Yes, it's definitely the same couch," she said, running her palm over the dark green cushion. "I can't believe it's still here." She took a seat and rubbed her hand over the multicolored red, orange, yellow and white quilt made with old clothes her mother had saved over a period of time. "I watched my mother make this. It took her quite a long time." She held back tears by sniffling. "She was so proud when she laid it over this couch."

"It's beautiful," Bryce said, standing in the room. "I'm surprised how much you remember?"

"So am I," Patricia said softly, still stroking the quilt. "Everything in this room has a story, and I know every single one of them."

"Maybe one day you can tell them to me and our daughters."

"Yes, but I wouldn't know where to begin. This is all so over-whelming - I need time to digest it all."

"I understand."

They were interrupted by Savannah. "This place is tiny. There's only two bedrooms at the back and one bath. Where are we all going to sleep?"

Patricia stood and walked away from the couch, "I'm not sure yet. Can you show me the bedrooms?" Patricia said, taking her daughter's hand, even though she already knew where they were.

Savannah quickly led her mother down a narrow hallway lined with knotty pine boards. She stopped halfway and looked at a large picture on the wall. It was of her as a baby being held by her mother, and her father sitting next to them supporting Patricia's head. "I look like my mother," Patricia whispered.

Savannah squeezed her hand. "What did you say, Mom?" Savannah asked, stopping in the hallway.

"Nothing, sweetheart," Patricia said. "Lead the way."

Savannah took her to the room on the right at the end of the hall-way. "This looks like it's a girl's room, Mom."

Savannah was right; Patricia took a deep breath before entering what was once her room and sucked in a sharp breath when she saw Jewel sitting on the bed covered with a red quilt, her legs crossed and, in her hands, she held Sally, the blonde-haired doll that Patricia took with her everywhere when she was a child.

Patricia stood in the entranceway of the room, hesitating to go in. Just like the living room and kitchen, her room was exactly how she'd left it when she walked out the door 20 years ago. The single bed was lined with her favorite stuffed toys that her mother had bought at yard sales. Her lamp with a fish stand sat next to her bed on two blue milk crates covered with a green tablecloth. Next to it was the wooden dresser her dad had gotten from one of the neighbors. Patricia wondered if it still held the clothes she'd left behind. She wasn't ready to look yet. On top of the dresser was an Atlas, some encyclopedias, and some classic children's books including Tom Sawyer, Little Women and Nancy Drew. Across from the bed was an old wooden desk and chair, as well as another small lamp with a white shade and brass stand. Patricia held her chest. "My god this is eerie," she whispered, looking at the wooden chest at the end of the bed. "Everything is still here."

Jewel looked up, holding up the doll. "Look Mom, I found a doll. She's really pretty."

Patricia took a seat on the edge of the bed. "Can I see her?"

Jewel held out the doll. "Sure."

Patricia took Sally and ran her fingers over her face and through her hair before clutching her to her chest. Sally had been her only friend for years. She'd had many tea parties with her outside on the front porch. At night they'd read books together by flashlight under the sheets of her bed. Her father had attached a wooden crate to her bike so that Sally could ride with her. "Hi Sally," Patricia whispered, stroking the doll's hair, her eyes misty with tears. Even when she became a teen, she never outgrew Sally and the stuffed animals.

"Does someone live here?" Savannah asked. Why is all this stuff here?"

Bryce entered the room and looked at Patricia holding the doll. "Old friend?" he said.

"Why would the doll be an old friend?" Savannah asked, picking up a stuffed lion from the bed. "This is cute? Who do all these stuffed animals belong to?"

Still holding Sally tight against her chest, Patricia took Savannah's hand. "I think we need to make some lunch and have a talk." She looked at Bryce and gave him a weak smile. "What do you think?"

"I think that's a good idea."

CHAPTER 32

Savannah and Jewel took a seat at the table. Jewel had brought a white stuffed polar bear from the bedroom and was walking it across the table as Savannah tried to grab it. Their giggles filled the cabin.

Patricia didn't realize until she had reached the kitchen that she was still carrying Sally. She placed her on the counter before grabbing some plates from the cupboard and the roll of paper towels they'd bought at the store.

"I'll go ahead and make us some turkey sandwiches," Bryce said, unpacking the bag of groceries.

"Do you need some help?" Patricia asked.

Bryce didn't want to make her feel uncomfortable; he'd never witnessed Patricia offering any help in the kitchen. This was a definite change in her, and he believed she was unaware of it. Being in Alaska in the cabin where she grew up brought her back to her natural self, how she used to be before she'd left – a side of her he'd never known.

Stunned by her offer, Bryce hesitated. "Err, sure. Do you want to wash the lettuce? Oh, wait you can't do that with just one hand."

Patricia laughed at his comment, taking the head of lettuce from him. "I'm sure I'll manage just fine."

Bryce thought for a moment. "There's running water here, right?"

"Yes, and a running toilet and shower as well."

"Oh good, that never crossed my mind until we needed water," he laughed.

Bryce smiled to himself as he and Patricia made lunch together in the small space of the kitchen, occasionally bumping into each other, their bodies touching, their eyes meeting before a subtle smile was exchanged between them. He hadn't felt this close to Patricia since he'd been married to her. Seeing her in this environment expressing her emotions was affecting him in a way he'd not expected, and, like Patricia, who was unsure of how to react being back where she grew up, he was also unsure of how to react to what was stirring within him.

Once the sandwiches were made and Patricia had emptied a bag of chips into a red plastic bowl, she and Bryce joined their daughters at the table, carrying the plates of food and bowl of chips. Bryce made a second trip to the kitchen and grabbed a gallon of milk and four plastic cups.

"So, do you like this place?" Patricia asked the girls, wondering how to begin her confession.

Savannah nodded while chewing her food.

"It's kinda small, but I like it," Jewel said, taking a bite of her sandwich.

"I like it too, but yeah, it's really tiny," Savannah said. "You never did tell me if someone lives here, "she added. "There's so much stuff here."

Patricia took a deep breath and looked over at Bryce who gave her a slight nod. Patricia knew it was time.

"Someone used to live here, but they don't anymore," Patricia said, looking at her daughters.

"They left all their stuff behind when they moved?" Savannah asked, her brow furrowed.

"No, the man that lived here sadly passed away," Patricia paused, taking in another deep breath. "He was my father."

"He died a long time ago. This stuff has been here all that time?" Savannah asked, wearing a look of confusion.

"Actually, he died a few months ago. When I moved away from here, I never stayed in contact with him."

Savannah set down her sandwich on the plate and looked at her mother. "You used to live here?" Before Patricia had a chance to answer, Savannah spoke again. "Wait, you told us that your dad died a long time ago. Why did you lie?"

Patricia reached for Savannah's hand and was crushed when she pulled away. "I didn't lie, sweetheart. I just never talked about him. I told you that my mother had died in a car accident; everyone assumed my father did too. I'm sorry I never told you he was still alive."

Patricia looked over at Jewel who continued to eat her sandwich, not asking questions like Savannah. Maybe she's still too young to understand, Patricia thought.

"He was my grandpa, wasn't he?" Savannah asked.

"Yes, he was, sweetie," Patricia replied, softly.

"And he never wanted to see me or Jewel? Why?" Savannah asked.

Patricia's heart dropped; guilt swept through her. Savannah believed their grandfather had abandoned them and wanted nothing to do with them. She couldn't have them thinking that and shook her head. "No, no. He never knew about you; he had no idea he had two beautiful granddaughters. If he did, trust me, he would have been on the next plane to New York to meet you. This is all my fault, sweetheart. I never told him about you."

Tears filled Savannah's eyes, crushing Patricia's heart. "Why, Mom? He was our grandpa. Why didn't you tell him about us? Are you ashamed of us?"

"Oh, no Savannah, I love you very much. I could never be ashamed of you."

Jewel finally joined in on the conversation. "Who was our grandpa?"

Savannah looked at her sister. "The man that used to live here. He was Mom's dad, and Mom never spoke to him after she moved out. It's all her fault we never had a grandpa," she cried, pushing back her chair and storming out of the room to what used to be Patricia's room and slamming the door.

"Why is Savannah crying?" Jewel asked.

Patricia looked over at Bryce. "Can you stay with her? I'm going to go try and talk to Savannah. I can't have her hating me, I need to fix this."

Before heading to the bedroom, Patricia stopped in the kitchen and grabbed Sally the doll. Funny how she still brought her comfort during tough times. With her chest heaving she cautiously approached the bedroom door and knocked gently. "Savannah, can I come in sweetie? I need to talk to you."

There was no answer. Patricia slowly opened the door. Her heart dropped when she found her daughter, curled up on the bed in a fetal position, sobbing.

"Oh Savannah, I am so sorry," Patricia said, walking over to the bed. She took a seat on the edge, resting her hand on Savannah's side. "Please forgive me. It was wrong of me to deny you a relationship with your grandfather. I thought I was doing the right thing, but I see now what a terrible mistake I've made."

Savannah continued to sob. "Go away!" she cried, scooting her body closer to the wall and away from her mother's touch.

"Savannah, please, talk to me. I lived an extremely poor life here and I only wanted a better life for you and Jewel. I was convinced that if I had any ties with my father or this house that I may end up back here, and I refused to have that be a possibility. Please forgive me."

Savannah turned and narrowed her eyes at her mother, her jaw tight. "But he was our grandpa."

Patricia rested her hand again on Savannah's side, "I know sweetheart, and I promise you, I will share many stories about him while we're here, and show you pictures. I know there are some old photo albums here that my mother put together. If you want, you can pick out some things that belonged to them and take them back to New York." She patted Savannah's side. "Would you like that?"

Savannah wiped her moist cheeks and nodded. "Yes, I would. What was his name?"

Patricia gave her a weak smile, relieved her daughter was talking to her. "His real name was Billy Matts, but after an accident where he lost an eye, everyone called him 'One Eye.'"

"How did he lose an eye?" Savannah asked, sitting up and leaning her back against the headboard.

Patricia leaned back on the bed, taking Savannah in her arms, and told her the story of her father's accident. A few minutes later, while she was in the middle of the story, Bryce quietly entered the room, holding Jewel's hand. He sat on the end of the bed as Jewel crawled up to her mother and snuggled her head on her chest.

"Are you talking about Grandpa?" Jewel whispered.

Patricia nodded, gave her a loving smile, and continued with her story as Bryce listened in with a warm heart.

"Do you miss him?' Savannah asked after hearing the story.

"I never knew him. Once I moved to New York I never spoke to him again. It's hard to miss someone you don't know. I only found out he passed away a few weeks ago." She looked at Bryce when she spoke again. "But I miss him now."

"Why are we here if he's dead?" Savannah asked, handing Jewel a stuffed toy she was pointing at.

"Because we have to sell everything, and there's a nice attorney in Anchorage that's going to help us with that."

"Are we going to stay here the whole time before we go home?"

"Yes, we are," Patricia told her.

"Good, because I want to hear more stories," Savannah said, finally smiling.

Patricia pulled her in close and hugged her. "I have many more to tell you."

CHAPTER 33

$\mathcal{B}$ryce rubbed the goosebumps on his arms as he stood at the end of the bed and saw Patricia in a different light, one he could only describe as motherly - humble and real. He was witnessing her evolve from the heartless, corporate lioness which had consumed her since leaving Alaska, and now her true roots were reminding her of how she once used to be.

He had been expecting some sort of revelation, but this was beyond anything he'd hoped for. She was ready to open up and share her history which she'd suppressed for so many years. She showed a genuine desire to tell their daughters about her side of their family, and the grandparents they'd never known. They'd only been at the cabin for a few hours, and already so much had been revealed. What more would their trip unveil, he wondered.

His heart was full as he listened to Savannah ask many questions, and Patricia gave her a loving smile before answering.

"So, this was your room?" Savannah asked.

"Yes, it was. My mom made this red quilt." She smiled again. "She loved to sew and quilt." She picked up Sally the doll lying on the bed, pulling it into her chest. "My parents gave me this doll for Christmas when I was five years old, and she was my best friend up until I left. She went with me everywhere."

"Why didn't you take her with you when you left?" Jewel asked, stroking the doll's hair.

"Because there was no room in my suitcase. I cried when I left her behind."

"Can I take her home with us?" Jewel asked, taking her from her mom's hold. "I like her, and I like her name, too."

Patricia stroked Jewel's hair. "Yes, of course you can. I think that's a great idea."

"I want to take the photos home of grandpa and grandma so I can look at them every day," Savannah said, sitting up.

"I love that idea," Bryce replied, smiling. "We can keep some at the farm as well as the apartment, if that's okay with your mother."

"That's fine with me. We'll find a special place to display them." Patricia agreed.

Bryce's ears perked up. "Was that a knock at the door?"

The room fell silent and a few seconds later, they all heard a second knock.

"Who could that possibly be?" Patricia said, her brow furrowed as she stood up. "I don't know anyone here."

"I'm coming with you," Bryce said, following Patricia as she approached the door. "Let me answer it," he said, grabbing the handle before Patricia could open it. "It might be some crazy person."

Patricia chuckled. "This isn't New York, Bryce."

Bryce slowly opened the door and was greeted by an elderly man with a head of grey, mangled hair and a grey beard in dire need of a trim. His eyebrows were also grey and thick. He stood with a stoop, holding a wooden cane, and wearing blue jeans held up with black suspenders and a red and black checkered shirt. He had on black rubber boots and gave Bryce a friendly smile when he opened the door.

"Hello there, my name is Tom and I live next door. I saw you pull into the driveway earlier today, and being the nosy neighbor that I am, I wanted to ask what brings you here? The fella that lived here passed away a few months ago and I've been watching the property."

Patricia pushed past Bryce and stared at the elderly man. "Tom? From next door? I'm Patricia, One Eye's daughter."

Tom stood back and smiled. "Patti? Is that you?"

Bryce was stunned and whispered to Patricia, "he called you Patti."

Patricia waved her hand to silence Bryce. "Shh," and then looked at Tom. "Yes, It's me. Please come in," she said, ushering him in with her hand.

Tom entered the cabin, continuing to stare at Patricia. "Well, I'll be. Look at you, you're all grown up." He looked over at Savannah and Jewel. "Are those yours?"

"Yes, these are our daughters Savannah and Jewel, and this is my ex-husband Bryce who accompanied me on this trip. It's a lot to deal with." She turned to Bryce. "This is Tom. He and my father were good friends for decades."

Tom's smile disappeared and was replaced with a frown, "So One Eye was a grandfather?" Tom asked, his tone no longer friendly.

Patricia avoided Tom's stare. "Yes, he was." She pulled out a chair from the table. "Please have a seat."

Patricia noticed he walked with a limp when he accepted her gesture and sat on the chair. "What happened to your leg?" she asked

"Oh, a silly accident on the dock. I slipped and did some permanent damage to it."

"So, I guess you're no longer fishing?" Patricia asked.

"Oh, I'm still in the business; I have a bigger crew now and stick to just driving the boat most of the time. It'll take more than a beaten leg to get me to quit fishing, just like your old man. He fished up until the day he died."

"I only found out a few weeks ago about his passing. I can't believe how everything here is exactly how I remembered it."

"You broke your daddy's heart when you left. He swore you'd be back and wanted everything to remain the same for when you did. But you never did. I have to say, he was never the same afterward. He kept to himself. Hazel would bring him homemade pies and soup because she knew he wasn't eating well. When you left, so did a part of your dad, I'm afraid."

"I'm sorry Tom, but there was nothing here for me. I had no future here."

"I know, you traded in your dad for a career. That aunt of yours filled your head with nonsense," Tom said in a condescending tone.

"That's a little harsh, Tom," Patricia said with an edge.

"Sometimes the truth is," Tom said, using the same patronizing tone.

Looking over at Savannah and Jewel standing in the middle of the room, Bryce interrupted. "Hey girls, why don't you go in the bedroom for a bit while we talk to Tom, okay?"

"Okay, Daddy," Jewel said, taking her sister's hand and leading her down the hallway.

"Sorry, I didn't want them listening in on our conversation," Bryce said, taking a seat at the table.

"Thanks," Patricia said. She looked at Tom. "Where is Hazel anyway?"

Tom leaned back in his chair. "She passed away ten years ago from cancer."

"I'm so sorry Tom, she was a like a second mother to me after my mom died. She even homeschooled me when I couldn't get to the schoolhouse in the winters."

"Yes, you broke her heart, too. You never even said goodbye to her. You *do* know that you were the daughter she never had. We love our two boys, but Hazel always wanted a girl, and you filled that void she had."

Guilt swept over Patricia. "I had no idea, I'm so sorry." Patricia looked away for a moment. "I didn't realize how many people I'd hurt when I left, but I see that now."

"Of course you didn't; you were only concerned with what you wanted. It was very selfish of you if you ask me."

Bryce remained silent as Patricia and Tom talked, and even though he knew Tom's words were harsh and stung Patricia, he was convinced she needed to hear them.

Patricia tried to reason with Tom. "I was young, only eighteen. I didn't know how much I'd hurt him."

Tom shook his head, not buying her excuses. "But you never came back, Patti. You're a grown woman now. You have been for years. Why did you never come back, or even pick up the phone?"

Patricia shrugged her shoulders. "I don't know. Fear I guess."

"Fear? Fear of what? He was family, the only one you had - I might add - and you were all he had."

Patricia sniffled back her tears. "I don't know, Tom. I don't know what I would have said to him if I had returned. I was afraid he'd hate me."

Tom raised his voice a notch. "There you go again. Always thinking about yourself and how you'd be affected. Screw the people you shit on. What you did was wrong, and I don't care if you hate me for telling you exactly what I think of you. Your dad was a good man, and after your mom died, he did the best he could raising you, even with a broken heart. But it wasn't enough for you, was it? His heart was already broken, and you had to finish it off by crushing it. He died alone in his bed from an aneurism that burst while he slept. I found him the next day when he didn't show up on his boat. Your dad never missed a day of fishing. It's all he had after you left him. In case you're interested, he was buried at sea. Me and some fellow fisherman took him out on his boat for a final farewell and scattered his ashes. The ocean befriended him and provided him with a decent living. More than I can say for his daughter."

He reached into the top pocket of his shirt and pulled out some keys. "These are the extra set of keys to his boat and storage shed in Whittier that he entrusted to me for years, I've no use for them now. I've been running the boat a couple of days a week since he's been gone. Can't leave it just sitting there at the dock." He placed them in Patricia's hand. "I'm not sure what plans you have for the boat; I imagine you'll be selling it. If that's the case, I know of a couple of guys who are interested. They knew One Eye well, and we'd like to keep it in the fleet if you don't mind."

Patricia avoided his stare. "Thank you. I'll keep that in mind."

Tom stood up abruptly and leaned on his cane. "Now, if you'll excuse me, I must get going. I've said what I wanted to say to you. I had to wait over 20 years to do so, mind you, and I have nothing more to say." He walked to the front door and opened it.

Patricia stood. "Please Tom, can we please talk some more?"

"I'd rather not, if you don't mind. I'm done here. I'll leave you to your business," he said, stepping out of the cabin and walking over to his white Ford truck.

Patricia stood up and walked over to the entranceway of the cabin and watched Tom turn his truck around in the wide driveway and drive away without acknowledging her. When he was out of sight, she closed the door and leaned against it, closing her eyes.

"I'm sorry you had to hear that," Bryce said.

Patricia pulled herself away from the door, shook her head, and returned to her seat at the table. "I deserved it. Everything he said was true and he had every right to be angry with me. How did I forget about him and Hazel so quickly? They helped us so much after my mother died." She shook her head again. "God I'm an awful person."

Bryce was shocked by her words. "Hey, that's enough, I won't have you talking like that. I know you can't see it now, but coming back here was a good thing. I'm already seeing so many changes in you." He gave her a kindhearted smile. "You actually have *feelings*, and watching you tell our girls stories of your father was beautiful. They will carry those stories with them for the rest of their lives."

"I hope you're right, Bryce, because right now I'm not feeling too good about myself."

"Give it time." He leaned back in his chair and folded his arms. "You know, we need to figure out where we're all going to sleep in this cabin. Do you have any ideas?"

Patricia leaned forward, resting her good hand on her knee. "There's one room I've not been in yet. I thought the girls could sleep in there."

"Your parent's room?"

Patricia nodded. "Yes," and then got up. "I think it's time I see it."

"Do you want me to go with you?"

Patricia nodded again. "If you don't mind."

CHAPTER 34

*B*ryce followed Patricia down the hallway and waited behind her as she slowly turned the handle and pushed the door open. As she stepped into the dimly lit room with the green curtains drawn, she turned and looked at Bryce. "Just as I thought – nothing's changed. That's the same brass-framed bed, and the pine end tables on either side that my father made."

"It's dark in here, shall I open the drapes?" Bryce asked, as Patricia continued to scan the room.

"Sure," she said, walking over to the large wooden dresser and mirror. She picked up a bottle of perfume. "Look at this. These were all my mother's things. Her perfumes, hairbrush, and glasses." She returned the bottle of perfume and picked up a white plush teddy bear. "My father won this for her at a state fair. I can't believe he kept all of her things? Why? He knew she was never coming back..."

"Looks like he could never let go," Bryce said, approaching the dresser.

Patricia opened one of the drawers and lifted out a beige sweater. "These are all her clothes." She looked at Bryce, her eyes misty. "This is so sad. He refused to move on, and I had no idea," she confessed, walking over to the door across the room. "This is the closet," she said, opening the door. "Look at this, my mother's clothes on the left, his on the right." She walked to the bed and sat on the edge. "When my mom died, he sat right here where I am now and cried so hard while he held me tightly in his arms. He told me *as long as her things are here, your mother will always be with us.*" Patricia looked at Bryce. "He never stopped believing that did he?"

Bryce took a seat next to her and took her hand in his, "I guess not. I think that's what kept him going, and he left your room untouched too, thinking you'd always come back to be here with him like your mother."

Patricia removed her hand from his, stood up and scanned the room. "I think you're right. Everything in this house has my mother's fingerprints on them. No wonder he didn't change anything. How are we supposed to remove all of these things and get this place ready to sell? That would go against everything my father has done; he was preserving my mother's memory and keeping all her things."

"We don't have to think about that now," Bryce replied, changing the subject. "I think the girls will be fine sleeping in here, but what about you? Where do you want to sleep?"

Patricia rested her hand on the dresser. "As strange as it may sound, I want to sleep in my old room."

"Okay, I can sleep on the couch, it looks long enough."

"Sounds good. Speaking of which, we should go check on the girls."

Bryce hesitated before opening his mouth, wondering if she'd had enough of childhood memories. "What do you want to do about dinner? We don't have much food here. Do you want to have dinner at the Seaview Cafe?"

Patricia didn't answer right away. "The last time I was in that restaurant was the night before I moved away. My father took me to dinner there and told me he would drive me to Anchorage Airport. I had told him that morning when my ticket arrived from my aunt that I was moving to New York. He didn't try to change my mind, he just said, "*I'm not surprised. I knew this day was coming, but mark my words, Patti, you'll be back because you belong here.*"

"I was determined to prove him wrong. I had no idea how I was going to get to the airport, it hadn't even crossed my mind. I spent the day packing my one suitcase, deciding what to take and what to leave behind. It wasn't easy, and my father worked out in the yard while I packed. That evening he told me he was taking me to dinner. When he told me he'd take me to the airport, I was shocked and told him he didn't have to. I remember his loud laugh and then him folding his arms and smirking. *"How else are you going to get there? You're my daughter, and I want to make sure you get to the airport safely. Any father would do the same. I may not agree with what you're doing, but I'm not going to abandon you."*

She looked at Bryce, "He was there for me up until the minute I left. He's right, he never abandoned me." She paused and looked at Bryce with sadness in her eyes. "I abandoned him." She gave Bryce a weak smile. "Yes, we can go to the restaurant tonight."

After spending the afternoon unpacking, they each took turns taking showers and changing into clean clothes.

Jewel was the last to bathe and came out of the bathroom wrapped in a navy-blue towel. "This is weird having one bathroom," she said. "I had to wait ages, it's tiny."

Patricia handed her a clean pair of jeans from the ones she'd set out on the queen-size bed in what was once her parents' room. "I know you miss your big, heated bathroom. It's just for a few weeks. Now, come on, get dressed, we're going out for dinner in town."

Jewel took the jeans. As she was dressing, she said, "it's okay. I like this house because it was my grandpa's and grandma's house. I wish they were here," she said, sitting on the edge of the bed sliding her leg into her jeans.

"Me too, Munchkin," Patricia said, softly.

They arrived at the Seaview Cafe a little after 6:00. The sun was still high in the sky with just under four hours of daylight left, and it was a cool 38 degrees. Patricia stepped out of the SUV dressed in jeans, a black polo sweater, a long, black wool coat, and the laced boots she'd worn for most of the trip. She looked out at the waters of the Turnagain shores, closed her eyes and inhaled deeply. "God, the air is so fresh here," she whispered. "I'd forgotten how good the slight breeze feels on my skin and in my hair."

Bryce smiled. "It sure is beautiful here, and so peaceful. I thought Connecticut was remote, but that's nothing compared to this. I've only seen two cars on these roads since we've arrived, and they're parked in front of the restaurant."

"It's why my father lived here for most of his life. He had no desire to see other places or even the world. He always used to say he had everything he needed right here."

"I think he was right," Bryce said. "I've seen a lot of the world, and this is quickly becoming my favorite place."

Patricia chuckled. "I think my mother must have felt the same way. She arrived on a cruise ship in Whittier, met my father, fell in love and never left."

"The more I learn about your parents, the more I see what an incredible love story they had," Bryce said, looking down the desolate street then at Savannah and Jewel swinging from the white wooden railing leading up to the entrance of the Seaview Cafe. He turned and looked at Patricia. "Come on, let's go inside, I'm getting hungry."

Patricia nodded. "Me too."

"Oh, well something *has* changed. This place is completely differ-ent," Patricia said as they walked inside. "I'm actually glad it is," she confessed. "I've had enough of childhood memories for one day," as she looked at the wooden bar to the left lined with barstools and a flatscreen TV high on the wall to the left.

All the walls were pine, decorated with many pictures of the locals and most likely tourists too, looking proud of a fish they'd caught. Wooden tables, chairs and benches filled the rest of the room, and soft country music played in the background.

Patricia walked over to the wall of photographs while Bryce talked to the friendly young blonde hostess about getting a table. Jewel joined her mother and took her hand. "Look at all those *fish*, Mommy! I hope we get to go fishing soon."

Patricia looked down at her and smiled. She had to admit, she was enjoying this time with the girls. "We will Munchkin, but don't forget, you're going to have to help me because of my broken arm," she reminded her, holding up her arm in the cast.

As they continued to look at the many photos, Patricia came to an abrupt stop when a photo of an elderly man with a long grey beard and grey hair caught her attention. He was dressed in blue jeans, a black sweatshirt and rubber boots standing on the banks of the Turnagain shore behind the restaurant, holding a nice-sized Salmon. She immediately knew It was her father when she saw the patch over his eye. Guessing from his age, Patricia believed it was taken within the last five years. It was the latest picture she'd seen of her father – all of the ones in the cabin were of him when her mother was alive. She now had a sense of what he looked like in his older years. He had aged well, and, like Tom had said, he spent most of his days fishing, whether it be for a living or pleasure.

"Look Munchkin, that's your grandpa," Patricia said pointing to the picture.

Jewel's eyes grew wide. "It is! Look at the massive fish he has."

"Yes, he was quite the fisherman."

Jewel turned and yelled at her sister. "Savannah, come see! There's a picture of Grandpa here and he has a gigantic fish."

Savannah immediately left her father's side and joined her mother and Jewel. "Wow, he's a lot older there," Savannah said, looking closely at the picture.

"Yes, that was probably taken just a few years ago," Patricia told her.

Bryce soon joined them. "That's your father? It looks like he aged well."

"Yes, it is. I'm glad I got to see this. I now know what he looked like as an older man."

"And that's a good thing, right?" Bryce asked.

Patricia nodded. "It is. I feel like it's one of the final pieces of the puzzle. There's so much going on in my head. So much of my past I'd forgotten because New York and the corporate world seemed so much better."

Bryce gave her a caring smile. "Do you still think that way?"

"Honestly, I don't know. Being here with the girls and even you," she chuckled, "feels good. I thought I'd never be able to stay in the cabin. I had it set firmly in my mind that it was dirty, run down and pretty much a shack, but it's completely the opposite. It's homey and very charming."

"I think this place is changing you." Bryce smiled. "I'm liking the new you," he said before the hostess came by to lead them to a table overlooking the water.

After taking a seat, Patricia scanned the restaurant and saw there were only two tables taken and then gasped when she noticed the man sitting alone two tables away was their neighbor, Tom. "Oh, great, he's here."

Bryce turned his head. "Who?"

"Tom, our neighbor," Patricia whispered, hiding her face behind her menu.

"I think before we head back to New York we should try and make amends with him. What do you think?" Bryce suggested.

"I don't think he wants to talk to me anymore. You heard what he said at the cabin; he even said he had nothing more to say to me. He hates me."

"Give him a week to calm down and maybe he'll give you another chance," Bryce told her.

After feasting on a seafood dinner and ice cream for dessert, Jewel looked out the window. "Can we go down to the water after dinner?"

Bryce looked at Patricia. "Sounds like a good idea. What do you think?"

"Sure. I'd like that," Patricia agreed, smiling.

After paying the check and leaving a generous tip, Bryce took Savannah's hand as Patricia took Jewel's, as they headed down to the water's edge. The temperature had dropped to a chilling 35 degrees, and the wind had picked up a bit, blowing the girls' long hair into their faces.

"Button up your coats, girls," Patricia called out as they let go of Patricia and Bryce's hands and raced down to the shore.

"They're having so much fun here," Bryce said, walking alongside Patricia. "They really do enjoy the outdoors."

"Yes, they do. I see that now, and it's sad that it took my father's death to realize it."

Well, I've been telling you for years how much they enjoy being on the farm, but you, stubborn as you are, wouldn't listen," he joked.

They approached a large rock and Bryce took a seat. "There's room for two and we can see the girls from here."

Patricia took a seat next to him and attempted to fold her arms to keep warm, but the cast on her arm made it uncomfortable.

"Are you cold?" Bryce asked.

"A little, but it feels good to sit out here."

Bryce removed his jacket and draped it over her shoulders. "Here, this'll help."

Patricia smiled and pulled the jacket around her neck. "Thanks."

"I like that we're getting along on this trip," Bryce smiled at her. "We haven't spent this much time together since before our divorce."

"I must admit, I agree with you. It's nice that we can be civil with one another, and watching the girls enjoying this lifestyle has really been an eye-opener for me. They're just being themselves. I see now how I've been trying to mold them into something they obviously aren't," Patricia confessed.

"So does that mean you're going to end their ballet and music lessons once you get home?" Bryce joked but meant what he said. Jewel had told him many times that she hates ballet.

"Oh, I don't know, but I foresee some changes being made in my parenting skills," she chuckled.

"That's a good start. I think being here, away from the strangulation of the city and the corporate elites, you're able to see things from a different perspective."

"Your right about that." She looked at Bryce. "You know, since we've been here, I've not thought about the firm. I haven't even checked my messages or my emails. My laptop doesn't work at the cabin anyway, but I did see they had wi-fi at the restaurant."

"I've never seen you this relaxed, even when we were married. You were always behind your laptop or on the phone, but if you need to, we can always bring the laptop to the restaurant."

"No, I like this freedom away from the office. Like you said, they'll manage without me, and will call me if there's an emergency."

"Wow, I'm really liking the new Patricia!"

Patricia laughed. "Well, don't get too used to it. Once I'm back in New York, the old me shall return."

Bryce gave her a hard stare. "Are you going to allow that to happen? After what you just said about how you like spending time with the girls and the freedom you're experiencing?"

"This relaxed, carefree woman sitting on a rock in Alaska would never survive in New York. I must be the way I am to be successful; it comes with the territory."

"Then you're not being you," Bryce said softly. "It's why I left. Maybe you're in the wrong place, too."

"Bryce, I don't want to have this conversation. Let's enjoy the view and the girls."

"Of course you don't. All I ask is that you give it some thought. Ask yourself, after being here for just a day, are you genuinely happy with your life?"

CHAPTER 35

They arrived back at the cabin, a little before 10:00, just as the sun was setting.

"We're going to go to bed Daddy, we're tired," Jewel said, taking off her coat and draping it on the recliner.

"That's fine, you've had a long day," Bryce said, giving her a hug and then Savannah.

Patricia came over and gave them both a hug. "Goodnight girls, we'll see you in the morning."

After the girls had closed their door and were down for the night, Bryce removed his jacket and headed for the kitchen. "Do you want a cup of tea? I packed some teabags. An Englishman never goes anywhere without his tea," he laughed.

"Yes, I would, thank you," Patricia replied, taking a seat on the couch.

Bryce filled up the kettle on the stove with bottled water, unsure if the water was drinkable in the cabin, and set it back on the stove to boil.

"So tomorrow we're driving to Whittier to go check out your father's boat?"

"Yes, I guess so. I'd like to find a buyer before we leave rather than let the attorney deal with it. What Tom said stuck with me."

"What was that?" Bryce asked, handing her a mug of tea before taking a seat next to her.

"That he'd like to keep the boat in the fleet. I think I'd like that, too. My father's fished these waters most of his life. I think he'd agree with Tom's suggestion." She leaned back. "But then, that would mean we'd have to make amends with him."

"Nothing wrong with that. Needs to be done anyway," Bryce noted.

"I know, but I'm not particularly good at apologizing. In fact, I suck at it," Patricia confessed. "I may need your help."

"I'll be right by your side when the time comes." He took a sip of his tea before continuing. "I looked up Whittier; it's about 50 miles from here, and we have to go through some sort of tunnel that is only open certain times of the day, because apparently, it's shared with the trains."

"Yes, that would be the Anton Anderson Memorial Tunnel. We'd have to take the train into Whittier," Patricia told him.

Bryce shook his head. "No, we don't. Cars can drive through it. It was opened up to cars in 2000."

Patricia's jaw dropped. "Really? How come I never knew that?"

"Well, it's not like you've been keeping tabs on this place since you left."

"My dad had two trucks because of that tunnel. He'd park one on this side and take his supplies on the train to the Whittier side and load an old beaten truck which he only used for transporting and getting to and from the boat. It never left Whittier. He must have been happy when they finally opened the tunnel to cars."

"I'm sure he was," Bryce said with a nod. "I downloaded the timetable onto my phone of when the tunnel is open to cars. It's open at 9:00 am if we want to make that one, and I also saw they have lodgings in Whittier and thought it'd be a good idea to spend the night there instead of driving back and forth in one day. What do you think? I'd like to check out the town, and I'm sure Savannah and Jewel would, too."

Patricia chuckled. "From what I remember, it's not much of a town. Maybe a few stores and restaurants, but sure, it'd be a wonderful experience for the girls to see where their grandpa fished."

Bryce picked up his phone from the coffee table made from a slab of wood with a tree stump for the base and checked the time. "Well, we have a big day tomorrow, we should call it a night."

Patricia sat up and looked around the room. "We need to find you some blankets for the couch."

Bryce got up. "I saw a chest in your room at the end of the bed, maybe there's some in there," he said, walking towards her room.

Patricia followed him, standing behind him as he opened the chest. "If I remember correctly, I think I had stored some magazines in that chest," she said, looking over his shoulder as he grasped the metal latch to the chest.

Bryce lifted the heavy wooden lid and saw that she was right. It was full to the brim of elite magazines - Vogue, Elle, Bazaar and Cosmopolitan. Bryce picked up a handful and combed through them. "Where did you get all of these? There are a ton of them. I know there's no place in this small town that sells these kinds of magazines."

"Aunt Cassie used to send them to me every month," Patricia told him, picking up a copy of Elle.

"For how long?" Bryce asked, combing through more magazines before picking up a letter that fell out of a copy of Bazaar.

"Since my mother died, and until I moved to New York."

"So, since you were eight years old and for the next ten years she sent you this garbage," Bryce said, holding the letter. "This fell out of one, and I see more letters tucked into the side. Are these from your aunt also?"

"Yes, she'd always included a letter."

"Can I read one?" Bryce asked.

"Sure, they're just letters full of her dreams for me."

Bryce took a seat on the edge of the bed, pulled out a letter from the envelope and read it.

My Dearest Patricia,

You know I'll never call you what your father calls you. It's such a common name, and when you come to New York, Patricia will be the only name everyone will call you.

Here are some magazines for you showing you what our wonderful city has to offer. Just imagine, my sweet Patricia, you can have all these things. Beautiful clothes, a luxury home furnished with the best and most exquisite furniture that your heart desires, expensive cars, and lots of money.

I know you're only ten, sweetheart, but when you turn eighteen, your life will begin when I bring you to New York and get you away from that horrible place where your father can offer you nothing but a life of poverty. I am sending you these magazines to let you see what you have to look forward to.

I love you, and I will take care of you. It's what my sister, your mother, would have wanted.

Love,

Auntie Cassie

Bryce stared at the letter. Numbed by what he'd read, he looked at Patricia with a blank stare. "Can I read some of the others?" he said, as he stood up.

"Sure," Patricia said, leaning over and pulling out a handful of letters.

After reading four more, Bryce had seen enough. They all said the same thing about how she was bringing her to New York when she turned eighteen. "My god, for ten years she was brainwashing you, convincing you that your father was a horrible man and couldn't provide a good life for you." He held a letter in his hand, holding it out while he spoke. "You were a child, and for ten years were told you had to get away and that she'd be your savior." He shook his head. "Did your father ever see these?"

Patricia shook her head. "No, Cassie said it was our little secret."

Bryce released a sarcastic laugh. "Of course she did. That woman stole you from your father, brainwashed you and indoctrinated you, making you believe you had no future here and that your father was a terrible man, unable to provide for you. I know she sent you a plane ticket to New York when you turned eighteen and you lived with her; was she the one that told you not to talk to anyone about your past?"

Patricia took a seat on the bed next to Bryce. "She offered to pay for me to go to law school and I couldn't refuse. It's what I've always wanted, but she said she would only pay if I completely forgot where I came from, because if it were known that I grew up in a shack in Alaska raised by a fisherman, it would smear my reputation and I'd never get anywhere in the corporate world. Cassie said I would be a laughingstock, so I agreed, and for over 20 years I've kept my promise. She was right! Look what I've accomplished."

Her words angered Bryce. "Don't defend her!" he yelled. "Because of that woman, your father lost his daughter and died alone. His granddaughters never got to know him, and your priorities of having the best home, the best car, lots of money, and only friends and clients in the elite circle are selfish, and it's completely put you out of touch with the real world."

"That's not true!" Patricia snapped, standing up to her feet and narrowing her eyes at Bryce.

"Yes, it is, and you bloody well know it. We've only been here for a day, and in that brief time, you're finally getting to know your daughters. You've spent more time with them in the last few days than you have in their entire lives. You even said so yourself how much you love seeing them being themselves and enjoying the outdoors."

"Stop it, Bryce, I've heard enough! Cassie did what was best for me," Patricia yelled.

"No, I won't stop it. You need to face the truth and come to terms with it. You have been brainwashed by an evil woman since you were a young child, trying to mold you into something that she approves of and can showcase to her rich friends, but it's not you, Patricia, it never has been. My god, don't you see that? Since we've been here, I've seen who you really are, and you want to know something? I like her. I like her much better than the stuck-up snob in New York. Here in Alaska, you're *real* - you show your feelings, you talk about them, and you're a mom to your daughters - spending time with them, making them lunch, going out for dinner with them and getting excited, planning a day of fishing." He stood and approached her, seeing that her eyes were misty. She turned away to avoid his stare, but Bryce lifted his hand, cupped her chin, and gently pulled her face toward his. "I never thought I'd say this, but we are so much alike in many ways. We both grew up in small towns. Our parents weren't rich, but they did the best they could. Do you see the similarities?"

Now calmer, Patricia briefly closed her eyes. "Now that you mention it, yes."

"Take away all the corporate garbage that you've been fed and you're not bad," he joked, then smiled. "I fell in love with you when I was a corporate brat, and when I saw what that evil world was doing to me, I left, and I admittedly fell out of love with you because you represented everything that I had come to hate."

"But you just said you like me."

Bryce smiled again and brushed his fingers gently over her cheek. "Now that I've gotten to know the real you, yes, I do like you. Seeing you in this environment has stirred up emotions I thought I'd never feel towards you again. It's mind-boggling, but I'm not going to pretend they're not there. I spent decades pretending I was living the life I thought I wanted in New York. I don't pretend anymore." He leaned in, looked into her eyes, and kissed her gently on the lips. "I don't know what I'm doing, but I had the urge to kiss you," he whispered, his nose touching hers.

"I'm glad you did, I had the urge, too."

He smiled, leaned in, and kissed her again. This time the kiss was longer, and, with his eyes closed, he pressed his body against hers and felt her good arm embrace his waist, pulling him in closer. Her body felt good against his. Her lips felt soft - the kiss was sensual and slow. He wrapped both his arms around her waist and held her tight as the passion of their kiss increased.

She welcomed him, kissing him harder, exploring his mouth with her tongue. "My god, what are we doing, Bryce?" she whispered between bated breath.

He kissed her fiercely before speaking. "Starting over as the real us." He then kissed her again, using his tongue to search every inch of her mouth. Panting, he spoke again. "I told you this trip would be good for you, but I see now it's good for the both of us."

CHAPTER 36

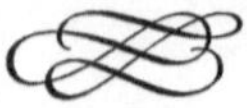

*P*atricia closed her eyes. Her heart was racing as she released her hold on Bryce and raised her hand to her brow. "This is all happening so fast. I wasn't expecting this, and it makes no sense," she said as she pulled away, pacing the room.

"It makes all the sense in the world to me." He approached her and rested his hands on her shoulders, stopping her from pacing. "I've never stopped caring about you, Patricia. You are the mother of my daughters, and seeing this other side of you has stirred up all kinds of feelings." He paused and gazed into her eyes. "I think I'm falling in love with you again."

Patricia pulled away. "Bryce, please stop. We can't do this. What about the girls? They're right next door."

"What about the girls? I'm their father. You think they'd object to me showing their mother affection again? I think they'd be overjoyed that there's a possibility that their parents might be getting back together again." He smiled. "We'd be a family once more, just like we used to be."

Patricia's jaw dropped as she pulled away. "Bryce! Now you're just talking nonsense. We are *divorced*. We lead separate lives, and once we leave this place, this will all be forgotten. It was just a silly kiss, we got caught up in the moment."

Bryce stood in front of her, his face lowered, giving her a hard stare. "Is that what you think it was? A silly kiss? I'm sorry, but I disagree with you. Why are you fighting this, Patricia? You can't honestly stand there and tell me you didn't feel anything? Why do you continue to lie to yourself? For god's sake Patricia, be yourself for once."

Patricia raised her hands to her chin, the cast on her arm was heavy. "I just need some time, Bryce."

"Time for what?" His lips narrowed, showing his anger. "Well, you know something? You have all night to think about it. I'm going to find some blankets and call it a night." A few seconds later he was gone, leaving Patricia standing alone in her room.

Subconsciously, just like when she was a child, Patricia walked over to the bed, picked up her faithful friend Sally the doll and hugged her before closing her eyes. Sitting on the edge of the bed, repeating Bryce's words in her head, the doll brought her comfort just like it did many years ago. *"For god's sake Patricia, be yourself for once!"* His words struck a chord, and she wondered who she had been for the last 20 years? She hated to admit it, but he was right - her life had been molded to Cassie expectations and approval. She was actually beginning to see things clearly now for the first time and she owed Bryce an apology. Something she'd never have admitted to before this trip.

Holding Sally close to her chest she stood up and slowly opened the door, thankful to see there were lights still on in the front room, which meant that Bryce was still awake. She crept down the hallway and called his name out softly - her anxiety peaked - remembering his anger when he left the room. "Bryce are you still awake?" she said, entering the living room where she found him laying a blanket over the couch.

"Yeah, what do you want?" he said gruffly, not looking at her.

Patricia approached him with caution, unsure if his anger was still present.

"Can we talk?"

"I thought we were done talking," he mumbled, throwing a pillow on the couch that he'd found in the hallway cupboard.

"Please, I can't sleep with this hostility between us. I owe you an apology."

Bryce stopped and looked at her, his brows furled. "Wow! I never thought I'd hear those words come out of your mouth. You owe me an apology? I gotta hear this," he said, folding his arms.

"Please Bryce, stop. After you left the room, I couldn't stop thinking about what you said."

"What was that?"

"That I should be myself for once. You're right Bryce, it never occurred to me before that I had been living a lie until you said that. It's all making sense now."

She had Bryce's full attention; he sat on the couch and patted the space next to him. "Come on, sit down and tell me what you mean."

Patricia accepted his invitation and took a seat next to him, still holding the doll. "When you said that, I saw everything different. Cassie never forgave my father for falling in love with her sister, my mother. She hated the man, telling me time after time how he stole her sister from her and made her live a life of poverty. She blamed him for my mother's death, stating that if she'd never met the man her sister would still be alive today. It was, sadly, a freak accident. It was no one's fault. My father wasn't even with her when the accident happened." Patricia paused. "I strongly believe she brought me to New York for revenge. She took me away from my father because my father took her sister."

Bryce took her hand and gave it a gentle squeeze. "You just might be right. What an evil thing to do, but it would explain why she was so upset last week when you told her we were coming to Alaska. A place she has managed to keep you from and *brainwashed* you into believing it's the worst place on earth."

"She was strongly opposed to us coming here, afraid we'd never come back. She even ended the call saying she'd lost a sister, and she wasn't about to lose a niece." Patricia lifted Bryce's hand, still entwined with hers, and rested it on her cheek. "Oh, Bryce, I'm so sorry, I believe I have been wronged by my aunt and not you. Please forgive me."

Bryce gave her a thoughtful smile, wrapping his arm over her shoulder and pulling her in. "It's okay. She had me fooled too; I thought she genuinely cared for you, but you've been nothing more than her pawn to get revenge on your father."

Patricia leaned her head on his chest, his heartbeat in her ear soothing her. "Sadly, I think you're correct." She looked up and smiled, gazing into his eyes. "Thank you for bringing me here."

He matched her smile and leaned in to kiss her. "Does this mean you're going to start being yourself?"

Patricia kissed him back. "I'm slowly getting to know her, and I think she'll be here permanently very soon."

CHAPTER 37

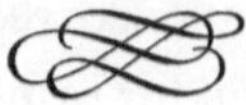

s much as Bryce wanted to seduce her and make love to her right there on the couch while he held her in his arms, he restrained himself. Maybe he'd come on too strong in the bedroom with his fiery kisses and needed to take it slow. Let everything that's happened over the past few days unfold in Patricia's head and not overwhelm her with the fact that yes, he was falling in love with her again, but this time it was with the real Patricia, the one he'd wished he'd first met; if it had been, he was certain they'd still be together today.

Soon after Patricia had laid her head on his chest, Bryce heard faint snoring a few minutes later. He chuckled to himself; she'd fallen asleep. Carefully moving his arm very slowly, he gently removed the doll she was still holding in her hand and placed it on the coffee table before kissing the top of her head. "Goodnight, Patricia," he whispered, leaning back and closing his eyes.

Bryce woke the next morning to the sound of feet running down the hallway. The first thing he noticed was that Patricia was no longer in his arms and he was covered with a blanket.

"Daddy, are you awake?" he heard Jewel say.

He rubbed his eyes and saw her standing next to the couch, looking over him. "I am now. Where's your mother?"

"I guess she's still sleeping, her door's closed. Savannah is too, and I'm hungry."

Bryce removed the blanket, stretched his arms above his head, and pulled himself up off the couch. "Let me go use the bathroom and then I'll fix us all some pancakes and eggs."

When Bryce returned, he found Patricia in the kitchen making coffee as Jewel stood behind her, eating a banana. "Hey, you're up!"

She looked over her shoulder and smiled at him. "Yes, I heard voices," she said, pushing the button on the coffee machine.

"When I fell asleep last night, I was holding you in my arms, and this morning you weren't there," Bryce said.

"I woke up in the middle of the night with a stiff neck and decided to go lay down in bed."

"Daddy, can I have some milk?" Jewel asked, handing him the banana peel.

"Sure, Munchkin. Go sit at the table and I'll bring it to you. Your mom and I are going to make you breakfast."

"Mommy's going to cook?" Jewel said, walking over to the table and taking a seat.

"Hey, I can cook, Letti's just a better cook than I am," Patricia said, grabbing an egg pan from one of the cupboards. "Besides, I only have one good arm to cook with. I'll be glad when this cast comes off," she said, handing Bryce the pan.

Ten minutes later, Savannah joined them holding a large photo album. She placed it on the table.

"What do you have there, sweetie?" Patricia asked, taking a seat next to her.

"It was under my pillow. It has a bunch of pictures in it."

"Can I see that?" Patricia asked, sliding it in front of her while the two girls stood on either side as she opened the album.

"I want to see too," Bryce said, leaving the kitchen.

Patricia stared at the first page showing four pictures of her standing on her father's boat wearing jeans, a checkered shirt, and a baseball cap. It was after her mother had passed away, and she believed she was around ten or eleven.

"Is that you?" Bryce asked, leaning over her shoulder.

"Yes, it is. We'd just come back from a day run and were back at the dock in Whittier."

"Wait, you used to go fishing with Grandpa?" Savannah asked.

"I did, after my mother passed away," Patricia confessed.

"Wow, Mom went fishing!" Jewel squealed, looking closer at the pictures. "But I thought you didn't like fishing?"

"When I left Alaska, I was tired of fishing. I wanted to do something different."

Bryce looked at the pictures on the next page showing Patricia on the dock holding buckets, standing next to her father who had his arm around her shoulders. "How long did you fish with him for?"

"Since my mom died and until I left Alaska, almost ten years. Not every day, mind you. Our neighbor Hazel, Tom's wife, homeschooled me and watched me when my dad went out fishing after my mother died, and on weekends I would go out on the boat with my father." She leaned back in her chair. "God, no wonder Tom's so angry with me. I'd forgotten just how much they helped us out."

Bryce sat next to her and smiled. "I can't believe this. You were out on a boat and went commercial fishing with your dad? Every day I'm learning something new about you. Who are you?" he joked.

Savannah turned more pages and pointed to a picture of Patricia, a bit older, maybe in her early teens, standing on the shore holding a fishing pole, her dad standing next to her.

"Where are you here?" Savannah asked.

"Right behind the restaurant where we had dinner last night. My father and I used to go fishing after dinner many times on those shores.

Patricia continued to thumb through the pages of the album - all the pictures were taken after the death of her mother - and she was touched that her father had kept it under her mother's pillow all these years. She pictured him in bed after she'd moved away, looking at the photos, reminiscing on the family he'd lost. Sadness crept in. She realized now how alone and hurt her father must have been.

Before the tears could fall, she closed the album and sat up straight. "Okay, we can look at more pictures later. Let's eat breakfast and get on the road. Today you get to see your grandpa's boat," Patricia told her daughters.

CHAPTER 38

When everyone was in the car and buckled up, Bryce put it in gear and was able to turn around in the wide driveway and head down to the street towards Hope Highway. It was a chilly morning with cloudy skies that were threatening rain.

"Let's hope the rain holds off today," Bryce said, turning onto Hope Highway. He looked at Savannah and Jewel through his rearview mirror. "Did we all bring jackets? It might be chilly in Whittier."

"Yes," they both echoed from the back seat.

Whittier was around 50 miles away and Bryce expected the drive to be under an hour. Patricia leaned back in her seat and took in the glorious views of snowcapped mountains and tall trees lining the two-lane highway, immensely enjoying the lack of traffic and people. "How could I ever forget how good this place makes me feel," she said, smiling and looking out the window.

"Beats me," Bryce replied. "No matter where you look the views are breathtaking, and the mountains seem to follow us everywhere." After driving seventeen miles on Hope Highway, Bryce turned left on Seaward Highway which would take him to the famous tunnel, the only way into Whittier.

After driving 22 miles, he pulled up to the kiosk where he was greeted by a young, friendly man who took his $13.00 one-way fee to use the tunnel and handed him a flyer on the rules while driving in the tunnel.

"You've got about a fifteen-minute wait before the tunnel opens up for vehicles; go ahead and drive into lane number one," the man in the kiosk told Bryce, pointing to the lane.

Bryce smiled, nodded, and took the flyer, put the car in drive, and slowly pulled up behind a white Subaru before shutting off the engine.

"That must be the tunnel," Bryce said, pointing to an A-frame structure on the outside of the mountain. "It looks like it cuts straight through the mountain," he observed.

"It does," Patricia agreed, lowering her head and looking out the window on Bryce's side.

"My father would park his truck somewhere over there, then we'd take the train," she said, pointing to the empty fields.

Bryce read the flyer. "It says the tunnel is two and half miles long. Wow, and that the speed limit is 20 miles per hour, and we need to keep 100 feet back from the car in front of us. I guess that's in case of some kind of emergency or something."

"Probably," Patricia said, turning her head and smiling at the girls.

"What are we waiting for?" Jewel asked.

"We have to wait for them to open the tunnel to the cars. Just a few more minutes, okay?" Patricia told her.

Soon after, the cars in front of them began moving. "Here we go!" Bryce said, putting the car in gear.

"Yay!" Savannah and Jewel yelled, leaning forward.

"It looks dark," Jewel said as they approached the entrance.

Once inside the narrow one-lane tunnel, they were surrounded by darkness. There was a continuous row of lights above them, illumi-nated just enough to not cause a glare.

"Whoa, this is really cool," Jewel said, sitting in the middle of the back seat, her body squished between the two front seats and her neck strained forward to look out the front window.

"This is really weird," Bryce said, looking straight ahead, keeping his distance from the car in front. "We are actually driving on the train tracks. They weren't kidding when they said the tunnel is shared with the railroad."

Six minutes into the ride, Jewel squealed. "I see light!"

"There is light at the end of the tunnel," Bryce hollered, laughing. "We're coming to the end of the tunnel."

"That was awesome!" Savannah yelled as they exited the tunnel onto Portage Glacier Road.

"Can we do it again?" Jewel said, her voice excited and loud.

Bryce laughed. "When we leave tomorrow, we have to go through it again."

"Cool," Jewel said, looking out the window.

Bryce drove for a few minutes until he came to West Camp Road, where he made a left turn, and within seconds he saw the ocean and harbor tucked away amongst the surrounding mountains. "Wow, this is incredible."

"I see boats," Jewel, said." "Is Grandpa's boat there?"

"Yes, it is," Patricia said, recalling the last time she was in the harbor with her father. It seemed so long ago, and she couldn't help noticing the many tourist attractions close to the cruise ship terminal that they passed, including jet ski rentals, gift shops, charters, and a yacht club. They were all new additions to the harbor which was now a tourist attraction.

Bryce turned onto Harbor Road and looked out at the many boats lining the docks to his left. "Any idea which dock your father's boat's on?" he asked Patricia.

"It used to be on the dock at the end," she chuckled. "Funny how I remember that."

Bryce found a parking space near the end dock and parked the car. He looked at Patricia and gave her a tender smile before taking her hand. "How are you doing? Are you okay?"

She smiled and squeezed his hand. "Actually, I am. I can't explain it, but it feels good to be here. I didn't think it would, but I feel my father's presence here. This was his life. He spent more time here than at the cabin. When I think of my dad I see him here, walking the docks, fixing the boat, repairing gillnets on the dock, and hanging out with the other fisherman telling fish tales." She looked out at the boats, gently rocking on the surface of the water. "Every time I came here, I was with my father. It feels strange being here without him."

"Are you ready to go down to the boat?" Bryce asked, opening his door.

"I am," Patricia said, her hand on the door handle.

"It's colder here than Hope; grab your jackets, girls," Bryce said, stepping out of the car and breathing in the salty air. "Man, it's gorgeous here," he said, looking at the spectacular views. "Is there anywhere in Alaska that isn't?" he laughed.

Savannah and Jewel exited the car and quickly put on their coats. "Where's Grandpa's boat?" Jewel asked.

Patricia took her hand. "I'll show you," she said, leading all of them down one of the docks towards the boats. She stopped at the slip that was second from the end. "It's still here," she said, pointing to a 32-foot white fiberglass Beaver gill-netting boat. "And it still looks the same." When she saw it, she gasped. On the side of the bow was the boat's name. She read it aloud. "*Patti*. He changed the name of the boat to *Patti*." She strolled to the end of the dock and looked at the stern where it also said *Patti*.

"What was her name before?" Bryce asked.

Tears pooled in Patricia's eyes. "I can't believe he named the boat after me. It was always called *Hope,* after our town, and how he always started his trips by saying, *let's hope it's a good day.*"

"You would never let me call you Patti. When I did, you almost bit my head off. That was the first and only time I did," he laughed.

"I know, and I realize now that Cassie had drilled it into my head that I should only go by the name Patricia to protect my image." She shook her head in disgust. "You can call me Patti anytime you want," she added, smiling.

Bryce grinned. "Good, because I like Patti better."

"Wow, this is Grandpa's boat?" Jewel said, her eyes wide open as she stood on the dock in awe. "Can we go on it?"

"Yes, of course," Patricia said, holding out her hand. "Let me help you."

The boat had a large working deck with a gillnet at the stern and a small cabin at the front of the helm. She had spent many hours on this deck when she was in her teens, helping her father and his deckhand fish for Salmon. Standing on the deck, she looked out at the other boats, surprised by the variety. No longer were there mainly commercial fishing boats, now there were pleasure boats, charter boats, jet skis and kayaks. It was April and the Salmon run didn't begin until June, so, like her father, many of the fishermen went out for Halibut this time of year. The harbor was busy with many fishermen on their boats, either doing repairs or getting ready for their next trip. Tourists were abundant; strolling the harbor, dining at the restaurants, or shopping at the variety of gift shops.

"This is a nice boat," Bryce said standing next to her, his hands in his jacket pockets.

"It was his pride and joy. He bought it in the eighties after my mother died, trading in his wooden boat," she told him, scanning the deck and allowing the floodgate of memories to consume her.

"And you'd help him fish for Salmon?" Bryce asked, watching the girls giggle, at the helm pretending to drive the boat.

"After I turned twelve, my father would bring me down here to help him. He had a deckhand, and I'd help them with the gillnet and put the Salmon in the tanks where we'd cover them with chilled water." She looked over at Savannah and Jewel and smiled. "God, I wished he could have met his granddaughters. Seeing them on his boat with their big smiles makes me feel terrible."

Bryce wrapped his arm around her shoulders. "Don't. They're here now, and you're doing an excellent job telling them stories about your childhood and their grandfather. It's wonderful that we're here experiencing this together instead of leaving everything up to the attorney."

"Well, coming here was *your* idea, and I'm *glad* you suggested it."

Jewel left the wheel of the helm and skipped over to them. "Can we go in the cabin?"

"Sure, the keys are in my purse, hold on," Patricia said, removing her purse from her shoulder and handing it to Bryce. "Can you grab them? This cast on my arm makes it difficult."

Bryce took her purse and rooted through it in search of her keys. "Here they are," he said, holding them in the air. "Let me open the cabin door for you."

Jewel and Savannah stood behind their dad, eagerly waiting for him to unlock the door to the cabin. Patricia walked over to the wheel at the helm and saw a picture taped above the dashboard. She leaned in to take a closer look and saw that it was a picture of her and her father standing on the deck arm-in-arm. She was older, maybe sixteen. She remembered that day; they'd spent three days on the boat, fishing every day and sleeping on the boat instead of going home. It was one of his best fishing trips and they had worked hard.

"Are you ready?" Bryce asked, snapping her out of her thoughts.

She nodded and then suddenly stopped when she saw her father's fishing boots on the deck at the doorway of the cabin. "I want to take those home," she said before entering the cabin.

"Wow! This is like a little house," Jewel said, spinning around in the small floor space before checking out the dual sleeping quarters where Savannah had walked over to.

"Just like his cabin in Hope, everything looks the same," Patricia said, stroking her hand across the surface of the small, wooden dinette table. "We used to play cards at this table before going to bed." She looked above the window at a collection of family pictures taped to the wall. Some of her mother and father standing on the dock, and some of the three of them. "He took us fishing every time through these pictures," Patricia said, her eyes moist. "Even after we'd left him, he kept our pictures close to him."

"He never forgot either one of you. I think it was his memories that kept him going," Bryce said in a gentle voice before taking a seat next to her on the bench where she sat.

Patricia looked out the small window at the other boats. "He always said I'd be back because I belong here. I believed that also kept him going." She looked at Bryce, tears in her eyes. "He was right." She stroked the surface of the table again. "We can't sell this boat, Bryce.

It's his legacy, and we need to keep it alive," she insisted, tears trickling down her cheeks.

Bryce pulled her into his arms where she rested her head on his shoulder "What are you saying?"

She pulled away and looked at him. "I don't know, but I do know I can't sell this boat."

CHAPTER 39

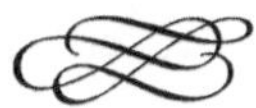

Bryce was taken aback by her confession. "Patricia, we can't leave the boat sitting at the dock rotting away after we leave."

Patricia stood up and began pacing around in the small cabin, her hand to her brow. "I know that Bryce, but I can't sell it. I just can't."

Bryce stood up quickly and took her in his arms. "Okay, okay, we'll figure something out. You don't have to sell your father's boat if you don't want to, no one is making you. You've said all along you'd wanted to sell it; I'm just trying to go along with your wishes."

Patricia rubbed her brow again. "Well, that's all changed. I don't want to sell any of it, including the cabin."

"You don't?"

"No, I don't," Patricia cried, shaking her head. "He kept everything. All of this, the cabin was his life. I can't just sell it off to the highest bidder like his life meant nothing, and then return to New York like none of this existed. I had no idea being here would have this effect on me, but it has, and I can't just ignore it. Look where ignoring and pretending about things has gotten me in the last 20 years."

Bryce was unsure of what to say; she was opening up to him like never before. "So, what do you want to do?"

Patricia pulled away and called the girls who were stretched out on the bunks giggling. "Savannah, Jewel, come here please." She looked at Bryce. "I know what I want to do, come up to the deck and bring the girls."

"Okay," he said, his brow furrowed. He called the girls. "Savannah, Jewel, your mother wants us up on deck."

Within minutes, Bryce heard the roaring of the diesel engine blast through the boat. He quickly raced to the deck where he found Patricia at the helm. Savannah and Jewel quickly joined them.

"What are you doing?" Bryce yelled in a panicked state.

"I need you to grab two life vests from under that bench," Patricia shouted above the roar of the motor, pointing to the other side of the dash, "and put them on Savannah and Jewel. That's where they were always kept, and I'm sure they're still there."

"Patricia, *what do you think you're doing?*" Bryce yelled again.

She ignored him. "Get the life vests, Bryce, then I need you to jump on the dock and untie the lines. We're going for a boat ride."

"Mom's going to drive the boat!" Jewel squealed.

Bryce shook his head, "this is insane! You need to stop Patricia, right now! You can't drive this bloody boat," Bryce hollered above the noise of the engine.

"Oh, but I can. My father was a good teacher. Tom said he'd been taking it out and maintaining it since my father's death, he said it even has a full tank of gas. This is something I need to do. You can either stay here or come with me, but I'm taking this boat out. I told you that I feel my father's presence here; it's everywhere, and I must do this."

"Okay, then I guess we're going with you," Bryce replied resignedly, knowing she couldn't be stopped. He proceeded to put life vests on Savannah and Jewel.

"Wow, Mom! Are you sure you know what you're doing?" Savannah asked as her dad jumped onto the dock and began untying the lines.

"I do, sweetheart. I drove this boat many times with your grandpa. It's like riding a bike - you never forget."

Once the lines were untied, Bryce and the girls stood in awe next to Patricia as she slowly managed to steer the boat away from the dock - even with one arm in a cast - headed for the open ocean. There was a slight breeze, and the waters were calm with clouds still lingering above them, but the skies remained dry.

"My god! I can't believe you're driving the boat!" Bryce hollered.

"Yay! Go mom!" Jewel screamed, her long hair blowing away from her face.

Patricia kept her hands on the wheel as she turned and looked at her daughters. "I was your age, Savannah, when my father taught me how to drive this boat."

"No way!" Savannah yelled. "Will you teach me?"

"And me!" Jewel added.

"Me too," Bryce laughed, shaking his head. "This is insane. I wasn't expecting this at all; I'm blown away!"

Patricia laughed. She couldn't remember the last time she'd felt this happy and content. A warm feeling rushed through her body as she steered the boat out of the harbor. Once they'd reached the open ocean, she managed to push the throttle forward with her casted arm to gain more speed. It had been a long time since she'd experienced this kind of freedom; in fact, the last time she felt this way was her last day in the state of Alaska. Unbeknownst to her, her life had been planned and dictated by Cassie. Beaming and feeling the wind in her hair, Patricia looked up at the skies and closed her eyes. "I'm home dad, and yes, I do belong here," she whispered. "I know what to do, Dad," she added, before slowing down the boat and putting it in neutral.

"Are you okay?" Bryce asked, noticing the tears in her eyes.

She left the wheel, allowed the boat to idle in neutral, and wrapped her arms first around Savannah and then Jewel. "I'm fine," she said, tears streaming down her face.

"But Mommy, you're crying!" Jewel said with a look of confusion.

"They're tears of happiness, sweetheart. Your mommy is so happy. In fact, she's never been happier."

She looked at Bryce and sauntered over to kiss him softly on the lips.

"Whoa, Mom is kissing Dad!" Savannah yelled; her eyes as wide as saucers.

Patricia looked into Bryce's eyes and smiled, tears streaming down her cheeks. "I'm home."

Bryce wrapped his arms around Patricia's waist. "You're home?"

She nodded. "Yes, I'm home, and I love you," she laughed through her tears. "I've always loved you, but I believed that I needed and wanted something different. I'm home, Bryce, and I never want to leave."

"What are you saying, Patricia? You want to live here?"

"I belong here, Bryce. This is my home, and you and the girls are my family. I want us to be together again, here in Alaska. I want to bring my family back to my father."

Bryce pulled her in close and kissed her hard. "Oh Patti, I want that too. I love you so much." He squeezed her shoulders. "Do you think we can do this? Is this what you really want?"

"Yes! I've never wanted anything more in my life. I belong here, Bryce! We can do this, I know we can," Patricia cried excitedly.

Bryce couldn't believe what he was hearing. "But what about your law firm, your home in New York?"

Patricia laughed, tossing back her head. "I'll sell it all!"

Bryce's eyes grew wide. "You're serious, aren't you?"

Patricia nodded her head vigorously. "I am."

Bryce smiled and pulled her into his arms before kneeling on one knee and taking her hand. "Patti Levenick, will you marry me?" he paused and laughed, "again?"

Savannah and Jewel squealed as they watched their father propose to their mother. "Mommy, Daddy, are you getting back together?" Jewel asked, clasping her hands in front of her chest.

"Let's see what your mother says," Bryce remarked, not taking his eyes off Patricia.

Before answering, she wiped her cheeks and nodded. "Yes, I will marry you again."

Savannah and Jewel raised their arms in a cheer. Bryce stood up and both girls embraced their parents.

With their daughters hugging his waist, Bryce looked into Patricia's eyes, his heart full. "I think I'm the happiest man on earth right now. How about we spend a little time out here on the ocean and then go check into the lodge, order pizza, and talk about mapping out a future for our family?"

Patricia smiled, "I like that idea."

CHAPTER 40

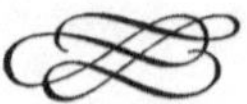

Patricia had never felt closer to her two daughters and Bryce than she did now, spending the last two hours drifting on the ocean on her father's boat, telling them fishing stories about their grandpa.

Sitting on top of the fish hold with a daughter on each side curled up in her arms with Bryce listening as he kept watch for any nearby boats, Patricia told them what she should have told them many years ago. With pride she told them that their grandpa was an amazing man who loved his family and worked hard to provide for them, making a living off the sea, while her mother, Grandma Louise, remained at home to raise her. She explained to them how their grandpa caught Salmon using gillnets, and how she'd help repair them on the docks, as well as helping his deckhand unload the fish when they returned to the harbor. She talked about having campfires on the beach around the point from the harbor when they were spending the night on the boat because the run of Salmon was so good. They would sit around the campfire, drinking hot chocolate and roasting marshmallows, while he told her tales of the sea.

"I know your grandpa would be enormously proud of you both, and I'm sure he's watching over us while we're sitting here on his boat. It's only right that we keep what he loved to do going," she smiled, squeezing her daughters tight. "What do you think?"

"Will we get to go fishing like you did, Mommy?" Jewel asked.

"Well, I'm sure there'll be times we can fish as a family, and your father and I have a lot of details to work out as far as running the boat, but it's ours, and we can use it whenever we want."

"This is so cool," Savannah said, beaming. "So, for real, you and Dad are getting married again?"

Patricia laughed. "Yes, for real, sweetheart. Do you like that idea?"

Savannah looked up and smiled. "I *love* it. And we're going to live in Grandpa's house?"

"We sure are, but we may have to make it a little bigger. I don't want to tear it down; his original cabin will be the heart of our new home."

Since there were no boats nearby, Bryce joined them. "I like that idea of the cabin," he said, kissing Patricia on the cheek.

"Me too," Savannah said. "It would be sad to tear it down."

"That will never happen," Patricia remarked, pulling Savannah and Jewel close to her sides and kissing the top of their heads. "I love you both very much. I'm sorry you never got to meet your grandpa, but I'll make it up to you, I promise." She squeezed them again. "Now, let's get this boat back to the harbor and order some pizza."

~

After checking into the lodge and getting settled in their two-room suite, the pizza arrived.

"Pizza's here!" Bryce hollered, tipping the doorman and placing it on the coffee table next to the two couches.

"Yay!" Jewel screamed, running over to the coffee table and plunking herself down on one of the couches. "I'm so hungry."

"This is getting to be a regular thing," Patricia laughed, taking a seat next to her. "Family pizza time in hotel suites."

"Are you complaining?" Bryce said, handing her a plate.

"No, not at all. I could do this every night," she said, smiling at her family. "I love you all so much."

Bryce sat next to her on the other side of the couch while Savannah knelt in front of him in front of the coffee table. "And we love you. I can't wait for you to be my wife again," he said, kissing her on the lips before picking up a slice of pizza.

Patricia couldn't believe the sudden change of events that were happening - not just in her life, but Bryce's and their daughters, too. She didn't have any doubts that she was being impulsive or caught up in the moment of being in Alaska where she had so many forgotten memories. Everything felt so right. She knew now that she had been living a lie, just as Bryce had realized when he'd left her; now she understood why he'd had to leave.

After spending the rest of the day being a family and loving every minute of it, Patricia kissed Savannah and Jewel goodnight. Once the girls were tucked into bed, before turning off the lights she joined Bryce in the master suite where she found him propped up on pillows on the king-size bed dressed in a white bathrobe.

"Hey," she said, smiling and closing the door behind her. "Mind if I join you?"

Bryce patted the empty side of the bed. "I've been thinking about this moment all day," he said, patting the bed again.

Patricia smiled at him. Engulfed in her corporate life, hating everything about Bryce and his farm, she'd forgotten or was blind-sided by how handsome he was. Walking over to the bed, she sat on the edge and removed her boots and jeans, leaving only her shirt and white lace panties and bra on.

"Man, you're even sexier then when I first married you," Bryce said holding out his hand. "Come here, I want to kiss you."

Patricia moistened her lips and crawled onto the bed with her knees, melting into his arms. He smelled fresh after his shower, his blond, curly hair damp. "Kiss me," he whispered, pulling her on top of him.

Their lips met; the kiss was hard and passionate. Five years of resistance suppressing their true feelings for one another, they exploded in seconds. While exploring her mouth hungrily, Bryce stripped her of her shirt, lace bra and panties within minutes. Empowered by her scent and soft skin he held nothing back. Smothering his naked body with hers, their lovemaking became unhinged.

Patricia's skin was on fire from his sensual touch – she'd never wanted Bryce more than she did now. For five years since their divorce, her body had not felt the touch of another man. Like Bryce, she held nothing back and became unleashed, falling into his arms after her explosive orgasm.

Between the panting and her heart racing, Patricia collapsed onto the pillow, her brow damp with sweat. "Wow, you never made love like that to me even when we were first married!"

Bryce lay next to her, his hand on his brow, his chest heaving. "I am turned on ten times more after getting to know the real you," he laughed. "Expect more of that during our second marriage."

"Bryce, I need to ask - you're not having any second thoughts, are you? You're as sure about this as I am, right? I mean this is all happening so fast. You won't change your mind once we leave here?"

Bryce took her in his arms. "You have nothing to worry about. I'm not going anywhere, I promise. It's me that should be worried," he joked. "I'm afraid once you return to New York, the corporate world will swallow you up again and I'll lose you."

She patted his naked chest. "That will never happen. In fact, I want to come back to Alaska as soon as possible." She rested her chin on her hand and lay on her side, looking up at him. "How long do you think it will take to dissolve our lives in the city?"

"Well, I've been thinking about how we can do all of this, and I'd like to give it a year."

Patricia's jaw dropped. "A year? That's a long time. Can't we do it any sooner?"

"Okay, what ideas do you have? One of mine is to have my brother Darren run the farm. Instead of him being a 30-70 partner, I'll make him a 50-50 and he'll be in total control. He can even move into the main farmhouse; I'm sure he'll like that." He paused. "Were you serious when you said you wanted to sell your law firm?

You've worked so hard building up the practice and your reputation."

Patricia cracked a laugh. "A life that wasn't me, and yes, I want to sell it, but the first thing I want to do when I get back to New York is call Cassie and tell her the good news. It'll be epic." She released a mischievous smile. "You know what? I'm not going to wait until we get back, I'm going to call her first thing tomorrow."

"Ooh, can I listen in?" Bryce said with a big smile, his eyes bright.

"You can say hi if you want," Patricia giggled. "We can call her from here in the bedroom and have the girls watch TV. I don't want them to have to hear the choice words I have for my Aunt Cassie."

"I love the idea. And, not to change the subject, but I also like your idea of building onto your father's cabin and not tearing it down. It's a wonderful idea, and I think your father would have approved."

"Yes, it would be heartbreaking to erase everything he'd worked so hard for, as well as all of the memories that I have growing up in the cabin."

"And what are we going to do for a living once we move to Alaska?" Bryce asked, his eyebrows raised.

Patricia laid her head on her pillow and didn't answer straightaway. "Do we have to work? I mean, between me selling the law firm, the income you'll get from the farm, as well as the money we already have, there should be enough to live off of for the rest of our lives. I want to make up for lost time and be a family." She suddenly sprung off the bed, spread her arms like an eagle and began spinning around in the middle of the room. "I want to homeschool our girls, bake with them, cook dinners as a family, play board games around the table, take them fishing and hiking, and explore the beautiful Alaskan mountains."

Bryce joined her in the middle of the room, pulling her in close, smiling before kissing her. "I want all of that, too. Oh, and one more thing."

"What's that?"

"We need to plan a wedding."

CHAPTER 41

*P*atricia woke up early, anxious to start the day. After losing sleep from planning what she'd say to Cassie, she quickly pulled back the covers and grabbed the white terrycloth bathrobe draped over the chair. She heard the shower running from the bathroom and suddenly changed her mind. Smiling, she turned the other direction and entered the bathroom where she heard Bryce whistling from inside the spacious shower.

"Is there room for two in there?" she hollered, removing her bathrobe.

Bryce slid open the glass door now covered in steam and smiled. "Hey, beautiful. Come on in so I can soap you up and kiss you all over."

Patricia walked over to the shower and tiptoed in, being careful not to slip, and was immediately pulled into Bryce's arms. She wrapped her good arm around his neck and kissed him hard on the mouth. "I can't get this cast wet. We have to be careful," she said, keeping the cast away from the spray of water.

"Hold onto my neck while I ravish your body," he said, dropping to his knees, his arms around her waist as he began to taste her.

Patricia immediately melted to his touch and the warmth of his tongue. She leaned against the cold tile while he devoured her, exploring every inch of her body, not leaving any part untraced. Their lovemaking was more passionate than ever before. With the walls of her corporate attitude now broken, she was able to let herself go and be free to embrace the passion between them. It was magical and real.

"Bryce, don't stop," she moaned, as Bryce continued to taste her, spreading her legs a little further apart before bringing her to an explosive climax.

"My god, where have you been all my life!" she said, still leaning against the tile, her eyes closed, chest heaving.

Bryce rose to his feet, leaned his body against hers and kissed her forcefully. "And where have *you* been all of *mine*? I don't know what you're doing to me, but this feels incredible. I just want you all the time. I can't stop thinking about you, and if we didn't have two daughters who are probably wondering where their parents are, I'd drag you over to that bed and keep you here all day so I could make mad passionate love to you."

"I want you all the time too, and I feel the same way. This is amazing, I don't ever want it to end."

He kissed her again. "It never will, I can promise you that."

Bryce turned off the shower. His ears perked up, "I hear the TV, the girls must be up. I bought some instant oatmeal and orange juice at the store yesterday. I'm going to fix them that while you get dressed, and I'll also make you some coffee."

"Then I want to call Cassie," Patricia said, stepping out of the shower and wrapping her body in a towel.

After Bryce had dried himself off and put on a pair of sweats and a t-shirt, he left Patricia to go tend to Savannah and Jewel.

Fifteen minutes later Patricia joined them dressed in jeans and a navy-blue t-shirt, no makeup, her hair damp.

"Here's your coffee," Bryce said, handing her a Styrofoam cup.

"Thanks," she said, smiling as she joined the girls at the table.

"How are you two doing this morning? Did you both sleep okay?" Patricia asked her daughters.

They both nodded before taking a spoonful of oatmeal. "Are we going back to grandpa's cabin today?" Jewel asked.

"Yes, we are," Patricia told her. "But first your father and I need to make a phone call in the bedroom. Will you two be okay watching TV while we do that?"

"Sure, Mom," Savannah replied.

After making sure Savannah and Jewel had everything they needed and had a show on TV they liked, Bryce and Patricia went to their room, closing the door behind them.

"Are you sure you want to do this now?" Bryce asked, sitting at the small table in front of the window overlooking Whittier harbor.

"Oh yes, I'm sure," she said, joining him at the table wearing a devious smile.

Patricia placed her phone on the table, located Cassie's number and hit the speaker button after she heard it ring.

"I hope she answers," Patricia whispered after four rings. She looked at Bryce and smiled when she heard Cassie's voice.

"Hello, Cassie speaking."

"Hello Cassie, this is Patti."

Bryce held his hand up to his mouth and laughed.

"Who?" Cassie replied.

"Patti, your niece."

There was a moment of silence. "You mean Patricia."

"No, I mean Patti. I prefer that name much more. Why didn't you want me to use that name Cassie?"

Cassie spoke in a sharp tone. "What has gotten into you? Your name is Patricia. Stop using that common name. I knew you should never have gone to Alaska. Please, Patricia, don't use that name, it's horrible."

"Well, get used to it Auntie, because I never want you to call me Patricia again. Why else didn't you want me to come here, Cassie?"

"What do you mean?" Cassie asked. "Alaska is *not* a good place. You know that."

"It's not a good place for what? For finding out who I really am?"

Cassie stuttered when she spoke. "What are you talking about, Patricia?"

"It's Patti!"

Cassie ignored Patricia's rude interruption. "You are making no sense. I brought you to New York so that you could have a better life. Everything I did was for you."

"What you did was brainwash me and made me believe my father was a terrible man, when in fact, he was the sweetest, kindest person that only loved his family. When my mother died, you did the most despicable act of turning his own daughter against him. Why, Cassie, why? Because of your selfish acts and making me believe that I could NEVER talk about where I came from, his granddaughters never got to know him. Why did you hate my father so much that you did this to him?"

"I saved you!" Cassie screamed into the phone. "I gave you a life. What would you be doing today if I didn't do what I did?"

"I know for sure that I would have had a special, loving relationship with my father, which you deprived me of. How could you? My god!" Patricia said, shaking her head.

"That horrible man that you call your father stole my sister from me; she was only 20 years old. He ruined her life and she died because of him. If she had come back to New York with me she'd still be alive today. I was not about to let him ruin my niece's life, too. I couldn't let that happen."

"No Cassie, you ruined my father's life, and you destroyed what family he had left, which was me. You destroyed any relationship my daughters would have had with their grandfather. My mother fell in love; she made her own choices and followed her heart. My father had nothing to do with her death, it was a freak accident." Patricia took a deep breath and held her chest.

Bryce reached across the table and squeezed her arm. "You're doing good."

"I will never forgive you for what you did. I've been living a lie for the past 20 years. Bryce knew that, it's why he left me. We were both living a lie; it just took me longer to see it, and being here in Alaska with my family opened my eyes." She paused and smiled. "I belong in Alaska, Cassie."

"What are you saying, Patricia?" Cassie said, her voice shaking.

"I'm saying my home is here. I'm home, Cassie." She squeezed Bryce's hand and smiled. "Bryce and I are getting married again and we are coming home."

"What?" Cassie screamed, "you can't do this, your life is here! I won't let you do this, Patricia. I won't lose my niece."

"Oh, but Cassie, you already have. I never want to see you again, and I sure as hell don't want you anywhere near our daughters. You did a horrible thing, and there's nothing you can do to make me forgive you. I have said all I want to say. Bryce is sitting here next to me, and we're going to plan our lives together with our daughters, and I don't want you to be any part of it. Goodbye, Cassie."

Before she could reply, Patricia quickly ended the call. "God, that felt good," she said, breathing heavily, her hand still on her chest.

Bryce stood up and strode over to her as she got up, taking her into his arms. "I am *so* bloody proud of you. Come here and give me a kiss. You really gave it to her - well done."

"I'm going to put her out of my mind, just like she ordered me to do with my father." She gazed into his eyes and smiled. "Come on, we have our future to plan."

CHAPTER 42

ONE YEAR LATER

Do you, Bryce Levenick, take Patti Levenick to be your lawfully wedded wife?" The priest paused and released a slight chuckle, "again?"

Laughter erupted amongst the guests sitting in the small rustic church in Hope, Alaska.

"I do."

The priest looked at Patti. "Do you, Patti Levenick, take Bryce Levenick to be your lawfully wedded husband, again?"

Holding Bryce's hand, she smiled and looked into his eyes as their two daughters looked on from the front pew. "I do."

The priest gave them both a caring smile. "I now pronounce you man and wife. Bryce, you may kiss the bride."

As Bryce leaned in to kiss Patti, their guests cheered and clapped their hands.

Savannah and Jewel left their seats and raced up to their parents and hugged them. "You look just like Grandma and Grandpa in their wedding pictures," Savannah said, grinning.

With tears in her eyes, Patti hugged her girls. "We do? They got married in this church two years before I was born, and they were as much in love as me and your daddy are."

Patricia looked out at the guests mingling in the church, all of whom were locals from the town that she'd gotten to know since they'd returned to Hope four months ago after dissolving their lives in the city.

Everything had gone according to plan. Darren, Bryce's brother, agreed to manage the farm after the initial shock had worn off after learning of their plans, but after hearing the entire story of how their lives had taken a sudden turn, he was overjoyed and excited for them. Bryce was happy for his brother, too, whom he learned was now dating Kittie, the owner of Kittie's Kitchen in Easton.

Patti got top dollar for her law firm, and renovations to the cabin started almost immediately, building out from what Patti called the heart of the cabin, her father's home. They added three bedrooms, two baths, extended the kitchen out, built a large wrap-around porch, and doubled the size of the living room. Appliances were upgraded and some of her father's furniture which had seen better days was replaced. Photos of her parents and childhood hung proudly next to pictures of Bryce and their daughters.

After removing some trees behind the workshop, they had a large barn and corral for Savannah's horse, Cleo, who was successfully transported to Alaska just two months ago, much to Savannah's delight. Goldie and Jack weren't left behind either, and traveled with them on their final flight to Alaska.

When the dogs settled onto their beds that were waiting for them in front of the fireplace, Patti felt her family was finally complete. She had grown extremely fond of Goldie and Jack.

Their neighbor, Tom, approached Patti, who was standing arm-in-arm with her family. "It's good to have you back, Patti. Your daddy would be mighty proud of you and would thank you for saving his boat from savages."

"Tom, I couldn't have done it without you. When I came to you to apologize that day and tell you our plans, it was your idea to hire a crew and ask the local fisherman that knew my father to fish his boat. It was a brilliant idea. My father's boat is still out there fishing, and my family can use it, too."

Tom smiled. "Welcome home, Patti."

Tears trickled down Patti's face. "It feels good to be home, Tom."

ABOUT THE AUTHOR

Award-winning author Tina Hogan Grant was born in England and moved to the States in 1979. After moving to California, she became a commercial fisherwoman and spent ten years fishing off the southern coast of California with her husband Gordon. After retiring from fishing, they moved to a small mountain community in CA and spent the next ten years building their dream home, doing most of the work themselves.

Grant enjoys writing suspense romances, stories with strong female characters who know what they want and aren't afraid to chase their dreams.

Favorite quote: "There's no such word as can't "

When Grant is not lost in her world of writing she enjoys riding ATVs, hiking and discovering new trails, and going on long road trips.

Grant's book Better Endings won a gold medal award for Best Fiction Adventure 2020

And The Reunions won a Gold medal award for Best Fiction Adventure 2021

Grant has had appearances on FOX NEWS Bakersfield, Bakersfield NOW NEWS, HOMETOWN -KVPA Radio Santa Clarita, Voyage LA Magazine, and The Mountain Enterprise Newspaper, and BOLD Magazine.

Keep in the loop with Tina and receive Davin The Sabela Series Prequel for FREE by signing up for her newsletter https://www.subscribepage.com/tinahogangrant

ALSO BY TINA HOGAN GRANT

THE TAMMY MELLOWS SERIES

<u>First Fall - The Prequel</u>

<u>Reckless Beginnings - Book 1</u>

Better Endings - Book 2

The Reunions Books 3

Waves And Memories - A Short Story Collection

THE SABELA SERIES

Davin - Prequel

<u>Slater - Book 1</u>

<u>Eve - Book 2</u>

Claire - Book 3

Jill - Book 4

All Of Us - Book 5

Vegas Bound - Book 6

Open Arms - Book 7

Dream Big - Book 8 (Final book in the series)

THE SECRETS SERIES

Secrets Told - Book 1